Written by Claudia Blood
Cover design by Sunset Rose Books

Copyright 2021 by Claudia Blood

Paperback ISBN: 978-1-954603-40-0

BOOK OF SECRETS

THE MERGED SERIES
BOOK 1

CLAUDIA BLOOD

DRAGON BANE PUBLISHING

ABOUT BOOK OF SECRETS

The human world and the world of myth have merged. Ordinary individuals must become extraordinary if they hope to save it.

Joshua Lighthouse never wanted to be a hero, but now, he has no choice.

For three hundred years, the human world and the world of Myth have lived as one. The cataclysmic Merge forced those who survived – both human and Others – to form factions.

As leader of the Human Protection Agency, Joshua is charged with maintaining the safety of the humans in his city. But he secretly protects an artifact more powerful than even he knows...

The Book of Secrets.

With the anniversary of the Merge approaching, the Book of

Secrets is stolen and Joshua finds himself at the center of a plot to unmerge the worlds.

Stripped of his position, betrayed, and with a bounty on his head, Joshua must outrun the organization he once served and legions of Others in a race against time to locate the book and prevent the inter-species war that will end the world he knows forever.

Can he find his way to salvation when everything he believed is a lie, or will his distrust lead to another epic cataclysm he can't stop?

Book of Secrets is the first book in The Merged urban fantasy series. If you love stories full of desperate rescues, unexpected twists and tragic betrayals, you'll love this installment of Claudia Blood's epic series.

Trigger warning:
This book contains death, violence, off screen torture (victim is rescued), non-main character self sacrifice, and self-defense that ends in death.

1

JOSHUA

<u>1AM, August 11, 2016 - Earth before the Merge</u>

Joshua Lighthouse's plan was simple. Sneak out the window, climb to the roof, and watch the meteor shower. Nothing was going to stop him.

Not even the strange heavy feeling which still hung in the air. The feeling of a storm coming. The forecast had been for clear skies, but he'd been unable to shake the feeling that something was coming. That something was wrong.

Every year the Perseid meteor shower came close to his birthday. This year the peak fell on his twelfth birthday and the peak of the meteor shower would happen at his birth hour and there was going to be an outburst. Double the normal number of meteors.

He tightened his hand around the backpack's handle hidden under his Star Wars bedspread. The details of his room were lost in the darkness. His new star projection clock didn't project enough light to chase away the dark shadows. Instead, it filled his bedroom with a steady clicking like the mandibles of a giant ant.

The digits on the clock took about a century to flip to two AM.

It was time.

He pulled out the remote control from the side pocket of his bag. A button turned on the camera on his spybot hidden on the top of his parent's wardrobe. The lever made the spybot crawl out from behind the discarded baseball caps, cups, and change. The camera focused on his parents in their king-sized bed.

His father's mouth opened wide, his arms flung out with one touching the nightstand and the other over part of his mom's pillow. His mom was hidden under the quilt with just the tips of her dark hair sticking out. Her arm hung over the side and twitched in time with father's snoring.

His parents were asleep.

The remote snapped back in place in his bag. He kicked off the covers. His toes sunk into the plush carpet as he crept across the room to open the window. The screen already sat hidden behind his dresser.

He scanned his neighborhood. The streetlight stood silent guard between dark houses.

He pulled out the second remote and sent Betty, his other little robot, from her hiding spot on the roof. She rolled to the edge and lowered the rope already around the chimney. It slithered down next to his window.

The climb took a moment. From his vantage point on the roof, the neighborhood spread out beneath him. The neighbor's black lab, Petey, lifted his head from his paws, snorted and curled back up in his kennel.

Joshua pulled up the rope, tucking it and the robot back in

their hiding place. Fifteen steps brought him to the faint chalk X which marked the spot where the best view would be. In that spot, the chimney would block the light from downtown Rochester, and a gap in the trees would give him a wide view of the sky.

He sat on the spot and unpacked. Snacks – check. Binoculars around his neck – check, a blanket for his legs to ward off the chill – check.

Then he settled back on the roof. The trees in the backyard swayed gently in the slight breeze. The roof was rough and warm on his back. The faint smell of backyard fire hung in the air.

His eyes adjusted. The stars twinkled in swaths in the sky looking like spilled salt on his mom's black granite countertop. Lines traced the first passing meteors. Only the faint hum of mosquitoes and the flutter of a bat broke the quiet.

The Perseid meteor shower would go on for an hour. His parents were sound asleep so they'd never miss him. He'd be able to watch the whole thing.

<u>Bong.</u>

<u>Bong.</u>

The deep distant note of a gong tolled. He flinched and covered his ears, but it made no difference to the loudness of the noise.

The gong had a deeper tone than the bells of Assisi Heights up the hill. When the bells at Franciscan Sisters rang, his chest lightened. No, this was something different. That seed of worry that had been nagging him sprouted.

He tucked his blanket in his backpack and stood, walking towards the chimney, and braced his shoulder against it. His binoculars out, he scanned the horizon.

Nothing seemed amiss. The neighborhood lay quiet and

dark. Too quiet. Silence, so loud it echoed in his ears. The winds hid, the animals waited. But for what?

To the south, the pink and blue lights of downtown Rochester glowed. The feeling of a storm approaching deepened and his bones responded with an ache. He did a full circle scan, but saw nothing but cloudless, star speckled sky. Was he imagining it?

His eyes were drawn back to downtown, the stars behind the buildings disappeared. Not blocked by clouds, but gone, as if they had been drawn on an etch-a-sketch that a kid had shaken. The pit of his stomach gave another harder twist.

Dark splotches swarmed the Mayo building, army ants overrunning its prey. The darkness faded and left a gaping hole in the skyline. The building was gone.

The hairs on his body stood up as one. His heart drummed and he grabbed the chimney. The stone cut into his fingers.

The Plummer building floated up into the air, water and sparks trailed after it. What was he seeing? It made no sense. He pinched himself and the sharp pain made even less sense. He wasn't dreaming. But how could it be real?

<u>Wump-boom-ba-boom</u>.

The roof shook. His foot slipped from under him and only his hold on the chimney kept him upright. His heart skipped and he turned toward the sound.

A stone tower crushed the Miller's house next door, leaving Petey howling in his backyard kennel. Black spots swarmed the kennel fence and it disappeared. Petey tucked his tail and ran to the front of the house, yipping and whimpering.

From across the street, Mrs. Lake banged open her door. Petey huddled at her bare feet hiding his head under her checkered robe. She gaped at the new stone building, mouth wide, hand to her chest. She seemed about ready to faint.

At the bottom of her porch stairs, a single blue light grew until it looked like a swarm of fireflies. When they fizzled out, a skinny woman with a green-feathered body and long black feathers cresting from her head appeared. Her feathers fluffed up, making her seem bigger. Her long wailing cry broke the silence.

Mrs. Lake fell back against the door, clutching her blanket. She took one deep breath, her mouth hung open, eyes bulged.

Joshua leaned closer to the chimney. If Mrs. Lake looked ready to freak, then this was all real. He pushed down his fear and scanned again. Black swarms took things away, and blue light brought them. What made things move? The stone tower and the Plummer building had moved.

Another blue shimmer in the middle of the street and a large hedge appeared, blocking his view of Mrs. Lake and the green bird-lady. A deep fog rolled in ushering in the stench of rotten cabbage.

The fog made it easier to see faint orange lines which crisscrossed the street looking like a basket that was unraveling. Every third or fourth one brightened into a bolt of flickering orange lightning.

A faint hum brought his attention to an orange bolt inches away from the corner of his house. Stones and plants from the garden drifted up in the orange lightning. The orange lines must be what moved things. It thickened as he watched, embedding the orange bolt inside the edge of his house. If the lines caused movement that meant–.

The house beneath him shook and lifted, leaving the rest of the neighborhood, the hedge, and the fog all shrinking away. The orange light pulled his house higher and higher until everything on the ground was dollhouse sized. He was flying. A strange exhilaration gripped him.

Around him more and more orange bolts brightened, dragging along objects. The bolts were not straight, some turned and twisted around other bolts.

A grove of trees flew above him raining black dirt caught in another orange bolt. When they sped past, a worm landed on his shoulder. He jerked. The worm squirmed on his shoulder just before it fell. That woke him up. He was in danger, just like the worm.

<u>Bap-Bap-Bap</u>

The trees smacked like machine gun fire into a floating grey castle. The castle must've appeared like the bird lady and the fog. The trees splintered into chips and left cracks in the stone. A man in armor held onto the buttress which shook each time another tree hit. The castle sunk following its orange line down.

The air thickened with debris. The pops and bangs of a hundred such battles assaulted Joshua's ears. He felt a sting on his arm. He slapped it, and his hand came away bloody. He must've been hit by some broken glass.

Something pinged the roof sending a shingle flying. The house shook each time an object battered it. His house had stayed together, which wasn't what should've happened. Houses weren't meant to float and stay together, no matter what kid's movies might show.

He had no idea why, but so far buildings acted like ships on the sea and only when they crashed into something else, did they break. So far, his house hadn't been hit by anything big enough to break it apart.

The sharp tang of ozone and then a blue shimmer mid-air birthed a long wooden tower that pierced the air like a spear that punctured his house. A mortal wound, the house shuddered and pieces of Joshua's life fell away. His dresser, his train set, his clock plummeted. Where were his parents? He pulled out the monitor.

The video cameras he'd placed with such care showed

nothing but splinters and blood. The tower filled the whole floor. "Mom? Dad?" he whispered. His gut twisted like he had eaten that worm and all its brothers.

He wrapped his body around the chimney, cheek pressed against the brick. The feeling of displaced air made him look up. A pyramid, blotted out the sky and rushed toward him.

Adrenalin came online and pulsed through his system. His heart picked up speed.

Maybe if things came out of the blue light, he could use the light as a door to get out of here. He had no idea what was on the other side. It could be even worse. But he'd die for sure if he stayed here.

He focused on the blue light still at the far end of the towers that had pierced his family's home. He let go of the chimney and grabbed the rope attached to it, sliding down the way they did in the movies. Gravity no longer pulled just down. It pulled down at first and then shifted to the right causing him to slip and hit his shoulder on the house. The pain of hitting his shoulder blurred the edges of his vision.

If he didn't move, he'd be crushed.

He pulled hand over hand until he stood on the tower just outside his room. The tower had pierced his bed, obliterated his room.

The last of the tower pulled out of the blue light and the light shrank. The rope in his hand loosened. A brick from the chimney grazed his cheek.

He had one shot to run across the tower and leap into the blue light. If he missed before the light disappeared, he would fall to his death or be crushed.

The grinding of the rest of his house battling and losing against a stone pyramid faded as he focused on the ten paces between him and the end of the tower.

He stepped. His heart thumped a hundred times for each step.

His breath panted out.

On the tenth step, he leapt at the blue light now the size of a paper plate, diving like he would off the high board.

And fell.

2

JOSHUA

Joshua fell out of bed, landing in a tangled mass of blankets on his floor. The wooden floor was nothing like the one in his bedroom before the Merge. Thank God. He wasn't reliving the Merge again. His breaths sounded like terrified gasps. The sweat chilled across his body. He must've forgotten to bank the little stove.

He took a deep shaky breath. The Merge had been almost three hundred years for the world, but only fifteen years ago for him. And yet he woke up every morning with nightmares of the past. That nightmare always left his scars aching.

He untangled the blankets and pulled them tight over the bed. He ran his hand over the top to make sure there were no wrinkles.

He dropped to the floor to start his push-ups. The first set of fifty gave him different pain to focus on. The familiar rhythm eased his panic.

After leaping through the hole between worlds, he'd fallen and landed in a pile of hay in a small human community. The second set of fifty had his arms burning. If the HPA (Human Protection Agency) hadn't rescued him and brought him to New Nadezhda, he'd have been sacrificed. His first run-in with Others hadn't gone well.

Standing, he assumed burpee position and did a set of twenty. The full body exercise always made him think of the HPA Archive. That's where he'd gotten in the habit of exercising. The other orphans had joined him. No one else wanted to be in the HPA, but he'd known even then that being an agent was what he wanted. He could be the one to rescue people in trouble and make a difference. At the end of the second set, he took a deep breath and focused on the present. He was not only an HPA agent, but now he was the head of the organization. And they were in a crisis over a serial killer.

Eighteen bodies had been discovered in five different locations. Five little girls had been drained in a way that didn't fit the usual pattern: no teeth marks on necks, no ripped-out jugulars, no headless bodies, just mummified corpses. The other thirteen had been the girls' guardians and their bodies hadn't been mummified. They'd been torn apart. This new pattern fit none of the identified species' habits. Which meant they had an unknown killer on the loose.

Rose had a lead on the murderer. She needed him to meet her before dawn at a human neighborhood at the western edge. He did his final set of sit-ups and stood. It wouldn't take long to get ready.

His stomach rumbled in warning. He'd grab some food, and head out. He walked to the other side of the room to his tiny kitchen and opened his homemade fridge.

Snowball needed snacks as well. When he lifted the cover on

the box at the bottom of his fridge, a brown, furry, frost covered head poked out.

"Hey Snowball. How you doing?" Joshua stroked the winter bug until Snowball made his fingers too cold. He dug out some pellets and dumped some in Snowball's tray. Snowball squeaked and poked his head into the tray. The fridge was noticeably colder from Snowball's prancing around.

Most would think him crazy taking an old fridge box and getting a family of winter bugs to nest inside to make it cold, but it meant food right here. And because winterbugs looked like hamsters they reminded him of before.

He grabbed something from his section of the fridge and popped it into his mouth. Fig and crust melted in his mouth. Chewing got his brain focused.

This killer wasn't like anything the HPA'd seen. Two full crews had been dismembered, just like the girls' guardians. There weren't many things that could take out a full crew, let alone two. The crews had still had most of their ammo and equipment intact. The attack must've been a surprise or happened so quickly that they hadn't had time to defend themselves.

He closed the fridge and opened the wardrobe just a step away. Inside, his collection of a dozen wooden stakes, two silver daggers, a cold iron rod, and cuffs. The shelf had a bowl of salt, holy water, holly, garlic, anything that might help him protect humans from the Others the Merge had brought together. This world was full of the creatures of myth and legend.

His bow seemed the best weapon. It would allow him to hang back and assess. It should mean less chance of getting ambushed too, since he would be farther away from anything suspicious. The arrows were silver-tipped, coated with a special mixture of his own making that had been blessed by one of the few remaining priests. The mixture would close a wound on a living person but would mean certain death to the undead. One of the arrows would stop a daemon-bound T-rex, and after the damage he'd seen done to the other HPA agents, he knew he'd need both its deadly power and its healing power.

His leather satchel hung on the hook by the door. He never left his room without it. Humans with no protection died quickly in this world.

The door locked behind him with a soft click. A green glow lit the next short hall. Twelve lights represented the status of each path that led from Kraft Tower and through the desolate zone. The mad wizard Kraft was said to live here and Joshua did everything he could to support that rumor. The best way to be safe was to have no one who wanted to be near.

The door opened to stairs going down and led to a circular stone room. Twelve doors like numbers on a clock face, led out in different directions. The green lights cast a soft glow in this room as well.

The roman numeral twelve marked the door he opened. He followed another short hallway and another green light. The dirt path that led away from his tower had its first pit trap under a tree. If he fell into any of these traps, only Rose and Bob would look for him.

The only people he trusted were Bob, his ex-partner, and Rose. Bob because you couldn't almost die countless times and save each other's lives and not learn that trust and Rose because she reminded him of Delilah.

Rose would search for him if he went missing, but she had no idea where he lived.

Around the next corner, he bypassed the tripwire and came out of the desolate zone on the west side.

He ducked between boards on a crooked fence and stepped onto the cobbled street. This area reminded him of movies about Sherlock Holmes and London. Fog hid the details of the mismatched houses and the haphazard way they stood. The fog made it look like this could have been a neighborhood from before.

From the center of town near the river, the fish processing plant whistled for day shift. A hundred townspeople were arriving to gut, scale, and divide fish to feed the town. Without the plant, everyone would starve. He could've been one of those workers, could've had a family, could've had a normal life. But instead, he was head of the Human Protection Agency. He dedicated his life to protecting the humans of this town.

He started at one end of the neighborhood, looking for Rose's sign. He passed house after quiet house. Then on the sidewalk he saw one of her signal coins. Head facing a suburban two story that could have been from his old block pre-merge. White house with black shutters on the windows. Everything seemed peaceful and quiet.

Too quiet.

He picked up the coin, the bottom was stained red. His heart thudded. Something had gone wrong.

He was too late.

3

SERENE

Wee Hours, Luminous twenty-ninth, 299 years post-Merge

The chorus of birds echoing through the rookery walls woke Serene of the Pack. Voices of a community. Some of the Aeros joined in, their more human sounding voices adding a layer to the tribute to the sun that was about to rise.

She stared at the curved ceiling of the oval nest room and then stretched, transforming from her small furry wolf form to her human one.

The feathers in her nest acted as a soft caress. Many of the Aeros had donated feathers, treating her like a fragile nestling instead of a grown woman of another species. They'd ignored her wolf-like appearance and had accepted her. Gratitude warmed her heart. She would figure out a way to repay their kindness for protecting her for over a year.

Her gaze caught on the paper on the ledge. Wren's guards had brought up the wanted posters from the HPA. The human protection agency only cared about humans. In theory anyway.

They never seemed to be involved with anything good for any other species. She didn't have to look at it to remember that the paper said she was number one on their list. She hadn't expected the HPA to help her seek justice for her pack, but being on their most wanted list sparked a slow burn of anger deep in her belly.

She had many distant memories of being with her Pack from years ago, but something had happened a little over a year ago. The last thing she remembered was a strange hissing inside the Pack's den.

A flash of cage bars and a mix of fear, anger, and desolation stabbed her heart. She rubbed away the cold chill that always came from probing that blank space. Despite the discomfort, she needed to start somewhere if she was ever to piece together the memories of what had happened that night. For the first time in over a year, she made herself think back to her last memory before the Rookery. To when she'd been rescued.

She remembered rain on her face, like tears, that cleared the stench of burning plastic. A female feathered face still covered in grime from imprisonment blocked the gray sky. Then the fragile-looking Alesia had picked Serene up and, in a voice full of authority, called out, "Help them all."

But nothing gave her a clue about where she'd been or why the HPA had targeted her.

She needed to go back further. Her heart thundered, bringing flashes of disconnected images. She tightened her eyes. A cage. Bent bars. Her mate's body on the stone floor. Splintered wood. Fire. It was too chaotic to sort out. Her breaths came out as harsh gasps. She had no idea where she and her pack had been taken. All she knew for sure was they were all dead. That space within that housed her Pack's bond was an empty void.

She swallowed hard, still not able to think of her pack

without pain. It remained a raw open wound even after all this time.

A deep breath cleared some of the tension. It had gotten easier to lock away the pain. She'd have to ask Alesia what had happened the night Alesia had rescued her. They never talked about that night. They'd had an unspoken agreement, but Serene was about to break it.

Serene's chest tightened with guilt. She didn't want to lose Alesia, but she had to find out why she was on the HPA's most wanted list. The only way to do so was to ask about that night.

Serene dressed and stepped out to an outer porch with large open windows, the breeze was cool on her bare skin.

Alesia sat cross-legged eyes closed, her wings open wide and her head thrown back in song. Her human-like face tilted back and a jewel dangling at her throat sparkled in the glow from the window.

The last note faded and her friend opened her eyes. Her normally cheery expression was missing, replaced by worry.

"What's wrong?" Serene sat next to her and stroked her head feathers down.

"It happened again." Alesia's voice was a strained whisper.

Serene's stomach dropped and she took Alesia's hand. "Tell me."

For the last month, Alesia had been showing signs that she might be a Seer. She'd forgotten things she'd said, and, most telling, the things she'd said had come true. Since Seers only took over women during times of trouble. The world must be approaching a time of trouble.

"I came to myself on the stairs with everyone looking at me." Alesia shook her head, pressing her lips together, desperation in her eyes, and then she looked away.

Serene knew Alesia's people mattered to her, but the only

person Alesia had ever been worried about letting down was Wren. "Your brother won't hate you."

Alesia's gaze snapped to hers. "Gammy went crazy when the Seer first came. She...."

Neither Alesia nor her brother would talk about what had happened to their grandmother, even a hundred years later, another bad sign.

"You aren't her. You're strong and will find a way to be both a princess and a Seer," Serene said.

Alesia's face grew red. "I am not a princess."

She was the daughter of the Aero King and part of her brother, Prince Wren's, delegation sent to New Nadezhda. Alesia was a princess whether she wanted to be or not.

Serene grinned. "You're my friend. My best friend."

Alesia's eyes widened; a shy, pleased smile played on her lips. But then she froze. Even her breath stopped.

A cold chill crawled up Serene's back. The feeling of old and powerful magic hit her. Could this be the Seer? Seers protected the world, but the right questions had to be asked to get useful answers. A Seer would give a hint, but never volunteer clear answers. There were even whispered rumors about angering a Seer by wasting questions or ignoring their answers.

Alesia blinked and her blue irises became iridescent and bored into Serene. "Purpose will give you power. It is time to leave the nest." The Seer seemed to be waiting. Serene took a breath. The Seer must be referring to her Pack. Finding who murdered them was the only thing that would give her purpose. She needed another hint.

"Lady Seer, I have no memory of that night. Where should I begin?"

Alesia's hand cupped her face and the otherworldly eyes blinked. "It is the head that has the answers you seek."

"What of Alesia? Will she break as her grandmother did?"

The Seer gave her a kind smile. "This vessel is strong when she believes."

Alesia's hand fell away, and the next time she blinked, her eyes returned to their normal blue. She shook her head, seeming dazed.

"It happened again didn't it?" Alesia asked. All the feathers on her back puffed and her hands trembled.

"Yes." Serene hugged her friend. "You need to tell your brother."

"No." Alesia shook her head. "I cannot, it would–"

"I asked the Seer about you."

Alesia gaped. "W-what did she say?"

"You're strong when you believe."

"In what?" Alesia whispered, closing her eyes. A moment later she seemed to shake herself. Alesia cocked her head in a very bird-like fashion. "What will you do now?"

The restlessness grew within Serene. She could sit here forever pampered and broken, or she could go into the world and try to get justice for her Pack. She might die in the process, but wasn't that a better way to live? "I must leave. The Seer agreed."

"Then so it must be." Alesia's feathers drooped and she looked at the ground.

It wasn't like her friend to be so dejected. Alesia's steady soft presence had brought Serene through so much. "What's wrong?"

"Will you still be my friend?" It was said so softly, Serene almost didn't hear her. The male dominated society, let alone being the sister of its leader, had left Alesia mostly friendless. Until Serene.

Serene lifted Alesia's chin and kept her gaze. "You are the sister of my soul." It was true.

"Will you hate me w-when I become a Seer?"

"Never. You'll be yourself most of the time, and when you're not, you'll be trying to save the world."

"Where will you go?"

Serene pursed her lips. She hadn't left the Aero's castle in over a year. Alesia and her kind had kept her safe and protected since that night. The head could be anyone. The humans used that term and so did some of the other species. Maybe if she knew where they'd been, she'd have another clue. "Where were we that night?"

Alesia paled and said nothing.

"The Seer told me I must go to the head to find my answers."

Alesia swallowed. "We were at an HPA research facility outside of New Nadezhda."

Serene had heard the talk of HPA raids and the heightened tensions between the factions. Hundreds of species formed alliances, but the Aeros, Lizardfolk, and humans were the biggest.

The Seer had said, "the head."

"Who's the head of the HPA?" She hadn't cared before who led the humans but The Seer had probably meant the head of the humans.

"Joshua Lighthouse."

Serene shivered and goosebumps rose on her arms. That name was the name they used to scare pups to behave in the Pack. If you were bad, Joshua Lighthouse would get you. She'd had no idea he was a real human or that he was head of the HPA. "Then I must find Joshua Lighthouse."

"The HPA is dangerous," Alesia said.

Worry knotted her gut. Alesia was right, but it made no difference. She tried for a joke. "I've seen their picture of me and there's no way they'd recognize me."

"The HPA has other methods to get information. Bribery and extortion." Alesia wrung her hands and her crest raised.

"I'll be fine." Serene soothed the raised feathers. Alesia had enough to worry about with The Seer. "I must discover who was behind the murder of my pack."

Alesia took Serene's hand in both of hers. "Serene." Her lips pressed together for a moment. "You saved so many from the burning lab."

Serene's heart picked up speed and she searched Alesia's face for a clue about where she might be going with this.

"You saved me from the lab. Thank you."

Serene flushed with embarrassment. She didn't remember a lab, let alone saving anyone. Alesia shouldn't be thanking her. It was Alesia and her people who had sheltered her and helped her heal.

Alesia met her gaze. "Many owe their lives to you. You are not alone."

The idea that she wasn't alone was the kindest thing Alesia could've said.

One last hug and Serene went back into her nest and grabbed the pack made for her wolf form. She stuffed in clothing and a few supplies before switching to her wolf form and slipping on the pack.

She would track down death himself if that's what it took to bring her Pack justice.

4

JOSHUA

<u>Dawn, Luminous twenty-ninth, 299 years post-Merge</u>

Rose's signal coin weighed heavily in Joshua's hand. He leapt up to the front porch of the marked house. The wooden door with chipped green paint looked so normal at first. The cold of the knob seeped through his glove; the door swung open at his touch. Not a good sign. The entry was still and dark, as it should be, but that edge of something amiss hovered near. Candles at the top of the stairs twisted the darkness, blurring the line between real and imagined monsters.

No sounds. No childish laughter. No hush from a parent.

No crunching of bones.

Sweat dripped from his temple, the room hot after the chilled air outside. His leather coat was suffocating, but he couldn't remove it. The leather and the weapons inside were his only protection from what might lurk inside the house. Rose was in here somewhere.

Something scraped above. The sound could be someone

using a chamber pot or could be Rose sorting through evidence or could be bait in a trap.

Adrenaline zinged, making everything sharper. He drew his knife and crept forward, scanning for clues. He watched for more of Rose's coins and evidence of a break in.

The stairs under him creaked and moaned. Pictures of the homeowner's family grimaced at him. The oldest images in titanium frames, from before the Merge, when humans could still extract titanium. Newer frames were clearly elven-carved, and magicked to give the pictures a lifelike quality.

The copper smell of blood and something rotten intensified with each step. At the top of the stairs, pieces of wood crunched underfoot. An open maw replaced where a door must've been.

He hit the wall with a gloved hand, leaving a hole. Dust puffed out. His guilt and anger mingled.

The Human Protection Agency was too late.

He was too late.

He was always too late.

He walked into the remains of the bedroom.

Rose's slender figure bent and snatched something off the floor. Her red ponytail swayed. The protective leather she wore didn't creak.

She stared down at the teddy bear in her hands. Smeared with blood, its ears worn, squashed flat around the neck from too many nights being clutched to ward off monsters.

This time the monsters had won.

"Why do we even bother fighting?" Rose's voice was flat, but her face was pinched, and her eyes blinked too rapidly.

"Because we do save some." He used his best I-know-exactly-how-you-feel voice. He had to believe they made a difference. She was his best agent. If she gave up on the cause, more people would die and he would lose a friend.

Joshua scanned the room, paused at the father's torn leg by

the window, then at the mother's bare feet poking out the top of the toppled wardrobe, the rest of her body hidden inside. Frustration burned his throat. He was meant to save people.

Maybe the parents had been in the room when the monster struck. Maybe they had run in when the girl had screamed. It had made no difference.

He forced his gaze to the mummified girl's body still in her frilly white nightgown at the foot of her bed. Pale, peaceful, exsanguinated. The fancy word for when someone bleeds out. The cuts on her neck matched that idea, but no blood pooled around her body.

His stomach sank, this site was like the others over the last two weeks. Another little girl and her guardians dead. This was no normal Other killer.

Something was off. The HPA's normal sources knew nothing. Even Rose's leads had been too late. They had no leads and no indication it would stop. He needed to do something extreme. Maybe he needed to ask The Book.

Fear and loathing twisted like snakes in his gut. He hadn't opened The Book in years. It was too dangerous. The Book would try to re-awaken the powers he'd fought to contain.

He shivered. The powers he had banished could be set free again. Fear skittered down his back. He'd never been sure how he'd banished them in the first place. There was no one to ask. He was the only one that had been thrown this far forward in time. Besides, who could he trust enough to tell that he was not quite human, that he was like the things they hunted. At best they would force him out of the HPA. At worst, they would try him for crimes and kill him.

Was avoiding that risk worth the life of another girl, another family, another team? That Book might be the only way to catch this killer before it killed again. All normal methods hadn't helped.

"Did you know you bite your lip when you're about to do something stupid?" Rose asked.

He closed his eyes. It was stupid. The Book of Secrets was locked up for a reason. Even so, in his mind, all he could see was yet another dead girl. Adding these three, that made twenty-one total bodies. Five of the twenty-one were little girls. How many would it take before the killing stopped?

He would go to his office and use The Book to find out what was going on. That meant he needed to ditch Rose. His gut twisted with the weight of worry and guilt. He couldn't put her at risk. He'd already lost Delilah and Marvin to his power. He couldn't risk Rose.

When he opened his eyes, Rose still stood next to him, staring at the bear.

"I won't let this killer drain and mummify another innocent girl, or take out another team. No matter what it costs." He held her gaze, hoping to show her how important this was. No matter what happened to him, he needed her to be strong. If he failed, it would be up to her to catch the killer. She nodded.

Rose dropped the bear on the canopy bed. "You are going to talk to that book. You remember how dangerous that is?"

Rose picked the bear back up and tucked it in the little girl's arms.

"There are some missions I need to handle myself." He didn't miss the flash of hurt in her face.

"Let me come with you." Rose stepped next to him, too warm, too near, and squeezed his arm. "You know I'll always have your back."

A spiny ball of regret clogged his throat. Rose was good people. The best he'd ever met. Her dark eyes forgave him everything, and she would always be there for him, but he could not offer what she wanted. Only friendship. Although his powers had been dormant, if they broke loose he didn't want her to die.

He needed to keep his distance. Even his big brotherly feelings might make her vulnerable.

He squeezed her fingers and removed them from his arm. "I need you here. You have a knack for understanding how the things that crawl in the dark think. Please."

She looked away and swallowed, but nodded. Her arms wrapped around her stomach.

He backed toward the door. He knew this might be good bye and he didn't want her to think that he didn't trust her. "It's not safe for you to be with me right now. Otherwise you would be the one I'd want to cover me."

She nodded; her face unreadable. "I'll bring the clean-up crew here."

He turned to leave.

"Be careful," Rose said.

The urge to have her guard his back grabbed him. He fought it down. It was too dangerous. He waved and left before he could give in.

He headed east toward downtown. The HPA tower cut through the still dark sky like the talon of a predatory bird cut through flesh. The double doors gaped open leading into the bowels of the HPA building.

Joshua walked through the front doors of the office. The lights flickered and his footsteps echoed across the empty lobby.

Ten of his fifteen years in this town he'd been walking these halls. It'd meant something to him to join the agency that had rescued him. Without the HPA he never would've survived his transition to this world.

Joshua approached the K2300 Detector that blocked the way to the main hall. A door would open on one side, and the inner chamber had technology and magic which detected if you were human. If you were human, the other door on the far side would open and allow access to the rest of the HPA.

Two new guards, a burly blond cop and his skinny buddy didn't stand as Joshua approached the gray box. They barely looked up.

The door slid open. Joshua stepped into the detector and placed both hands on the sensor. The light turned blue. When the book had released his powers, would he still be able to pass the detector? Would he still be human and not an Other?

The light turned green. A bell chimed. The door slid open.

Joshua strode towards the elevators. Furs, skulls and bloody weapons decorated the west wall of the long hallway. Under each item, stained placards explained their history.

The white fur was from a Yeti who'd been terrorizing the humans on the North at the edge by the mountains. Twitching green fingers held down with wire were from the great zombie escape from Malani Necropolis, the Central Graveyard, a couple years ago. To the left hung a cracked Axe dated from when the HPA had helped the Crylon's repel invaders from a rival town. That had been long before his time at the HPA.

On the opposite side of the hallway, the organization's motto sprawled along the wall in large gold letters: 'To protect humans from all manner of incursions.' Cracked and tarnished, the gold letters collected cobwebs.

Were things different now? Did the letters reflect the core of the organization? After he caught the serial killer, he'd come back here and clean the Motto. He'd do what he could to bring the HPA back to what it had once been.

Joshua waited for the elevator, legs braced apart, hands in pockets. His reflection in the elevator door showed the same red hair, same blue eyes and the same angry scowl which had greeted him every other day.

When he stepped inside, he pressed the button for the tenth floor. The mechanism rattled and shook. He'd have to find someone to service the elevator as well. Having something mechanical that worked, was a great honor. Even if no one but the HPA's people saw it.

The elevator door opened on his floor. Quiet and darkness spilled across the reception area. He turned right, moving past the empty offices. The majority of the agents would be home at this time of the morning, catching a few hours of sleep before starting again. He paused at the line of windows, staring out over the city.

Below, the city sparkled, the torches and electric lights indistinguishable from this height. Big Ben's face glowed to the east, one of the few buildings with electric power, but Ben was still stuck at 11:35.

With the sun just rising, and the height of the window, he could almost imagine that the city below him was a normal human pre-merge city. A place where there were just humans, and little girls were not drained of blood, and magic was only an illusion at kids' parties.

Something both feathery and scaley hit the window and landed, stunned, on the small ledge outside. Razor teeth gnashed, scales glittered, and feathers puffed. It curled for a moment, legs sprawled, tongue out, before it stood, and hissed at Joshua. It dove off into the darkness.

But that was wishful thinking, the city below was not pre-merge. From this height he couldn't make out the different districts, but they existed. Shifterville, Malani Necropolis, Rainbow borough, the five human sections and numerous other areas. Somewhere the killer was stalking its next victim. He had to make it stop. He ran a hand through his hair, he was delaying. If he was going to ask the book, he needed to ask his question and stop the serial killer.

He followed the hallway to the corner. The door to his office opened with his presence. He stepped into the office and the lock clicked behind him.

This was dangerous. Even opening the safe was dangerous. He pulled out his chair, checking the one place big enough for someone to hide. Stakes, organized from thin to thick, lined the back wall behind his empty desk. A bowl of fine salt stood in each corner. The old army cot leaned against the cabinet. Nothing looked out of place.

He wiped his palms on his pants and took a deep breath to steady his nerves. The book had almost killed him once.

He pressed six inches to the left of the doorframe. The embedded safe shimmered into view. He turned the knob to ninety and watched the clock hands for a full minute. Anything less than sixty and he would trigger the trap.

Once he realized the book was intelligent and evil and contained any number of deadly spells, he'd locked it up tight. Adding in layer after layer of protection so that no one else could open the safe without deadly consequences.

He switched the dial to thirty-two and waited two minutes.

No one knew he worked this hard as penance.

Penance for surviving the Merge when his family had not. Penance for becoming a freak with powers. Penance for the two innocent lives lost because of his powers.

He switched the dial then to sixty-five. Each turn and pause disabled more traps.

He clicked the handle and eased the safe door a tiny bit open to let the poison dissipate. The last trap cleared. He waited another thirty seconds and then swung the door wide. The faint taint of rotten egg held for a moment before dissipating into the room.

The safe held only three items. He pulled out the picture of three young boys. A narrow blond, Alex, stood at ease in the background, just behind and to the left of a redhead, a youthful Joshua. His grand-mum used to call him stocky. Even then, he had been bigger, thicker, different from the other boys.

A dark-haired boy, Marvin, to Joshua's right looked innocent with chubby cheeks and a wide smile, but he held two fingers behind Joshua's head.

The young version of himself slouched unsmiling in the middle. Haunted was the word that came to mind. Perhaps he still was. Of the three, only Marvin didn't have circles under his eyes. Only he'd seemed to be unconcerned about life.

Marvin had died soon after the photo was taken. He'd been the second person Joshua's powers had killed. The old pain flared, sending his heart crashing. It'd been his fault. He should've known better after Delilah. If only he'd realized that his powers were evil sooner, one of his best friends would still be alive.

Under the picture was the piece of glass he'd made into a necklace in remembrance of Marvin. The only surviving piece of a mirror that had once housed the Book of Secrets. He set it aside.

He lifted the Book of Secrets and laid it on his desk. Soft brown leather with twisted gold chains wrapped around the book interconnecting into a skull. He fished a silver chain with a key from under his collar.

He'd become guardian of the book that awful night ten years ago when he'd killed his friend. Red flickered from deep within the eye sockets and a black space between the fangs opened. Almost as if the book was asking to be fed.

At first, he'd fed it all the information he could find, thinking that maybe in this world of magic, the book could help him get his dead friend back. But the book never gave him the answer he sought. Instead, the book had turned on him, creating the obsession with an Other. Then it had tried to use his obsession to enslave him.

It'd been Rose, not his partner who'd found him unconscious in an alley in a part of town that was dangerous for humans. He didn't remember walking to the alley, but knowing the book, it must've planted that impulse. He must've walked like a sleep-walker until he passed out. He was lucky to be alive.

Once he opened the lock, the book would be free and would be able to undo his years of work chaining its powers. The book would be able to influence anyone who touched it. That was why he'd get the information he needed and then lock the book up again. The risk to himself was worth the people he might save. If he didn't survive or lost his place in the human world, so be it.

The key slid between the teeth and the lock snicked open, revealing the picture of a woman he had yet to meet in person. The long, dark hair and deep green eyes stared back at him. He'd forgotten how beautiful she was.

He ran his finger along the edge of the paper. When he'd realized the book had created his obsession for this woman, he'd looked closer and found the psychic hook into his powers the book had meant to control him with. That was the day he'd locked the book up for good. Or at least he'd thought so then.

Below the image was the question he'd written all those years ago. The script hadn't faded with time nor had the book's response. In his handwriting it said, "How do I protect my friends from dying because of my powers?"

The book's answer was still below in block print. "Find *the one* and protect her when no one else will. When the time comes, you must trust her to another."

He still had no idea what the book's response meant, but he needed to pen a new question.

On the last page was a space for a question. The killings were too important to leave to chance. With the pen from his drawer, he started writing, "Where and when will I find..."

The space below swirled with letters and words, a magic 8-

ball window. The book tried to answer, but the question wasn't complete.

He finished the question. "...the next serial killer kill site."

The book's response appeared as if being written by an unseen hand. An address appeared and then, at the bottom of the page, the book wrote, "Tonight. But beware, things are not as they seem."

The book slammed shut.

Joshua jerked back. The book hadn't ever moved on its own before. The book was stronger than it'd been.

As he locked the book, one of the teeth moved and gouged his finger. Blood welled and dripped into the mouth of the lock. A sharp pain behind his eyes caused tears to well and his breath to hiss out. The room dimmed.

He fought the feeling. The book had to be locked lest it control him. He forced the lock shut and leaned back. Was he too late?

A feeling of pins and needles, like when his leg fell asleep, filled his head. Something, not quite one of his five senses tingled.

The powers he had shuttered broke free.

5

SERENE

<u>Mid-morning, Luminous twenty-ninth, 299 years post-Merge</u>

Serene lifted her nose into the rancid breeze kicked up by the fish factory. Everything smelled so different now. Even the fish smell couldn't mask the strange tang of fear she'd never noticed in the air before.

She walked along the rooftop in her furry form, picking her way over tiles heading toward downtown. There were some places she might go for information that may not have been tainted against her. Being on the HPA list made everything more difficult. No one on the street would recognize her as the woman on the HPA wanted poster, but as soon as she started asking questions, she'd be at risk. Even good people had to give into bullies like the HPA sometimes. And then there were the desperate people who would turn her in for any advantage they could get. She needed to be very careful who she talked to.

Her son would help her. Her heart warmed. Her son had

come to visit her in one of his disguises while she was at the Aeros. Unfortunately, he hadn't been able to come very often.

Alesia had never asked and Serene had never told her that Daniel was her son. No one expected a grown son of a pack leader to visit his mom. The politics and magical bonds that connected a pack made that almost impossible. He had only been able to visit because he was packless, but that made him vulnerable. The world would consider him defective. Worry tugged at her. If he was caught helping someone wanted by the HPA, he would be punished harshly, perhaps even killed because they'd assume he was mad.

The Silver Folk had been her pack's allies. They had a lot in common and had even defended each other's dens.

A flash of a pale face, silver hair unrecognizable beneath the grime came to her. Perhaps there were some who might cooperate because of more than old pack ties. But would they have what she needed? The Silver Folk generally didn't have much to do with humans. And when they did, they tended to be jokesters. It seemed unlikely they would have connections to Joshua Lighthouse.

Maybe she should've asked Wren for help before she'd gone. They had never really talked. Not really, just the superficial chit-chat of people who have nothing in common. He seemed to put up with Serene because it made Alesia happy. But she got the impression that he wouldn't approve of her tracking down a faction leader, even Joshua. She'd been right not asking him for help.

The next roof had red tiles that remind her of Lizardfolk. She'd gotten to know Walter from the Lizardfolk. He'd visited the Aeros because he and Wren were friends. Or at least friendly. Walter was a savvy businessman so she would need something to trade with him before he'd help. She had little he would want.

A small tower poked up from the middle of the next house. She shimmied up the tower and surveyed the area. She was at the edge of West district.

It was a crossroads of sorts with shops that catered across species. The different sections of Shifterville surrounded one side and the outskirts of downtown on the other. Joe's was in the crossroads.

Maybe she should consider seeing Joe first. Joe was the center of the Hive, a group of people psychically connected. The hive was mostly neutral, but did have spies everywhere. The hive would have great information. The only issue was that they were always looking for new members to join their society. The center could create their psychic bond with any living creature. There was a chance that Joe would want to conscript her into the Hive. She shuddered. Their bond was a lot like the Pack bond and being forced into a bond once was bad enough. It'd taken years before she'd adjusted the first time and she'd almost died in the transition. Her mate would never have tried if the Pack hadn't been so desperate.

She'd never survive the process again. Hopefully, she was too damaged from her Packs' deaths to fall into that trap. Or maybe the rumor that Joe only took the willing was true.

Of all the options, Joe's seemed both the best and the most dangerous for learning about Joshua Lighthouse. Joe had spies everywhere and almost instant access to information. But she'd have to take her chances that he wouldn't insist on conscripting her into his hive.

Joe's was across the river that cut New Nadezhda in half. A few bridges crossed the river and they were mostly safe. The nearest bridge was next to a market. She'd need to talk to people to get information, so she might as well switch to human now. The picture on the wanted poster had been a made-up hybrid version that looked nothing like her human form, so she should still be safe. She skipped across a few more rooftops, and dropped down between buildings.

The alley didn't smell quite right. She hesitated, more alone than she'd ever been before. The pack had formed a unit. Each member took a position. One of the Betas would take point. Another would take rear guard. Members pooled their knowledge and shared their duties at the bond level. She'd been with them when they'd gone through hostile territory, so she had a vague idea what to do. But being a single member of the pack meant she didn't know all the dangerous scents. Still, huddling here afraid wasn't going to get her answers. There was no pack to come to her rescue.

She didn't hear anything alarming. There were the normal day sounds, the wind, a small animal rummaging for food. But where were the sounds of people? At the very least, the noises of the market should carry to this alley. Maybe it was a trick of the land that hid the noises from her. She retracted her fur and dressed in a tunic and leggings from her pack.

There was a constant haze over this part of town that diminished visibility. She padded across the stone walk and up the crest of a hill on her way to the bridge. Shuttered businesses and homes lined the square.

The last time she'd been here, vendors with umbrellas hawked wares. Children had raced between stalls. The closed windows and doors and empty street made her shiver. Perhaps it was the time of day. *Liar.*

She walked as silently as she could, wondering if it was better to walk in the middle of the road so she'd have reaction time if someone jumped her or whether it would be better to hug the edge and have some cover. Perhaps her furry form would've been better. But she'd wanted the ability to communicate in the common language of the city.

If only her mate was here. He'd know what to do to keep her safe and make her feel better.

She took a deep breath. The mental connection between the pack members made strong emotions contagious. Pups learned early how to control and focus their emotions, but her not being born to the pack had made such things harder on all of them.

A scrape sounded behind her. She jumped, but clamped her mouth shut to keep from squeaking. She couldn't sense anything so she kept walking.

A row of wooden crates blocked the road. Hundreds of spears, some with dark red tips, faced the river. As if they were trying to keep something out.

There was space against the building for her to get around the line. Once she did, there was another wall. Shattered boxes and broken spears lay scattered across the ground. The wall must've been stacked four crates tall before being demolished. Whatever had demolished the wall had to have been big and very strong.

She climbed over the next barrier. The bridge should be ahead, but the path was blocked by a mound. Had there been a mound before? She sniffed the air and that odd twist of earth and musk she hadn't been able to identify was back.

She slowed her steps. The breeze ruffled her hair and the grass of the mound, but nothing else moved. Or did it? Had the middle of the mound moved? She looked at the mound more carefully. A slight tremor in the middle could be a shallow breath. The green grass could be fur. The shaggy mound couldn't be an animal. Could it? It was too big. Big animals didn't end up in the middle of the city. She slowed even further, looking for patterns in the hill. The dip at the far end could be eyes and that strip that protruded just a bit taller than the rest of the mound could be its tail over its nose. Like a giant, green fox. She stopped.

The mound blocked access to the wooden bridge spanning the river.

The next bridge that was shifter friendly was half a day up the river. Of course, It'd been friendly a year ago, it might not be any longer. She needed to cross the bridge.

She swallowed back her apprehension and took another step toward the mound. The hill rippled, like an animal stretching and yawning, and big, red eyes opened and focused on her.

Maybe it was friendly. The thing lifted its head and gave a rage filled moan. She flinched back. Definitely not friendly.

She ran back toward the barriers. If she could get behind them, the long spears might stop it.

Thump, its tail whacked the ground blocking her escape. It yowled and glared at her. Fear had her scrambling sideways and heading along the building wall. The white stone wall towered above her, a smooth long line. There was no way she could climb it. The path narrowed with each step. The river gully pushed closer to the wall.

The bank going down to the river was rocky and steep at this part. A large branch that had become trapped between boulders and broken trees on each side of the river formed a makeshift bridge that was pounded by the churning water. She wasn't a good enough swimmer to cross the seething river. If she fell in the icy water would be deadly.

She needed a way out. She looked from the water toward the stone wall that was the backside of the shops she'd seen earlier. A drain hung down from the roof at the building's corner. Her heart gave an extra thump. If she could get to the roof, she might be able to get away.

The earth shook. She glanced back; six huge hairy legs supported an even bigger body with broken spear shafts poking from red seeping wounds. This giant foxlike creature must be the reason for the desolate marketplace.

She leapt and shimmied up the gutter.

She ignored her heavy arms and legs and kept moving. Lift pull, lift pull. Any moment she expected to be ripped off the pipe and popped into the beast's mouth as a mid-afternoon snack.

She was almost to the top when the building shook. The gutter squealed and jerked. This was bad.

She couldn't make the roof, but maybe if she hit the beast hard enough, she could stun the creature and make a run for the bridge. She wrapped her arms around the gutter and braced her feet against the wall. She pushed. Nothing. Then she kicked. The first kick loosened the gutter, the next kick popped it off the wall. It teetered and then swung back to the wall. She put every-thing she had into the third kick, launching herself backward toward the beast.

She held on tight and braced for impact as the gutter popped off the wall above. Her shoulder thudded into the crea-ture. Hot sticky breath steamed around her, but instead of teeth clamping down on her, she and the creature slipped and fell backward over the ledge and into the river.

Water rushed around her. She clung to the gutter, but opened her eyes. Water swirled around her. The monster doggie paddled toward her, but the current won, dragging the creature away.

The bottom of the gutter caught on the makeshift bridge and the force of the water surged up around her, cutting off her air. She reached up and grabbed higher on the gutter. Her lungs burned, but she kept inching her way up until she finally emerged.

She sucked in air and kept moving. The gutter was liable to break free and send her back into the water. She climbed until she reached the slippery rocks and then dry ones, pulling herself forward until she could feel grass under her fingers. And then she put her head down, panting, and shivering. That had been close. She was lucky to be alive.

A noise brought her head up. A line of Human and Other men held spears and stared at her. Was the monster behind her? She glanced behind, but the cliff was clear of the monster. One guard shouted something. Water sloshed in her ears, so she couldn't make out exactly what he'd said, but the angry tone told her it was time to run for it.

She switched forms and wiggled out of her clothing. Another of the men shouted and lifted his spear and the other men followed suit. She slipped under some brush and raced along a narrow, overgrown pathway along the river. She heard no sounds of pursuit. Her wolf form made her much faster and nimbler, making it easier to lose them.

The narrow trail opened up to a row of small houses. Wash hung on a clothesline strung between one of the houses and a tree. People in this world worked so hard for their possessions but, she needed to have clothing for what she wanted to do. She changed form and snagged a shirt and pants and held them up. Close enough. She'd have to come back later and pay them back for borrowing their clothing.

A few minutes of fast walking brought her to Joe's neighborhood. The buildings around Joe's subtly leaned away. The communication of the Hive fluttered just outside her senses. She knew it was there, but couldn't make out what they said.

She sniffed the air, but still wasn't able to identify all of its scents. It'd been a long time since she'd been here, but it looked the same. A silver box with large windows winked in the sun. A sidewalk led to the front door. On either side of the walkway clusters of plants and boxes littered the property. Her mate had used such boxes for defense of their den. The sidewalk was probably trapped and would open as another layer of defense.

She hopped across the sidewalk to Joe's. Knowing they

watched, she kept her pace casual giving them plenty of time to see she wasn't a threat.

When she opened the door, the bell jangled. The red topped booths along the windows were empty.

A brown-haired man sat behind the counter. Even sitting, he towered over her. He was almost as wide as he was tall. Joe looked up and nodded. The tension she hadn't known she'd felt, melted from her shoulders. Maybe she could get information about Joshua Lighthouse's location.

She pulled out one of the yellow vinyl seats lining the counter and sat across from Joe. "I used to come here years ago with my pack."

"You are pack?" He rolled silverware, wrapping the white towel around silver eating utensils. He didn't sniff, but seemed to be using a different sense to look at her. Almost as if he could read her thoughts.

She nodded. She was still Pack even if she was packless.

"You don't feel like Pack." He said the words slowly and frowned.

Maybe this wasn't such a good idea. Maybe he was thinking about converting her to hive, which would kill her. "Is that a problem?"

He kept looking at her with puzzlement clouding his face. Perhaps he was trying to break down her defenses. She didn't feel Joe in her head, only the hum of hive communication which didn't pause. The urge to flee raised the hairs on her back, but this was the best place to get the information she needed. She had to stay.

The silence stretched on. He might be waiting for her or talking to the hive. She'd just have to break the silence with her questions.

"I–"

The door behind her burst open. She jumped and squared off against one of the guards from the bridge. He dropped her clothing and backpack on the counter and stepped back. She glanced at Joe.

"You're still wet from the river."

She shivered. The guard must be part of the hive. He'd passed along the information that she'd been in the river without speaking. "Yes."

"Go change, Felix can return the clothing you borrowed."

She preferred being in her own clothing, but for a moment she wondered if bringing her clothes had been a trick. But what could Joe gain from her wearing her own clothing? She grabbed the clothes and fled to the bathroom.

The room was small with a mirror and lock on the door. The hive communication was muted here which made her feel safe. She changed quickly.

When she left the bathroom, the emergency exit sign beckoned. She could slip out the back door and probably get away, but she'd have to get information somewhere else and Joe had just proven that he had people in many places.

She headed back out.

Joe grinned at her. A warm fatherly smile she hadn't seen since she'd had to leave her own father.

The soldier bowed and took the clothing she offered.

"Besides vanquishing monsters, what was your plan today?"

Serene straightened her shoulders. "I need to find Joshua Lighthouse."

"Indeed."

Should she disclose more? "A seer said he can help me answer the question of who murdered my pack."

His eyebrows raised and then he nodded. "He comes in here sometimes."

Serene stopped breathing for just a moment. "What's he like?" Could Joe tell if he was a murderer? Did that type of evil leave a mark? It was odd that a man renowned for hating non-humans came to Joe's.

Joe shrugged. "Human. Lonely."

She waited for more, but he returned to rolling silverware. Lonely wasn't what she'd expected him to say about Joshua Lighthouse. Not that she thought he'd have friends. It was more that she hadn't expected him to care about not having any. She'd expected him to be so wrapped up in hate that he needed no one.

"Do you know how I might talk to him?" She asked hoping Joe could introduce them.

"There is a Gala tonight. He may go."

"A Gala?"

"A cross species affair where everyone has amnesty. You could mix and mingle and have a chance to see him before you do anything drastic." His voice was low and even, but the last part still struck her as odd.

"What drastic thing might I do?"

"Throw him in the river."

It took her a beat to realize Joe was joking. "All right. Fine. I'll talk to him before I push him into the river."

"You're getting quite the reputation for monster slaying." He caught her gaze. "And rescuing people." Had she rescued hive that night?

The hairs rose on her back. He seemed to imply he had knowledge of that night. "What do you know?" Her voice came out hoarse and strangled.

"You remember nothing." It was a statement more than a question. He watched her face closely.

She shook her head and then held her breath wondering what, if anything, he would tell her. Dread and worry mixed with hope, leaving her feeling confused about what she wanted him to say.

"If you don't remember, I can't tell you." His voice was gentle.

She rubbed at the ache in her heart. "Why not?"

He pursed his lips. "You are not ready. You will remember when you are ready."

He was probably right. She must not be ready. The parts she could remember were horrific enough. Even if she didn't remember, she still needed to find Joshua Lighthouse and get justice for her pack. "How would I get in at the Gala?"

"You need an invitation."

"Is that something you have access to?" Maybe one of the Hive could get her in.

He shook his head. "You will have to find one on your own."

"There must be another way."

Joe shrugged. "You could wait here until he comes back. He's in about once a month."

"You have no idea where he lives?"

He shook his head. "No. You could go to the HPA office."

There was no way she could go into the HPA office. They only allowed humans in. And besides, she was on their most wanted list. If Joe didn't know where Joshua Lighthouse lived, then she either waited here or tried for the Gala. There were few who might have the means to get her an invite, but she didn't want faction leaders like Wren or Walter to get into trouble if Joshua were to disappear. Perhaps her son would be able to get an invitation to the Gala without the fuss. But could he get her one without endangering himself?

"We don't take the unwilling into the hive. If you ever decide you want to join, there would be a place for you here."

She started, but tried to hide it. The last thing she'd expected was an offer from Joe. Perhaps the hive bond was as misunderstood as the pack bond was. Perhaps it was true that they valued a being for who they had been before joining the hive. Maybe she'd be able to keep her relationship with her son if she joined them. Perhaps when everything was done, she'd consider his offer. "Thank you."

But first, she had to get an invitation to the Gala.

6

JOSHUA

Joshua walked down the road in the brisk air. The book was back in the safe and the tingly feeling had passed, but had left him jumpy. Everything had an extra layer of feeling he didn't understand. The house that the book had indicated would be the site of the next killing was through two wards and on the other side of town. He'd have to hurry to make it to the house by dusk.

The first ward he needed to cross was where the rich people lived. With the tension between the factions, he'd only be able to get in if a resident invited him. He could send a request to Elder Martin, who would usually allow him through. But Elder Martin was busy with his committees and with the Gala coming up, he'd probably not be available.

If Joshua made it through the first ward, there was a mixed-species ward next. No one but residents were allowed in there. He could use his HPA credentials to get into that ward, but the more tense the factions, the longer it would take to gain entrance. That would require more time than he had to get to the house and prevent another child from dying.

He could take the ditches. The previous generations had built ditches in the lower elevation wards to handle flooding. In the dry season, they became a no-man's land between wards. Even with the dangers that lurked there, it would be faster than begging admittance at each ward.

The closest system entrance was between two buildings in the next block. He stepped into a dank corridor that served as the ditch entrance and twisted down into the shadowy gloom between the buildings. Along the walls witch's marks had been carved on the building's stone backs. He shivered. The people that lived near here tried to keep the evil spirits they believed lived in the ditch contained with such marks. He ran his hand along the scarred surface of the wall. The sheer number of marks showed how scared the residents were.

At the bottom, the ditch extended two directions, he walked up the slight hill west towards his destination. He walked as quickly as he could. The light faded and the shadows length-ened as he progressed, making the piles of refuse to the side seem bigger. The sharp cry of a night hunter waking up, caused him to hurry his steps. If he could reach the edge of the human neighborhood before nightfall, he'd probably avoid encoun-tering whatever was living in the ditch.

He strained to hear where the creature might live. A rustling to his left had him turning. A pair of Death Kitties, a weird combination of bat and porcupine, rummaged through the debris. They turned and looked at him with spines extended. They weren't big enough to be the monster in the ditch that everyone was worried about. They were probably its food. Them and humans who wandered through after dark.

A hiccupping chuckle and trilling singing started faintly, but then picked up volume as he went on. It reminded him of the pond at night when the frogs, bugs, and night birds sang. He could almost see the turn he had to take to exit the ditch at the closest point to the ward he needed to be in.

An off key note sounded behind him and silence descended. He glanced back, but saw nothing. His footfalls echoed loudly. A sharp crack and groan sounded closer behind him. The feeling of something hungry stalking him set his heart racing. He bolted, running as fast as he could to the exit. When he reached it, he turned and sprinted up the access tunnel.

He'd gotten lucky, crossing into the human neighborhood as the sun sank. He waited at the top, but whatever had been following him, didn't follow him out of the ditch.

A few more moments brought him to a quiet circle. A large moss covered oak towered in the center of the circle. The center trunk was split into two branches, each big enough it would take two people to wrap their arms all the way around.

The house he was looking for had candles in the windows, which hid rather than revealed the details of the room into which he peered. A childish figure rushed past the upstairs window, leaving him the impression she was hugging a bear. A bear that wouldn't protect her. He imagined her family must be tucking her into bed. Maybe reading her a story. Unless he could stop the killer, this would be her last night. Her last story.

He fought down the urge to go and knock on the door. He'd learned that the direct approach never went well. Especially in this case, where the only way to identify the killer would be to catch him or her just before the act. If the monster knew Joshua was here, it would hunt elsewhere. He couldn't go back to the Book for more answers because the next time the book might gain control of him as it had before. He'd been lucky to escape its dominance the last time.

That left him watching the front door, which was the most

vulnerable to attack. The massive oak tree would work as a place to hide. He could easily climb up and use the large branches as concealment.

He found a roost partway up the tree where the branches offered concealment. He settled on the branch, leaning forward so he could still see the walkway.

His power twanged his senses, making him uneasy. He couldn't figure out how to put them away. The extra sense kept sending him signals and distracting him. Snippets of thoughts and feelings bombarded him from inside the houses. With the distraction and scattered focus, he'd never be able to do his job against a killer that had already taken out two teams. Maybe he'd have to put his powers to use. No one he had feelings for was near. Maybe it would be safe to use his powers.

He could send his senses out to gather information, and could even focus on one area almost like a trap. If he did this, he'd have to time the use of his powers so that the fatigue that came after wouldn't prevent him from taking on the killer. He'd have to wait until just before the killer came.

The night crept closer. And silence descended. Nothing broke the deep silence that coated the dimly lit area. No footsteps. No animal sounds. Fear had emptied the street. Both the human and non-human had fled. The book was right, something stalked this place.

Waiting. He hated waiting almost as much as he hated his powers. So he played tricks with his eyes. He could blur the odd collection of houses across the street. Blur the space pod, blur the plantation house, blur the grass hut that huddled by the target's white two-story. A two-story house that looked like the one he'd grown up in. He'd been a kid before the Merge, riding his bike around the block, swimming out to Carvers Rock. But the Merge had catapulted many things through time.

Including him.

The street lights flickered on, looking like ghosts solidifying out of the misty air. It was time.

With his powers he could form what he called a Soul Wisp which were little bits of his essence he could detach and use as spies. Joshua mentally pulled a chunk from his essence, like shaping a ball out of mud, and formed a spirit foot soldier. Ghosts that couldn't affect matter. Sweat trickled down Joshua's face. He gritted his teeth. The mud clumped and stuck. His mental muscles ached from the effort. Joshua's eyesight faded with each clump of mud, until the target's two-story was muted to gray-scale. Six Soul Wisps were all he could manage.

Through his Soul Wisps' eyes he could see six tiny replicas of himself with red hair, dark eyes, and dark skin. The seams of their cloak bulged at their shoulders just like his did. Scars littered the exposed skin of their faces, necks, and arms as they did his. The scars were his trophies from surviving the Merge.

He sent each invisible Soul Wisp on its assignment. One circled the house, like a hound sniffing out a fox. One zipped through a wall to the girl snuggled in bed. Another checked the father sleeping on the couch. One checked the mother on a chair by the father's side, one bounced off a warded door in the attic while checking the house for signs of evil.

The house was clear. He merged the Soul Wisps. They flattened and formed a thin layer around the target's house. He tuned the area, connecting it directly to his nervous system – his skin tingled, his heart stuttered as it connected. The feeling should even out in a moment and then he'd be able to sense anyone that stepped in the area he covered.

A hooded man eased down the lane below him. Joshua tensed. The man's essence, though not human, had none of the prickly taint that came with torturing a family and sucking them dry.

The skulker crouched in a shadow near the house Joshua

guarded and ran a sleeve past his nose. His hood slipped, revealing light colored, spiky hair. His chubby cheeks gave him that boy-not-quite-a-man look. A look linked with a flood of testosterone that made so many so stupid. What was he doing here?

It didn't matter. Joshua's senses said this was not the monster. Just some innocent teen who could be caught in the crossfire. The boy needed to leave before he became another victim. Joshua couldn't chance warning him, so he would just have to wait and see what he did.

A few minutes later, footsteps echoed from beyond the grass hut. Joshua tensed and leaned forward to see. A lean man in a top hat and suit strolled down the lane. A gentleman, his cane twirled and tapped like he was performing on stage

The man crossed into Joshua's sensory zone and foul bitterness seeped through his link, making it hard to breathe. There was nothing visibly evil about the walker. If not for Joshua's powers, Joshua would've mistaken him for a normal human.

This was the killer.

A thrill coursed through him, making everything sharper. The kid was still there huddled by the porch. Just because the gentleman with the cane was evil didn't mean he was the killer Joshua sought. Joshua had to make sure.

He eased an arrow from his quiver. His special arrow since he was not quite sure what this creature was.

The gentleman cocked his head at the boy hiding in the shadows. The smile that spread across his face had nothing to do with happiness, nothing to do with kindness, and everything to do with a predator licking its chops before it pounced.

"What do we have here?" The man whipped a blade out of his cane.

Joshua hadn't expected a blade. He hesitated. A simple blade wasn't part of the MO of the serial killer. This could still be a different evil. Not the serial killer he sought, but another killer. If he attacked now with no confirmation, the real serial killer could escape and choose a different victim. He couldn't open the book again, so he'd be back to no leads. If he didn't act this boy could die at this killer's hands. One life against the rest of the lives the serial killer might take. Nausea rose to the back of his throat at the thought of sacrificing this boy. But He had to wait.

The teen scrambled back.

"I'll come back for you once I'm done with the girl." The killer stabbed the boy through the meat of his shoulder, pinning him to the stoop.

Joshua winced. Damn. But at least the boy was still alive. Joshua'd get him medical treatment. The monster had confessed his intent, it was time to act.

The sweat on Joshua's hands made the bowstring slick, but he shot the arrow in one smooth motion, and then readied the next.

The arrow struck the man's shoulder instead of his heart. The serial killer jerked and then shrieked, sending Joshua's heart racing for cover. That was unexpected. It reminded him of a banshee shriek. On instinct, he ducked behind the main trunk.

A swath of flame shot out of the killer's mouth and struck, scorching the tree and burning back the mist. Joshua struggled for breath. What the hell was that? How had a creature based on a human spewed fire?

He leaned out from behind the tree and shot. The second arrow thwanged and embedded in the killer's heart. The killer fell to the ground twitching.

Joshua caught his breath ready to jump down, but the sense of wrong didn't clear. Something else was out there. He hesitated, fighting down the urge to run and help the boy. Everything in him said he needed to wait.

He opened his senses, trying to find what held him back

The moments ticked by with no change to his sense of wrong. Dread roosted in his gut and dug in long talons of fear. The hairs, starting at the small of Joshua's back, stood like dominoes toppling in reverse. They craned to locate the evil.

The teen sobbed softly which twisted a knife in Joshua's heart. He had to help. He slid down the trunk and approached the fallen killer. Its smoldering remains bubbled and popped. The smell of burning meat bacon drifted up from the body.

The teen pulled ineffectually at the sword in his shoulder, spreading the blood around his white T-shirt.

The night remained quiet. Unnaturally so. There was something else hidden. Did the killer have an accomplice? Serial killers tended to be loners by nature but it wasn't unheard of for them to work in pairs.

Joshua toed the dead body, his back to the boy. He broke out a Soul Wisp and sent it to look around. There must be some other being responsible for the twang on his senses. But the only other being in the area was the teen. Joshua turned toward the boy.

"Hold still." Joshua knelt and pulled the sword from his shoulder with a wet pop. "Why are you here?"

"Ow. Margaret and her family need me." The boy's voice shook.

Joshua nodded and applied pressure. The wound didn't bleed as much as it should. Odd. Maybe the sword hadn't injured the boy as much as he'd thought. The dread in his gut snuggled in deeper.

"I need to check on Margaret," the boy said.

"How do you know her?"

"We are friends." The boy blushed and looked away. The girl was too young for a boyfriend, but a boy that was a friend was reasonable. The blush seemed out of place, but maybe he had a crush on her.

"Why are you here now?"

"I was going to throw rocks at the window to see if she would come out and play. Her Dad chased me away last time." He pouted.

The boy could've been working up his courage. It seemed a little odd, but not out of the question. Joshua could be overreacting. But in any case, he needed to focus on the boy's treatment and get the body back to the HPA. "Your wound needs treatment. The blood might upset them." Joshua waved a hand toward the house.

The boy gave a wobbly nod.

Joshua removed layers of fabric to expose pale skin and a gaping wound that oozed blood. "The sword went in clean. We need to prevent infection." Joshua pulled out his healing mixture. He wouldn't normally, since the mixture was very rare and he wasn't sure he could get more when this batch was gone. But the guilt layered with the dread. He could have killed the man before the boy was injured. Helping the boy's wound to heal seemed the least Joshua could do for putting him in such danger.

The boy tensed, but didn't protest.

Joshua needed both hands to bandage the wound. The unease still gnawing at his gut made him reluctant to drop his bow. But maybe his powers were feeding him bad information.

Joshua tightened his hand on the bow and set it carefully aside. The boy had suffered enough. No one else would be around at this hour. Which was probably why the serial killer had chosen it.

He pawed through the bag at his hip. One hand held the boy steady as he squirted his special mixture onto the wound.

Joshua glanced around again. The smell of burning wood had faded and the fog rolled in thicker than ever. Once he got the boy bandaged, he'd take the body back to the HPA. Why the killer had seemed human and yet been able to breathe fire was important. Maybe that was why he was still uneasy.

Joshua wound the bandage around the boy's shoulder, realizing that the boy must be in shock, because he didn't have any goose bumps in the chilly night air. He'd get the kid to the HPA first then come back for the body. He tucked the end of the bandage on the top of the boy's shoulder. Joshua leaned back. "Try your shoulder."

The boy moved it carefully. When his arm was straight up, he winced.

"You should see a healer." Joshua stepped away. The unease focused into a feeling of being watched by something evil.

The shadows bulged from between the buildings. Maybe Rose had been right and he should've brought back-up. But there was nothing concrete showing. He couldn't defend against shadows.

"I'll be fine if I just grab a snack." The boy leapt, landing on Joshua, and pinning him to the ground.

Joshua jerked his head back and tried to twist away.

The innocent boy's face fell away and something older, darker, and more evil took its place. The boy's skin turned grey and hung from his bones. Molten balls of fire roared to life in his eye sockets.

What the hell was this thing? How had it fooled his senses? Something or someone had cloaked the boy. The Soul Wisp picked up rage now, but the rage was restrained as if something had put a mental muzzle on a rabid dog.

It sniffed and then licked, leaving a hot slime trail on Joshua's neck. "You'll do nicely."

Joshua's heart raced. He'd never been so close to dying. This monster looked fully able to kill him. The healing solution only worked on the living, and it might kill the undead if given enough time. Maybe he could get the monster talking.

"What are you?" Joshua heaved his body up, but the killer had too much leverage.

"The great Joshua Lighthouse does not recognize me?" The sneer pulled back its nose so its brain showed, gelatinous and gray.

It had to be an undead. If he could just keep it talking long enough for the mixture to start working, he'd have a chance.

"Are there others?" The solution just needed a few more seconds.

"Stregs are back."

Joshua bit his lip in confusion. Streg was a form of madness that had only affected Trolls and certain giants as they transformed into undead. He had no idea what caused it and had never heard of a case where the Streg was lucid.

"We will convert many. There will be no stopping us." Its laugh echoed down the alley, ringing louder and louder. Its eyes wild and hungry. He knew without a doubt, the monster would kill him when it stopped laughing.

It stopped mid-laugh. With a gasp, it toppled off Joshua. "What did you do?" The Streg asked.

Joshua scrambled back. Would the healing solution be enough to kill the creature?

Its wound hissed and the skin around the bandage blackened. Smoke curled from the wound. The monster really was an undead or the solution wouldn't be affecting it this way, but it being a Streg was impossible. Stregs were mindless from the madness. If this was a Streg why wasn't it mindless?

Joshua rolled away, snatching his bow, ready to shoot. The Streg had said there were others. That could mean this wasn't the only killer and that another Streg might take his place to kill again.

"How did you know?" The Streg pressed its back against the wall. It panted. Darkness spread from its shoulder to its face.

The skin crumbled and fell into its lap. The Streg's eyes turned white and its head slammed back into the wall. "You will never, never, never prevent it."

"What can't I prevent?" Joshua grabbed the Streg's shirt, but it jerked back.

"The. Worlds. Undone. You. Will. Give. Him. The. Key." Its head slammed into the wall with each word.

The Streg slumped back, but not before Joshua's powers picked up the faint taste of a presence that was gone too soon for him to track. A presence the Streg had hated even in its final breath.

With a whimper, the Streg crumbled to dust. The first body gave a loud pop and oozed into the ground, leaving him no evidence.

The oppressive weight lifted off Joshua's chest and a warm glow replaced it. He'd won this battle. The family was safe. At least for now.

He pulled back his mental soldiers. Weariness covered him like a heavy winter cloak.

He swept his internal space looking for dark corners, cobwebs, and for the sickly-sweet smell of decay that signaled a Rider had entered. A Rider could enter when pieces of a soul were away, perhaps taking the place of a missing soul wisp. His old friend, Alex, had told stories of people who used their powers without training. Some of them had gotten lost and never returned to their body. Or worse, had allowed a hostile takeover. A hostile being could force the person to become a mute slave in their own body.

With shaking fingers, Joshua pulled a book from his pouch and wrote out the boy's last words and the powers he had possessed. He wrote his impression of the presence while it was still fresh. If someone had figured out how to make Stregs and control them, this wasn't over.

But his mind stumbled over it being a Streg. It couldn't be a Streg. The last Streg attack on humans had been eleven years ago, just before he joined the HPA. The MO was all wrong too, all the victims rather than just the children should have been drained and dismembered if it was a Streg attack. Stregs would go from living thing to living thing with an insatiable and voracious appetite for blood. And who or what was that presence he'd felt just as the boy had taken his last breath?

Using his powers had made him tired, but hadn't exhausted him like the last time he'd used them.

A black and white cat strolled along the fence line, and then sat and slid a pink tongue across its paw. A flickering light flared upstairs. Joshua pulled up his hood to look like any other person out in the mist.

With no bodies, he'd have a hard time proving whether the killers had been Stregs. He'd go to the HPA and look at the records. Maybe there would be a clue to what was going on. One thing was certain, if he didn't get more information on Stregs, he'd have won this battle, but would lose the war.

7

JOSHUA

<u>Evening, Luminous twenty-ninth, 299 years post-Merge</u>

Joshua headed back to the HPA headquarters. The moment he walked in, Bob was there as if he'd been waiting for him. Most of the HPA would be here late tonight in anticipation of the Gala.

Joshua greeted him with a brotherly hug. "Bob." It'd been too long. He'd missed his old partner and friend.

Bob was too tall to go undercover as a dwarf, but had the thick hair and beard and the thickness around the middle of one. He, like everyone else in the HPA, was human.

"Is it true we should be celebrating?"

"Celebrating?" How had Bob known already? Joshua was too tired to think. His thoughts ran like pudding.

"You got the killer, right?" Bob bounced a bit, acting like a puppy.

Joshua nodded and went through the detector first. "There was something weird."

Bob sighed. "There is always something weird." Bob got the green light in the detector and walked with Joshua to the elevators.

"I think the killers were Stregs."

Bob's finger hesitated before tapping the top floor button. "What makes you say that?" His voice sounded worried.

"I know it sounds unbelievable, but the creature told me under the influence of Holy Water."

"Holy water does not make all creatures speak truth." Bob's voice was flat and he seemed unimpressed by the news.

"True. But there was something else." What could Joshua say? He'd never told anyone about the powers he'd gotten from going through the Merge. How could he explain what he'd felt?

"What?" Bob pressed the pause button before the door could open at their floor.

Bob had been a harsh critic of anything not quite human. Even though they'd been partners and friends for years, Joshua wasn't sure how Bob would respond if he knew there was something not quite human about Joshua. Better not to risk it. "It's just a feeling," was the closest thing to the truth that Joshua could come up with. He would figure out how to lock up his powers again and he'd be a normal human without them.

Bob seemed to search Joshua's face and then shrugged. "The men need a celebration."

"I will keep the feeling to myself until I have some proof." He rubbed his eyes trying to purge the ache.

Bob nodded and released the button. The door opened and the forty people who currently worked at the HPA crowded outside the doors.

"Is it true?" Thomas ran his hand through his black hair, leaving it twisted. He'd asked Bob, but his gaze darted to Joshua for a moment and then back to Bob.

"I dispatched two creatures that were trying to murder a

family with a little girl." Joshua didn't need to say anything about the questions whirling in his own head. He needed proof first.

Murmurs rose in the crowd.

"What was it?" Paula, the floor secretary asked. Her eyes were wide.

"How did you find them?" Madeline in Copy shifted her bulging satchel. She'd probably bring her load of records to the Archive later today.

Bob stepped in front of Joshua. "I got this. I'll meet you in your office," he said it so only Joshua could hear.

Joshua nodded and headed toward his office. He shook a hand here and nodded solemnly there. Everyone seemed to sense that he really didn't want to talk. The room seemed so long. He just wanted to sit. But not out here where the noise and the movement added to his fatigue.

Bob stood on a desk. "All your questions will get answered, just know that the latest attack by Others has been stopped. We have time to celebrate before the Gala."

They cheered.

Bob mingled with the crowd shaking hands and smiling. Joshua rested a moment gathering his strength, watching Bob work the room. Thank goodness, Bob still used his social talents to help the HPA. He laughed at the right times and said the right things to keep things running smoothly. When the word had come down that the golden boy, Bob, wasn't the next head of the HPA, Joshua had been shocked. When Joshua had been chosen instead, everyone had been shocked. Joshua had a great bag record, but wasn't good with people. His now ex-partner hadn't seemed to care about being passed over and had continued to cover the social aspects.

Thomas stepped up and Joshua shook his hand. "I need to get home to the wife and family. I'm glad you stopped them."

"Me too." Thomas was the one who'd done research on Streg. They'd each had to pick a topic before they could be promoted to full agent. Some of what had been produced had been a joke, but Thomas's research had been good. "Where is that research you did on Stregs?"

Thomas leaned back and blinked. "Why?"

Joshua shrugged. "Mind if I take it to read? I'll drop it back tomorrow."

Thomas grinned and shook his head. "I know my research is safe in that vault you call an office."

Joshua knew that Thomas had a young daughter. He didn't want to worry Thomas unnecessarily, but all of his instincts told him that this wasn't over. "You have a daughter about the right age. Be careful. Don't take down your protections yet."

Thomas's eyes widened and he glanced away. "I-I never can." It was an odd turn of phrase. The world was a dangerous place, but the way Thomas had said it implied his children were in more danger than most. "I-I have to go." Thomas fled.

The weight on Joshua's body tripled. He needed to get out of here. He'd figure out what Thomas had meant by his reaction later.

Joshua leaned against the back wall. Did he have to talk to anyone else?

Bob was occupied talking to Hugo on the other side of the room. Their heads were together and they both glanced his way. The rest of the agents mingled. Paula and the other secretary chatted. People he didn't quite know from the lab and research area patted agents on the back. Madeline, Thomas, and Rose were missing. Madeline had probably left for the Archive. Rose could be anywhere.

Joshua grabbed the files from Thomas's desk and left the celebration. He just needed to sit.

He opened his office and sunk into the leather chair. It

creaked in protest. Thomas's paper was a consolidation of the last ten years of confirmed Streg attacks.

In theory, any creature alive or undead could go Streg. But a giant or troll was far more likely. They were already brutal creatures, and when they got infected, they killed like mindless beasts and could only be stopped by being killed. And usually, the trolls or giants eliminated the Streg before they killed other creatures. The cause was unknown and there was no cure.

There were no recorded cases of two Stregs cooperating or of a Streg being anything other than a Troll or Giant. The boy had been a baited trap. No wonder he'd lost two teams to the killers. No one would've expected that tactic.

The paper had images of what Stregs looked like. Undead, but not quite. They came in all shapes and sizes and even had some wild uncontrolled powers. Which could be a match for the flame the man had thrown. But neither the boy nor man had been mindless killing machines. They'd been controlled, strategic even.

Thomas had copied the files from the cases he'd used as data. The files from Streg attacks within the Troll or Giant communities showed evil, crazy killing machines and the community dealing with it or reaching out for help.

His third time reading Thomas' research, Joshua spotted something unusual. In a case from about a year ago, a troll had gone Streg, but the family had reported him missing. Not returned to his ancestors, but missing. Joshua had assumed that they'd meant the infected troll was dead the first time he'd read it, but Trolls were very literal creatures. It could've meant the Streg was kidnapped.

The idea of kidnapping a blood frenzied Troll seemed ludicrous. Even if someone had managed to kidnap one and had smuggled the Streg away from the rest of the Troll tribe, then what? What possible use could someone have with a captive Streg? Unless someone was trying to cure the infection. Or learn how to infect another. He shivered.

He went through each report and found three records where an infected Troll or Giant had gone missing. What could they have in common? He laid them out on his desk. They were all Trolls.

A knock sounded at his door. Joshua flinched.

"It's Bob."

Joshua shoved the files in his desk drawer then went and opened the door.

Bob grinned at him. "You look like shit, Lighthouse."

"Thanks." Standing up was an effort.

"Sit." Bob waved Joshua to his chair. "I have news."

"Yeah?" Joshua sat and leaned back.

"I know the names of the non-humans who have invitations to the Gala. It's a long list."

"Where'd you get them?" Those lists were kept a strict secret. Bob had some of the best resources, but even so he must've used his charm to get such lists. Which meant he'd done it for a reason.

"I have my sources."

"So?" Joshua forced himself to relax.

"I heard that a certain member of a certain pack was invited under amnesty. Maybe we could set a trap for her. Like this." Bob snatched and crumpled a sheet of paper. He set it on the desk and slammed the upside-down garbage can to trap it.

Joshua jumped and let out a tired laugh. So dramatic. Bob was always so dramatic. "As much as I would love to catch Serene, that would break the rules."

"Just bend. If we do it right."

Joshua sighed and leaned back. "We talked about this. The

species tensions are too high to break the rules. It would make our job that much harder." Joshua knew Bob knew this, but sometimes Bob was able to smooth things over with charm and his contacts. The relationships were too volatile to chance that right now. One wrong move could start a war the humans would have a hard time winning.

"But in this case, wouldn't it be worth it? Catching the Other who's been taunting us for over a year?"

"Taunting us? No one has seen her. How is she taunting us? Besides, there's a right and a wrong way to do things. If we break the rules, we're no better than they are." Joshua gazed at Bob whose face went blank, like he was playing poker.

Then he sighed. "Fine."

"Anything else?" Joshua yawned.

"You really need to go tonight."

"To the Gala? You usually cover for me. Can't you go?" His stomach twisted. He was too tired to watch what he said and to tread carefully on delicate Other sensitivities.

"Elder Martin needs to see you."

Joshua closed his eyes. "I can stop by his place tomorrow after the Gala."

"You could...." Bob drawled, "but as your friend I am telling you to go to the Gala."

Joshua wanted to ask why tonight, but Bob's face seemed serious. Bob would have some smooth answer as to why Joshua should go. It may or may not be the real reason. Joshua was just too tired to spar. Now it was his turn to sigh. "Fine. Let me sleep for a couple hours."

"Don't forget your suit." Having got his way, Bob turned and left, closing the door behind him. The door locked automatically.

Joshua lurched out of the chair, knocking the garbage can,

still upside down on his desk, to the floor a crumpled ball rolled under his desk. He'd pick it up later after his nap.

He pulled out the suit he kept for emergencies from a drawer. The suit was rumpled and smelled faintly musty. Damn. He hung it up on a hook by the door and slumped into bed.

He had a bad feeling about tonight. Like he would come out the other side no better looking than his suit.

8

SERENE

Serene walked down the hidden walkways in Shifterville. She walked down a tunnel with an illusion cast so it looked like a wall, but was really hidden doors, and secret walkways that were easier to find with shifter senses. Humans and other creatures who didn't rely upon their noses would be lost.

She almost missed a turn because her sense of smell was not as good as other shifters, but she was able to re-find the scent. A healer's door would be open at all hours.

She found her son's door and knocked. A moment later, he flung the door open. Joy lifted her chest, bringing tears to her eyes. She reached up to hug him. He had his father's large, big boned build and easily lifted her off the ground.

She'd been unable to think of another way to get the help she needed. Still she worried that if she asked him for help, it would put him in danger.

She reminded herself that her son was an adult and knew

his way around more places than she did and he was one of the few she trusted completely. If she couldn't get an invite to the Gala, she'd have no chance to find Joshua Lighthouse. No chance to get justice for the pack.

"There you are." He growled as if he was the parent and she was the child. He ushered her in and closed the door.

She sat at a little table by the fire. "I need your help."

"Anything." He grabbed a plate with bread and butter and set a teacup by her plate and added tea. What he placed in her cup smelled of chamomile and something else with a light floral scent. Probably some calming mixture. He tipped the teapot closer to the fire to heat the water.

"I need to be invited to the Gala." She hadn't expected a response right away. This was an odd request, even for her, but his expression seemed thoughtful.

The pot whistled and he poured the steamy water into her cup and his. "I thought you said you needed an invitation to the Gala."

He offered her cream and sugar and sat, focusing his gaze on her.

"Yes."

Daniel raised an eyebrow. "Have you developed a taste for parties since living with the Aeros?"

She laughed. "No, it is my chance to get information from Joshua Lighthouse."

He sat back in his chair staring toward the fire. "I'd heard that you have an invite already. It's being passed along through shifters. So you will be able to get in, but why do you want to?"

She told him about what the Seer had said and her conclusion that the head must be Joshua Lighthouse.

"So you really want to get him alone somewhere private to find out what he knows."

Her mind blanked. Her son was right. Of course, Joshua

Lighthouse wouldn't want to talk to her. She would need some alone time with him. Maybe she could seduce him. But then what? That wouldn't get him to answer her questions. Maybe she could kidnap him. She was strong, but if he struggled and brought attention to them, especially on a night of amnesty, then she would have all the factions after her, not just the HPA.

If she was going to do this, she needed an ally to help kidnap him. The only one in the world she would trust with this was her son. But could she put him in such danger? If he was caught with her, the HPA would probably kill both of them. But if she did nothing her pack's murderers would get away and would strike again. She couldn't live with herself if that happened. She'd have to trust her son and hope the plan worked.

"I-I would try to seduce him. But I need your help."

"Indeed, I am an expert on seducing human men."

Serene snorted. "No, I'll do that part myself. I need a place to interrogate him and help moving him."

"I can help with that." He took a sip of tea, clearly waiting for her to continue.

"I will approach Joshua Lighthouse and draw him from the party. We will need to find a place to overpower him and a place to take him to ask him questions."

"You'll need somewhere close to the party to bring him, but someplace humans wouldn't look."

"You have an idea?"

"Yes, I need to go check it out, but it might work." He stood and ladled out some stew. "You eat and get ready here. We can walk to the Gala together."

She took the bowl and nodded. "I'll look through your closet to see if anything seems right."

He made a face. "I'm not sure I have anything Gala appropriate."

Serene laughed softly. "It will be fine."

He nodded and left.

Serene ate the stew. The hint of Sage in the chunk of meat reminded her of her time with the Pack. They'd had a rocky start, but she'd come to care about them. When her mate had discovered that she loved this stew, he'd made sure that this dinner was one of the communal meals once a week. Homesickness filled her chest and she closed her eyes. At least she had her son.

She left the half-eaten bowl on the table and ducked behind the curtain where her son slept. The low bed was made and a simple table next to the bed held a book. She knew in the corner a clever curtain hid her son's secret. He'd been disguising himself so he could bring his healing to those that would never come to him. A very dangerous thing for him to do with patients with sharp senses and even sharper teeth and a strong dislike for being tricked.

She tugged the curtain aside and walked into the tiny room. A mirror with makeup, and brushes sat in one corner, and on the other side of the room hung clothing. None of it was fancy, but the sturdy materials and colors were appropriate for blending into different shifter communities. Some pieces didn't seem to be shifter garb. They had too much sparkle or fur. She wondered how far her son had been pushing his luck trying to help others. He seemed to think the only way to show he had value was by helping others, even if doing so was extremely dangerous for him.

She pulled out a simple tan shift dress. It would be far too large on her. She held the dress to her front and then tied the straps around her neck. The dress dragged on the ground. She could belt the waist, but it would gape in the back. If she drew it over her head, she'd look like a kid in her mom's dress. This dress wouldn't help her seduce Joshua Lighthouse. None of them would.

Everything was too big. What she was wearing wouldn't be right either. She could go partially furred, but Joshua Lighthouse hated non-humans, so that would decrease her odds of seducing him. No she needed to look as human as possible. And as female as possible so his hormones would get the better of his brain.

She went back into the kitchen and finished off the stew. It was too late to get finery anywhere else or try to fix what he had. She'd had some special occasion clothing in her lair. Her mate had insisted. But she shuddered, there was no way she was going back to where the pack had lived. Not yet. What other options did she have?

If she couldn't find clothing, maybe she could go without. She could try for a more shocking look. If she could pull it off, going naked would show she was female. Might even help on the seduction front.

A few minutes later, Serene stood naked in front of the mirror. Maybe she should add a wig, since her own dark hair barely covered her tits. Her image was not Lady Godiva, more like Desperate Naked Chick. Did she look human enough?

Even though it'd been almost two decades since she'd been transformed from human to pack, the woman in the mirror didn't match the one still in her head. It was easy as a pack member to avoid mirrors. She was older, but still had coffee colored skin and small stature. The pointy ears, the extra hair in places it had no business being were part of the transition to Pack. So was her extra muscle and hopped-up metabolism. A transformation that now left her more alone. Her heart gave a warning thump and she pushed away the thought.

She needed to be seductive if she was to lure Joshua Lighthouse out of the party and interrogate him to find out if he'd murdered her pack.

"Really?" Daniel walked into the room and put a hand on his hip. "Just tackle him while you're at it. Not subtle."

She glanced over the changing screen at her son. "Do human men really go for subtle?"

"No, but is 'Ho for sale' better?" he asked in that dry tone he used when he was trying not to laugh.

"Fine. What do you recommend?" She held earrings up to her ears. She needed something else.

"If you want to lure him out of the party and find out what really happened, I'd tone it down." He sighed and walked out of the room, returning with a long, dark wig. "Try this."

"Why do you have a wig?" He didn't answer her teasing question. They both knew he used wigs as part of his disguises to bring his healing to the larger community. Even if it meant him dressing as a female, but she mostly pretended not to know his secret.

He rolled his eyes.

She tucked her hair up and let the wig drape around her body. It fell to block most of her butt. She could tuck it around her body and make it more artful, but still have some shock value. "Better?"

"I guess."

"Did you find a place?" she asked hoping they could work out the details of the plan.

"Yeah. It'll be perfect. You'll need to meet me at the south west corner of the Gala."

"The only way this will work is if we catch him unaware." A nervous flutter crept into her stomach. It was dangerous to hunt a hunter. This one was the worst of the hunters, but she had to hunt him. Joshua Lighthouse was the only lead she had.

"Are you sure this is the best way to accomplish what you want?" asked Daniel, handing her a long trench coat.

"Need." She said it firmly, which belied that tremble in her gut. She slipped on the coat. "What I need." It was a need or she would never put her son at risk.

"Fine, need."

"Yes, I need to know if that son of a human was involved with my pack's deaths." Her throat got tight and her eyes grew hot. Imperfect though they were, they'd been her family.

"Maybe we should try a different tactic. Something less dangerous."

Dangerous. Her laugh didn't sound happy or sarcastic, but sad. Her whole life was filled with danger as the only member of a pack. She was alone. More alone than she'd ever been, even before the transformation into part of the pack. The other shifters saw being packless as a symptom of a character flaw that meant that she was too dangerous or unstable to be in a pack. Her son was in much the same situation. "It's the only way I can be sure."

Her son put his forehead to hers. "If it's what you need, I'll help you."

"I know you weren't in the pack—"

"Which was the best thing for me." He said with conviction, his eyes meeting hers. "Besides, if I'd been in the pack, I'd be dead now too."

She nodded slowly and squeezed his shoulder, then had to look away. He'd bear the brunt of her mistakes. The Pack had transformed her in the hopes of changing the Pack's fate. She'd made the mistake of trying to go back to her human home while pregnant with Daniel. Instead of her boy bonding with the Pack at his birth, they were both cast out. Had she not gone; they would have killed Daniel for being packless so she'd been left alone to raise him.

It was only when the pack became desperate years later, that they demanded she rejoin the pack. Leaving Daniel alone, had been part of her demands for rejoining the pack.

Being raised outside of a pack meant he'd never know what it was like to have his own family. He'd always be seen as a menace because he was packless. "I better get going. I need to scout inside." Serene said.

"Do you really think you can seduce him? He doesn't like non-humans and none of my contacts can find anyone he's bedding."

He was right. Maybe it was a long shot, but it was her one shot to get to the head as the Seer had said. She needed to take this chance no matter how slim. She lifted an eyebrow and wiggled her hips. "Human men think with their dicks."

"Yuck, Mom." He grimaced and turned away.

She laughed and let the tension fly from her. Tonight, she would finally get answers or get caught trying. If she got caught, she'd sacrifice herself to get her son free.

"This isn't a way to die with the Pack...." He looked away. "You're not hoping someone will take you out?" His face looked serious.

"I need justice for them." She closed her eyes against the ache in her chest. She would focus on that need and after that who knows what might happen.

He touched her shoulder and met her eyes again. He looked so worried, so earnest. "You need to choose to live. Maybe someday choose to love."

Her son, the lone wolf giving pack advice. She squeezed his hand. "You are the only one I've done that for."

"Chosen to love?"

"With all my heart." She could see her own stubbornness in him. "Maybe when this is all over, you'll find a partner too."

"Maybe." His tone scoffed, turning his 'maybe' into a solid 'no'.

"It doesn't matter that you don't have a pack."

"Yeah, it does." He crouched down, hidden within his cloak.

The cloak fell to the ground and a far larger shaggy wolf slipped out from under. He gave a toothy grin and trotted out the door.

She had to find out who was behind her pack's deaths. The memory of that night was foggy, but the pack-bond burned the feeling of each member of her pack dying into her heart. The pack members had died to protect her and her unborn child. Her mate, the pack alpha, had been the last one murdered. Her heart clenched and pain radiated out, making it hard to breathe.

They, whoever they were, had to be stopped before they killed other families.

She closed her eyes and focused on controlling her heart rate, on slowing her breathing, on stuffing the black mass of guilt and anger back into the box.

It was time.

9

______

JOSHUA

<u>Night, Luminous twenty-ninth, 299 years post-Merge</u>

Joshua walked into the cool night air. Predators, both Human and Other, prowled the dark streets. Even tonight, with the amnesty in place between all the factions, there was still a chance of attack. He'd be careful rather than risk getting killed.

Twenty blocks and two double-backs later, Joshua skulked in the shadows across the street from Elder Martin's mansion. He took a moment to assess the target. A habit from years of stalking.

He counted at least five layers of protection. Good thing he wasn't trying to break in. The Aurora Borealis shimmer was a protective field that cost more than his whole division made in a year. The balls of light hovering like giant balloons acted as both illumination and a secondary defense system against air attacks.

Elder Martin wasn't taking chances. His ten-foot walls were fortified with six evenly spaced Giants that were some subtype of stone warrior, that spied on the crowd gathered in the courtyard.

A tall man rushed to the open gate and held out what looked like the invitation in Joshua's pocket to the monkey in the red suit. The guy was a set of cymbals away from a giant Charlie Chimp toy. Charlie didn't even glance at the invitation. The party-goer entered the front gate and disappeared inside.

Bob hadn't said why Joshua needed to see Elder Martin tonight. He saw Elder Martin in an official capacity once a month or so. Perhaps Elder Martin wanted to introduce him to someone. It was the only thing that made any sense. But why tonight? Introductions could be made at any time. Elder Martin knew how Joshua struggled at these events. He didn't mingle well and tended to make Others nervous. Then there were the tricks that were expected as part of intra-species politics.

His last event, there'd been an unfortunate incident with Walter, the leader of the Lizardfolk. That incident was the reason that Joshua didn't go to these things. Walter's last practical joke had left Joshua locked in the closet for hours. Joshua had lost political credit and would be expected to retaliate in just the right way or he'd lose even more face. The trick Joshua had to set up needed to be something that caused no permanent damage. Not his forte.

Maybe he could find Wren without Walter. Wren was much more reasonable to work with. Solid, dependable, and not quite as mercenary as Walter. Everyone kept track of favors, but Wren gave more for less. Joshua could ask him about Streg and perhaps even get a useful answer.

But, the longer he was there, the higher the odds he would offend someone or someone would try to play a trick on him to gain advantage. That meant his mission was to get in. Talk to Elder Martin. Get out.

He crossed the street and handed his invitation to Charlie who glanced at the invitation and said, "Weapons to the left."

The room had a single chest on the ground. They had something similar in the evidence area in the HPA building. When you locked the chest it would create a magic space that could only be accessed with the key.

Joshua put his bow, two knives, a half dozen stakes, and his bag of potions into the chest. He might as well be naked. A human without equipment was at a severe disadvantage to other creatures. Humans had no claws, fangs, or special abilities.

Joshua removed the key. If he were to open the chest with no key, his stuff would be gone and when he closed it a new key would appear. But if he put in his key, when he opened the chest, his items would be inside.

Charlie pointed to the right. "Elder Martin is in the ballroom."

He tucked the key in his pocket and scuttled past head-high hedges. These parties made him nervous.

He spotted movement in his peripheral vision. He ducked and rolled, taking cover under the hedge. His hand slapped where his knife should have been.

He took a deep breath. Man, he was losing it. This was a Gala. Every faction had agreed to peace for the night. He was behind serious defenses and every guest was divested of their weapons. Why was he so skittish?

Something felt off and wrong. Like the feeling of impending storm.

The movement had been living balls of light that zipped around to the music and seemed to pay him no mind.

He needed to calm down. Such foolishness in the Gala would open him up for tricks. He hadn't received too many tricks because he'd been feared. But now his political standing was unclear. Still, he'd rather react a hundred times and be susceptible to tricks than end up dead. God, he hated politics.

A softer lit area hummed with conversation. The lush scent of vanilla and musk hung heavy in the air. Moonflowers dotted the hedges. No immediate threat.

Joshua stood, brushed off, and headed through the center door.

Humans and non-humans flowed through the ballroom and sitting rooms, dressed in species-specific formal wear. They were all talking. Many were his enemies and what they said couldn't be trusted. He had no idea about the latest gossip which might be an innocuous starting place for a conversation. If he found someone he could talk to, he wasn't sure what it was safe to say. It was even worse than he'd imagined. He was completely out of his element.

He slid around the room's perimeter, his back to the wall. Something bad was coming. Glasses shook, voices were high pitched, and his nose flared at the sour whiff of fear. Was this sensation of impending doom his powers giving him a warning or his dislike of such parties? He couldn't be sure.

Joshua watched the crowd and a shot of red flagged from the sea of people. Walter's dewlap, a flag of skin that lizards have at their throat, extended. A beacon that led his eyes to the lizard man who was the head of the Other protection agency. Damn. He was here and Wren was with him.

Walter had been willing to sell information, which was very useful, but he'd been very mercenary. Even with his mottled skin, in his fitted suit he looked more like James Bond than Joshua ever would. Maybe Walter had some intel on the new Stregs. Joshua crossed the crowd and approached Walter like he would any other wild animal—at an angle.

"Nicccce sssssuit, Lighthouse," Walter said without looking away from his conversation with Wren, the leader of Aeros.

Joshua resisted the urge to tug and brush at his suit. It really did look sad next to their crisp clothing. However, pretty garb didn't do the hard work of keeping people safe.

"Perhaps he does not know this is a formal party?" Wren fingered the quick release on his chest harness.

Joshua stifled a sigh. Wren would be on Walters' side tonight.

Wren looked mostly human and male if you ignored the neck-down white feathers and the harnessed bird wings. His white, low-backed robe matched his wings and covered him from shoulder to floor. It pooled on the ground, covering his feet. The Aeros, for some reason, never showed their feet at cross-species occasions.

He needed to plot his trick now, or he wouldn't have a chance to ask anyone any questions tonight or potentially any night. Joshua wanted to kick up Wren's dress and see what was underneath. Bird talons or human feet? Or something else? But that wasn't the trick that was needed. The trick needed to be focused on Walter. Joshua couldn't back down.

"If you have something to say, you should just say it." Joshua invaded their space, crossed his arms, and fisted his hands. He leaned in and smelled the fish Wren had eaten for lunch.

The crowd opened a vacuum around them as if they could sense a trick. They didn't want to be drawn in, but wanted to watch.

"Nothing new. Merely the Human Protection Agencccy issss failing because of itsssss incompetent leader." Walter's tone suggested a lizard in wait for prey, practiced boredom, waiting to strike. He sipped his wine, still half-turned away from Joshua.

Joshua tightened his fists to keep his temper in check. Maybe there would be an opening if he stayed quiet.

"My people have a saying, if the head is bad, the body still follows." Wren's head feathers rose and flattened.

Wren was nervous. Joshua could use that. If he startled Wren as his fingers played with the quick release, Wren just might release his wings. His wings could connect with Walter and knock him down. It would be a worthy trick, if Joshua could pull it off.

He waited for the moment Wren tugged the quick release. Joshua jerked his hand at Wren's face, stopping it inches away, and ducked.

Wren startled, hit the quick release on his wing harness. His wings snapped out and extended ten feet. Wren's left wing whistled past Joshua's shoulder. His right wing smacked Walter in the face.

"Damn it, Lighthouse." Walter's tone was pained. He clutched his nose. Blood flowed between his fingers. His long, forked tongue flicked to the blood.

That trick should earn him some credit.

Joshua walked away, grabbed a glass of something pale from a passing waiter, and covered his grin with a small sip.

He'd find Elder Martin and once his credit spread, he'd see if any other faction leader would talk to him. He headed across the room.

The flash of a long, glowing dress left a white spot in his vision. A Silver Folk passed by with a small I-am-playing-a-joke-on-you grin on her face. Her dress must be spelled to be so bright. Silver Folk did love practical jokes which made them very popular. Her gaze connected with Joshua's and she headed toward him.

"Nice trick." She peered from under her swirling silver stream of hair. Hair covered one eye and merged with her disco ball dress. Green sparkled from both her eyes and from something lost within her mass of hair.

"Thanks."

She laughed, a small tinkling sound, a spoon against crystal. "You are not known for tricks."

Joshua stepped in closer. Blunt honesty was not the norm. This was not some random encounter with a vapid Other representative. "What do you want?"

She tilted her head and exposed a dangling owl earring with green eyes. "Even you may need help someday. You will have to trust someone with your secrets."

This was far more direct than Silverfolk spoke. She must really want him to listen.

"And then I would come to you with something sparkly or silver?" He said it softly so only she could hear. What was her game?

She leaned closer and tilted her head back even more. To anyone else it might have looked like submission, but the sideways glance and small uptick of her lip gave her away. She wanted him to get a good look at her pulse. Wanted him to believe her. "Silver is always good."

She wanted him to think she would be on his side and that there was a reason she could be trusted. "Why?"

She stroked the owl earring, sending the feathers clicking with the movement. "The psychics are going crazy. The signs are ominous. Even a human such as yourself should care about the signs."

The signs must be telling her to work with a human or him specifically. Her people were very superstitious. If it was a trick, she'd flinch if he confronted her.

"So you want me to gush my secrets because of an omen?" If Joshua had said it any flatter, he could've ironed on it. He watched her pulse. It remained steady. She was either a very good liar or it was true. If it was true then he was not alone with the feeling of doom and he might have an ally in this SilverFolk.

"Joe's is a place of Seers and secrets." She stepped back and moved away. "And answers."

"The diner over on 4th?" Joe's was his favorite place to eat, even if it was run by Others. For some reason he couldn't name, he felt safe when he went there.

Her head dipped forward. A nod. Maybe. She was swallowed by the crowd.

The crowd of people kept their distance as if he were the monster. Joshua may have made headway with his trick, but he was very out of practice. In the field, it was more black and white. In here, a whole different set of rules governed.

Bob would have a better idea if his efforts had helped. He scanned the room and spotted Bob. Joshua caught up with him. "How's the party?"

"People are talking about the Merge." Bob had braided his hair and beard. Glints of silver poked out.

Joshua shivered. Bob never said anything without a reason. "That's ancient history." Joshua used his most dismissive tone; maybe Bob would take the hint. Even Joshua knew, this wasn't the time to talk about such a divisive topic. Extremists and fanatics argued and died over something that could never be undone.

"The three hundredth anniversary is only days away."

"I guess that would get them talking." It was still hard for him to remember that the Merge was so long ago for this time-line, but just 15 years ago for him personally.

"Have you ever thought the Merge was the single most tragic event the earth has experienced?"

Joshua glanced around to see who was listening. Bob was a fool to say that in mixed company. Any event that ripped families apart and brought the worlds' monsters together was not polite dinner conversation.

"Bob. This is not the place to have this conversation. Even I know that." Joshua leaned in and put a hand on Bob's shoulder.

Bob shook his head. "Things would be much better for everyone, if we rid ourselves of the non-humans." Bob's voice boomed. Two vampires behind Bob snarled at him then stalked away.

Joshua drew back. Hearing something he might have said coming from Bob increased Joshua's unease. That statement was only part of what Joshua felt. The thought was incomplete. And very out of character for Bob to actually say, especially here at the Gala. "Send them away?"

Bob snorted and ruffled his mustache with a quick breath. "Yes, send them back to where they belong, to their own world."

The harshness and finality of that statement caused Joshua to pause. Was that what he sounded like? So bitter? So closed? He focused on Bob. Joshua knew that Bob didn't like others, they'd had conversations on that topic over the years, but only in private. Never in public and Joshua hadn't thought Bob hated Others enough to destroy the world.

The spell to UnMerge the worlds was in his book. Before he'd known how dangerous the book itself was, he had added research data going back years. He'd cataloged the vulnerabilities and strengths of the thousands of races and beings who populated this world. In the wrong hands, the book would bring large scale death and destruction. He could tell Bob, heck even pull out the book and show Bob that what he wanted wasn't just possible, but Joshua could help. As much as he distrusted Others, ripping the worlds apart wasn't a good idea. For that reason and many others, the book would stay locked in his office and the world would stay safe for another hundred years.

The shiny dresses and lovely art on the walls faded, as did the conversations around them. "Let's say that was even possible.

Do you know how much damage the Merge did to both worlds?" Joshua asked.

"The records—" Bob started.

The records were wrong, Joshua knew that. "Space and time twisted. No one born After thinks it is wrong to have Big Ben in the same city as the Egyptian Pyramids." But it was wrong. The Merge had devastated both worlds.

"Yes, but—"

"Do you know what it means, when space and time contorted? Imagine if every five feet gravity had a different direction. Imagine the flow of time swallowing buildings or spitting them out. Imagine the noise of a thousand grinders. Imagine how flesh fared in that crush. And if you were one of the few that survived, you awoke trapped in a caricature of what once was."

Joshua's mouth snapped shut and he fought down the swirl of emotions. Watching everything he loved get shattered had been bad enough, but having everything he thought he knew no longer be relevant to his survival had been even harder. The safe peaceful world he'd known had been destroyed and replaced with this dangerous and volatile one.

He'd shown too much. A deep breath helped push back the fear and anger that came with talking about the Merge.

"It was hard for drifters." Bob's smile and nod exposed how little he knew. "Hard for you."

"I saw Before and After." The words barely escaped through Joshua's clenched jaw. "I survived." The estimate in the old records was that only a thousand humans survived the transition. Bob had no idea what hard really was.

"But, if we reversed the Merge, things would revert." Bob softened his voice to a tone one might use to coax a pup away from its mom.

"Unlikely. It would cause another cataclysm." Ripping something apart didn't result in anything but more death. Even if it was ripped apart by magic. He slipped his hands into his pockets.

"We would be free to be human," Bob said.

"It was never free to be human."

The crowd swirled around them. A few Others looked on, perhaps wondering why the humans were not presenting a unified front. Joshua dragged in a slow breath. And another, letting go of the things he couldn't control. He relaxed his neck and shoulders, and pushed away the vivid images that haunted his dreams.

"Would you help UnMerge if you could?" Bob focused intently on Joshua's face.

A cold wind seemed to sweep through his body. That overly warm, there-are-too-many–people-nearby feel turned to a chill. His hairs stood up like prairie-dogs sensing a hawk. Who would support an UnMerging? Who would want the world splintered? "I need to find Elder Martin."

"He was on the patio." Something ugly flickered across Bob's face for just an instant before it was replaced with his normal jovial expression. He waved his hand, snatched a shrimp from a serving tray, and followed the waiter. The shrimp's discarded shell bounced off Joshua's boot and was crushed underfoot.

Joshua moved through the eddies of the crowd like a fisherman wading through a river. He caught snippets of conversations as people slid by.

A pink fairy flew by. She gave the human man wearing a tuxedo an I've-got-a-secret look. She landed on his shoulder and leaned close as if she was cleaning Mr. Tuxedo's eardrum, but her voice boomed. "The anniversary of the Merge is when the world is at its weakest."

Mr. Tuxedo winced. "Weak enough to be UnMerged?"

Pink Fairy nodded, her whole body twittering.

Bob was right, everyone was talking about the merge.

A few feet away, a tall lady covered with purple flowers, stood by a bark-covered man in a green suit and bowler. "I saw her myself."

"Was she really wearing nothing?" He covered his face with his hat.

"Nothing but the blush on her cheeks." The woman giggled and rested her arm on his shoulder.

"Which cheeks?" He lifted the hat just enough to ask.

They both laughed.

Joshua shook his head. The things people talked about were odd.

Joshua crossed the patio and walked back through to the bar. Elder Martin stood across the room in a blue suit and pink ruffled shirt. Despite his clothing, this man was not light and fluffy. Instead he was driven, deceptive, and dangerous. Every action calculated. Behind every Gala invite was a self-serving motive. Joshua's invitation would be no exception which caused him to wonder, what did Elder Martin want?

Elder Martin had his hand on the elbow of a towering man. The tall man's lanky body almost reached the ceiling. It was the same man who'd entered the party just before Joshua. The tall man smirked at Elder Martin. By the time Joshua reached Elder Martin, the man was gone.

Joshua decided he was being paranoid. Just because he'd noticed the man before, didn't mean the man was following him.

Joshua turned to look for the man and crashed into someone behind him, sending them both off balance. His arms wrapped around a warm, naked female body. The scent of lavender and peppermint tickled his nose. Joshua stared into green eyes.

The green eyes that had haunted him for years. His apology died on his lips. Time expanded, his heart contracted.

"Joshua, have you met Serene of the Pack?" Elder Martin asked.

"No." He sounded shaky to his own ear. This was the woman he'd dreamt about since he'd first seen her in the Book of Secrets all those years ago.

Not only was she here. But now he had a name to go with the face from his dreams. A name that went with the picture at the top of HPA's most wanted list, which looked nothing like her. A name for the Other heralded by every Other agency as a champion.

She was naked for all the world to see. In this form, she looked human. The only hint that she wasn't was the length of her canines and her small elfin ears. She was a petite beauty with her flashing eyes.

In spite of the fact that her hair strategically covered her nipples, the room grew hot, as if he had plunged head first into a dragon's maw. He forced his gaze up to her eyes.

"How are you?" Joshua asked.

She shrugged his arms off and stepped back. "Hunted. And you?"

Her piercing eyes stabbed his heart. His mouth opened to say something clever, but nothing came out. A strange brew of hunger, regret, and embarrassment filled him. Then hurt invaded. This obsession wasn't real. Whatever attraction he felt was because of the book. He focused on her eyes and avoided her perfect breasts, schooling his gaze not to go lower.

He found his voice. "Waiting to bag and tag you."

Her eyes narrowed. Her mouth slashed across her face. She lifted her chin and stalked away.

The crowd parted as Serene sauntered away; all the men stared as if they'd never seen a naked woman before. The sway of her hair brushed the edge of her perfect ass. Joshua fought the urge to chase her down and cover her with a cloak.

"The Pack have no self-consciousness." Elder Martin replaced his empty glass with a new one.

"I see." Joshua made it sound light even when he could still feel the silky caress of her skin. If only she'd been some hideous beast, then he'd know his attraction was all because of the book. But instead she'd been lovely.

"Here try this." Elder Martin handed Joshua a glass filled with what looked like pale wine.

Joshua sipped. It had a strange musky flavor he couldn't identify. "It's odd."

"The very best of the Silverfolk vintage." Elder Martin sipped his glass. "I got it just for this party."

"You throw quite the soiree," Joshua said. He tried to focus on Elder Martin. He still needed to know why he'd been required to attend the Gala.

"You have no idea how hard it is to pick a day for world peace." He waved like Queen Elizabeth to a subject across the room. "For a few hours everyone will play nice."

"That's why you hired armed guards with lasers." The amount of money this party must've cost was incredible. Guards armed in this way could mean Elder Martin thought there'd be trouble.

"Just encouraging good behavior." Elder Martin shrugged, a tiny movement almost hidden by his raised glass. "All the guards are Crylons."

A chill crawled up Joshua's back. Those stone men on the walls were Crylons. An army of Crylons. A small group of them had been used to decimate a rival city less than a hundred years ago. Crylons aged very slowly and any one of these guards could've been on that team.

"Why would the Crylons agree to be at a peace party? Don't they feast on strong emotions?"

Elder Martin hooked Joshua's arm and walked them deeper into the house.

He nodded. "They do. They fight for this job. Imagine the sweet tang of the bitterest of enemies sipping wine and making small talk." Elder Martin looked over his wine glass.

"Is that how you keep getting elected?" Joshua laughed to cover his unease. Elder Martin was good for the HPA. He'd always been willing to fund projects and lobby for things that helped humans. He didn't seem to have anything urgent to tell Joshua.

"That and all the bribes.," Elder Martin stage whispered and then his attention was caught by something across the room.

"Of course." Joshua raised his glass. "To employment... Speaking of which, what did you need to talk to me about?"

Elder Martin looked at him too long to be polite and pasted on his politician smile. "Nothing urgent. Why?"

How odd. A shaft of unease shot up his spine. Perhaps Bob had been confused. Or Elder Martin had forgotten why he needed to see Joshua. "Did you need me here tonight?"

Elder Martin shook his head and sipped his wine.

Joshua took a long sip of his wine still disliking its odd tang. Since he was here, he could ask Elder Martin if he'd heard anything odd. The man had many sources of information. "What do you know about the rash of human killings?"

"Bob said you'd eliminated the threat." Elder Martin's tone sounded bored, but something flashed in his eyes indicating his interest.

"There's an underlying pattern. I just can't see it yet." It was more than a pattern. It was too coordinated. Too meaningful. There was something going on. "Have you heard anything odd from your contacts?"

"Not really." Elder Martin sipped his wine and gazed around the party.

"Nothing about Stregs?" Joshua watched closely.

Elder Martin blinked and shifted his gaze to Joshua before glancing down. "Why would people talk about a Troll and Giant disease?"

If Elder Martin hadn't waited a beat too long, Joshua would've believed he didn't know anything, but that extra beat indicated Elder Martin knew more than he was letting on.

"Nothing at all odd?"

Elder Martin shrugged. "Strange monsters appearing in the city and killing. A surge of omens and psychic related activity across species. Teams of agents in all factions being ambushed and killed."

"What do you think is going on?"

Elder Martin seemed to choose his words very carefully. "The anniversary of the Merge is a highly volatile time. I fear that someone is looking to change what we have here."

Elder Martin was in a position of considerable power. If there was a plot to make changes, then he could lose his power. Could a man like Elder Martin lose everything? The worry about it might explain why he seemed nervous.

Exhaustion tugged at Joshua making him wonder why was he suddenly so tired? He widened his eyes but they were so heavy. He needed to get somewhere safe. "Good seeing you."

Joshua shook Elder Martin's hand and turned to escape.

The clang of an alarm-spell shrilled through Joshua's body. Someone had opened his office door. He wondered which idiot had broken into his office. They should know how dangerous his office was after Gilly'd broken in and had ended up dead.

His heart thudded as he waded through the ebb and flow of the crowd toward the front entrance. If he could make it to his office quickly, he might be able to save whomever had been dumb enough to break in.

He shouldered a man and woman apart and put his hand on

a broad back blocking his way and pushed. He may have been a bit rude as he shoved his way through.

The next alarm sounded in his head. The safe was now open.

The world stopped and then spun clockwise. His Book of Secrets was out of the safe. All of his protections had been bypassed. How had that been possible? His hands shook like a junkie in withdrawal and he stumbled. He couldn't quite catch his breath. His guardianship had always been two-fold; protect the book from others and protect others from the book.

He bulldozed his way to the garden, the closer of the exits, throwing elbows and shoulders to move the mass of beings.

A sharp crack brought his gaze up, a Crylon leaned toward him as he passed. He struggled to bottle his panic. The Crylons would crush him if he couldn't, but his feelings were out of control. Something was the matter with him. His heart pounded. Adrenaline raged, but his legs and arms felt heavy. He had to remember to open his eyes after each blink. His eyes just wanted to close. The room's colors swirled. He gulped air and focused on the door. He had to get out.

He dashed out the door, down the steps and across to the garden. The humid air swirled around him thick with lilac. His shoulder collided with the gate, forcing it open.

The cool air of the street slapped his face and woke him. His body still resisted the pace he was pushing it to, his mind snapped to the fact he ran headlong down the street. It woke him to the fact he had failed. The Book of Secrets was loose, ready to wreak havoc on the town.

10

SERENE

Wee hours, Luminous thirtieth, 299 years post-Merge

Serene found a quiet, shadowed doorway to hide in. She stepped back, the cold door against her behind, and hid in the shadow waiting to see who might follow her from the Gala. The air fogged and puffed around her.

When she was sure no one had followed, she walked to where her son was waiting.

Daniel stepped out of the alley and handed her the backpack. "Didn't go as planned?"

She shook her head, still feeling twisted up about what had happened. She shouldn't have fled, but nothing else had made sense in her response to the strange conflicted looks that crossed Joshua Lighthouse's face.

The first look was shock and maybe something akin to worship, which made no sense. It woke something warm and soft in her heart. A heart she'd thought long past feeling.

But, the next expression, one of dawning disgust had twisted his whole expression. Like she was no better than a bug on his dinner.

She'd seen enough of those looks, and it squashed the fluttering in her gut and killed the warm wisps of hope. And had left her wanting to flee.

Her son touched her arm, bringing her back to the here and now. "So, what is next?"

This wasn't the way it was supposed to go. She'd pictured it. He would be cool and reserved. She would use her feminine wiles to seduce him. Maybe that had been her issue; feminine wiles hadn't ever really been her.

"We wait." There was still some hope she could nab Joshua Lighthouse on his way out. She tucked the wig into her backpack grateful that she had some clothing if she needed it.

"Waiting is good." Her son focused on the ground. His stance when he was listening intently. "This is not the best place for you. I can hear agents all around."

"Amnesty lasts until dawn." She listened too. The soft scuff of a shoe. The stealthy tread of the creatures who stalked the night gave way to their louder human counterparts.

He shrugged. "All they have to do is hold you until dawn."

There were too many beings on the prowl tonight. She wasn't going to be able to seduce Joshua Lighthouse, so she needed to come up with a better plan. Attacking him or finding his lair had much lower odds of success even if her son was with her. None of those plans were worth the risk to her son. She needed to continue alone to protect him. "You're right. I'm going."

"Really?" He sounded skeptical and he was right to be. Giving up wasn't like her. But truth be told, she had no intention of giving up her quarry tonight. This was her one shot at getting to Joshua Lighthouse. If she didn't get him tonight, he would disappear again. The Seer had been clear.

Serene needed to find the head. Tonight was her best chance.

"Yes, smarty pants. Tomorrow let's talk about other ideas." She gave what she hoped was a convincing sigh.

He nodded, but his gaze darted away from her face. "You can stay with me."

"You're much better off if you don't know where I'm staying." The less she associated with him, the better off he'd be.

"Meet me tomorrow?"

She nodded. If she could stalk Joshua tonight, she'd have time to see her son tomorrow.

He gave his crooked grin, shifted, and took off in full fur before she'd left the alley.

The change had been harder for her, not having grown up a shifter. She'd practiced until it was smooth, but tonight it felt harder than normal. Ever since the night her pack had been killed, she'd had trouble shifting. Her conflicting emotions caused a variation of sizes and colors. She focused on what she wanted. To be small and furry and dark. The world grew taller around her. The walls shot up like weeds.

The cool night warmed with the fur that crept up her body. Her center of gravity shifted and her body flexed in ways it never had when she was human.

The scents in the night sharpened, deepened, became more meaningful. One deep sniff of the night air was like talking to all the neighbors. Not just polite small talk, but deep conversation. Peeping into their lives, because scent was rarely masked and blabbed secrets. Scent didn't lie.

She glanced at her paws. She'd gotten lucky. Her fur was a dark gray and she was the size of a small wolf. She slipped on the pack easily and then climbed up the side of the building, leaping from rail to ledge to roof. The upper ledge gave her a vantage point.

Her son would be fine. He was an expert at hiding. She was the one who needed to be extra careful. When Joshua Lighthouse came out of the party, she'd stalk him and find out where he lived. Only then could she plan her next move.

She shook off the unease and focused on the Gala. Elder Martin's mansion glowed. The light slashed the natural shadows and blocked the starlight. Her eyes watered if she looked directly at that harsh light. She watched the darker garden so she could see movement in the front, but wouldn't be blinded.

She had just settled her tail over her feet, when someone stumbled out the garden gate. He was male, judging by the broad shoulders and athletic build and human if the way he moved was anything to go by. Human and in distress. He looked vaguely familiar, but she couldn't see his face clearly. No weapons were visible, but the way he staggered and almost fell at the bottom steps was less graceful than even humans usually were. He might be drunk. When he wiped an arm across his pale face, he turned his face in her direction and the odd sense of familiarity settled into recognition. It was Joshua Lighthouse.

Then he collapsed. Her heart stopped. What was going on? Perhaps he'd drunk too much and had passed out defenseless on the street. He was her only lead. If he died her chance to learn what had happened to her pack would be gone. She needed to protect him until she could get answers.

Before she could move, a tall man stepped out of the shadows along the wall and picked up Joshua Lighthouse, and threw him over his shoulder.

Something was very wrong. She didn't know what his enemies might be planning, but it couldn't be good if it started like this. She could get caught up in his troubles if she wasn't careful. But, he was the only lead she had. If she wanted her chance to question him, she'd have to follow. She leapt down and tracked Joshua's scent down the alley.

Ahead, the man walked with quick steps, easily hefting Joshua's weight.

She followed, closing the gap and sniffing. He smelled wrong. There was human, but something underneath, something foreign and foul. Maybe he'd hidden in a dumpster. Maybe if she got closer, she could tell more.

One, two steps, closer and she kept pace trailing a few steps back. The man's steps didn't falter and he never looked her way. She took a deeper sniff.

Something human, magic and rotten. She'd never smelled that combination before. And there was a drug combined with Joshua Lighthouse's scent. Had someone poisoned him? That must be why he'd collapsed. Uneasiness made her slow her steps and let the distance build between her and the kidnapper.

Now that she had the scent she could easily follow. She scented until it led to one of the human prisons. She circled the building three times hoping that the scent would lead away, but it didn't. Joshua Lighthouse was in the building.

She found a spot nearby where she could keep watch. This was dangerous. If she was lucky, this was just a place they were pausing and she could wait here and catch them leaving. Reinforcements might come at any time. The other possibility was they were going to kill him here and she would never get her answers. If she went in, she would have to rescue him, which meant working with him and exposing herself to great danger.

She'd never broken into a prison. A flash of a memory of rage and grief and bending bars and smashing doors stole her breath. She shook her head and took a deep breath realizing she did have experience breaking out of prison.

The risks were the same whether she was breaking in or out. She could get caught and killed. But if she didn't get to Joshua before his enemies killed him then she wouldn't be able to figure out what happened the night her pack was murdered and would probably anger a Seer in the process. Breaking in might be easier. Keys would be on the outside of a cell after all.

If she rescued him, Joshua Lighthouse might be grateful enough to be cooperative.

Deciding she really had no choice but to help him, she hopped off the wall and circled a fourth time looking for a way in. An open window on the second floor beckoned. Her furry form could easily enter there.

A human prison didn't expect Others to break in.

11

———

JOSHUA

Wee hours, Luminous thirtieth, 299 years post-Merge

Joshua couldn't open his eyes. His arms wouldn't move. His body felt like a mummy with the wrappings tight and his brain felt so disconnected from the rest of him that it could have been in a jar on the floor.

He smelled nothing. The air didn't move. He must be inside.

Sounds echoed as if coming down a grand marble hall. The sounds slowly came together as words.

"What do you mean you don't have it?" The voice sounded familiar but it was pitched high in panic. A voice from long ago. The voice could be almost any species, but it seemed human. The question hummed at the edges of his mind.

"It was intercepted before we could recover it," A different, deeper voice that Joshua didn't recognize said.

"Who has it?" The voice sounded insistent, demanding, driven.

"We don't know."

Something crashed. Maybe the familiar voice had thrown something. He must be angry they couldn't get it. Whatever it was. More things crashed, reminding him of a kid having a tantrum.

"Change of plans. Keep him alive." The voice slid away, leaving the last words hard to hear. "For now."

The stab in his arm yanked Joshua out of the darkness. He shivered. Blue eyes hovered above him like spiders on a thread.

"I just gave you Elf-Blood. Do you know what Elf-Blood does?" The voice was the deeper one from earlier. He seemed familiar. Joshua had seen his tall form in the last day or two. "First you will sleep. When you wake up, Elf-Blood will make you responsive to my suggestions. You will be unable to resist the lure of female flesh. No matter the kind."

Joshua tried to pull away, but his body felt heavy. Panic rushed him. He'd have no choice or control. He knew too much. Had access to too many things to be responsive to anyone's suggestions.

"I think I will give you more."

All Joshua could do was watch as the thin man leaned over and stabbed him again with the needle. The room faded.

The distant splott-splott-splott of water matched the throbbing in his head and arm. Joshua opened his eyes. A cracked stone wall and the edge of a barred door came into view. He was in a cell. Dim and cold, but no rats nibbled on his toes, no flies circled his eyes. The stone work looked familiar, but that thought drifted away.

The mental fog lifted piece by piece until he was left without protection against his own senses. His harsh breathing – a wind tunnel, his heartbeat — a stately drumroll, the slightest movement electric along his nerves as if everything was wilder, rougher, more primal.

Some part of him knew he should be worried about how he'd gotten here and what was going on, but his rational and logical parts felt locked away. His primitive-self tested the air.

The scent of mold didn't interest him, but that hint of lavender and peppermint did and it drew his eyes to the cell door.

Serene.

His heart stumbled and then roared to life. The engine that fueled his body shifted to hyperdrive. He rose to his feet feeling more alive than he'd ever felt before.

She stood just inside the open door wearing a shirt and leggings that seemed to help her blend into the shadows. The dark green depths of her eyes engulfed him. They widened and she sniffed the air. "What are you doing?" Her voice was a throaty purr, her eyes dilated.

"I want you." His voice was rough, masculine, possessive.

"What trick is this?" She shook her head and drew away.

He brought his other hand to her cheek, and leaned in, and kissed her on the lips. For a moment, it was perfection, her lips so soft against his, her tongue delved into his mouth. His body responded, wanting to get closer. Her breathing became more ragged.

And then the world flipped over and spun. Cold stone floor pressed against his cheek. A grip stronger than handcuffs held his arms. It was good she was so strong.

His arms snagged up behind him. He knew pack were

strong, but feeling it first hand was different, more personal than facts from a report. He relaxed, there was no way he'd be able to escape.

"Up, lover boy." She helped him to his feet without ever relinquishing control.

He could feel the length of her body against his. His heart sped. He panted.

Color rushed from her cheeks down her neck. Her chest rose in time with his.

"You need to follow me but no touching." She used a stern I-mean-business voice.

"I can do that." He shook his head, trying to get some control. They had to get out before the drug worsened.

She released him and walked ahead to the open cell door. He couldn't help watching her. Anything she asked, he would do.

Her gaze shifted back and forth and she sniffed the air as if she were seeking something. Each foot landing with care as if she knew what it felt like to walk in a minefield. She seemed to sense things he couldn't. Every move was Other. He was both attracted and repelled. The drug made her more attractive, confusing him. She reached the corner of the hall.

Then she turned and smiled at him. It wasn't even a friendly smile, maybe mocking and something else, but the smile emptied his brain of anything but her.

He followed. How would it feel to have her in his arms? They needed a safe place to become one. At the next corner, He recognized the line of the wall and the way the cell doors looked. This was Drummer Prison and they were in cell block Seven.

"We should go right," he said. That would take them out a side exit.

She didn't even glance at him but went left at the next choice.

Her response annoyed him. He held onto the feeling and tried to push the urge to follow her away.

"Are you heading for the backdoor?" They needed to get out of the prison before the guards returned.

"Yes." Her voice sounded clipped.

"Take the next left."

She took the next right.

He ground his teeth. Frustration cleared his head even more. Her turn led to a small room with one door to a closet. No window. Dead-end.

A squeak of a shoe behind them, brought Joshua's head up. A guard. He rocketed past Serene and flipped the guard on his back.

Joshua gripped the man's throat. He looked down into the widened eyes of not a man, but a young man. A kid really. Joshua could feel the boy's heart struggling in his chest. Wrong, this was wrong.

A flash of movement, Serene waited at the top of the stairs like a ghost. Some otherworldly spirit meant not to just haunt him, but to judge him.

The urge to kill rose, like drums throbbing in some dark, ancient jungle. To sink his teeth in the wildly pounding throat and tear. To be the one she chose through blood and violence.

He fought this baser being and forced it back. It wasn't him. This was the drug. He wasn't a killer of the innocent.

Joshua pressed the boy's carotid just enough to black him out. When the boy went limp, Joshua checked the boy's heart still beat and then tucked him on his side under a desk. The young man would be out of the way of stomping feet, but still visible from the door.

Serene stood at the top of the stairs, waiting, watching, judging.

The primitive man inside him roared back out. He had to

touch her, make sure she was unhurt. He ran to her side and stroked her arm.

She flinched away from his touch. "They cleared out the guards." She pushed the main door out. The thick spell and fire resistant door that locked in all of the prisoners opened at that gentle touch. It led out of the cellblock. Out of the prison. "They left all the doors open."

"Your voice is heaven."

"It's a set-up." She turned to him and grabbed a handful of hair and pulled his head down to her level. "You need to focus."

The pain was nothing. "I am focusing." On the soft skin of your throat.

She snapped her fingers in front of his nose. "Want us to die?"

That pushed the lust and fog back for a moment. His gaze held hers, but what he saw made no sense. Dilated eyes, flushed cheeks, but she bit her lip hard enough to leave a mark. Her fist still clenched his hair. "We are in danger."

"You are in danger?" The drug muddled him, but protecting was something he did. Something he lived.

"Yes. Oh save me, save me. You big, strong human." She rolled her eyes and flipped her hair off her face.

Some part of him knew she was being sarcastic, but his world divided into Serene and not Serene. Everything took a faint red tinge. No one would touch her while he was on guard. She was his. His to protect.

Protect. His inner beast and his civilized-self agreed. He needed to protect Serene.

She walked ahead into the next room.

It was a guard station, with no doors or windows. Monitors showed the empty cell block. Steam rose from the tea on the desk.

How had someone gotten all the guards out this fast with no

bloodshed? This seemed important. He had no answers, but the thought poked him. It meant this was staged. They were letting him escape.

"We need a safe place." Serene looked at each monitor.

"My place is safe." Kraft Tower was safe. He'd made sure of it.

"Really?" She glanced at him.

"Yes." Images of what they could do once they were safe chased the moisture from his mouth. "We should go out the front." He pointed down a hall. Two turns and they could be out the front door.

She scrunched her nose as if she'd eaten a whole lemon tree and walked the opposite way from where he'd pointed. Why did she go the opposite way? Annoyance stabbed him.

Past a turn that could lead to a backdoor and into a hallway which had a single door to a bathroom. Single stall bathroom with one window.

What she did made no sense. There were a hundred different ways they could've left the building. But she chose the only one he hadn't directed them to. There had to be a reason for her contrariness. "Why did you go this way?"

"Your annoyance pushes back the drug." She went out the window and helped him through.

They crept along a fence line until it opened to a gap. Five steps and they were back on a normal street.

<u>Crack</u>.

He twisted to face the sound from the alleyway and pushed her behind him. He held her back and sniffed the air.

She laughed and shook her head. "Smell anything, human?"

He ignored her. She was right, but he needed to seek out and eliminate any threat. A lid fell off a garbage can in the alley on the right, he jumped and placed himself between Serene and the noise.

A cat waltzed out of the alley.

A touch on his shoulder. Her touch. He glanced back and nuzzled her hand.

She snatched her hand back and walked to the middle of the street. If they walked East and North, following Arch road, they could be to Kraft Tower within the hour.

She lifted the manhole with one hand. "Get in."

"We should stay above ground." Sewers were dangerous and he wouldn't be able to see, let alone protect her. But he couldn't let her go alone.

The manhole cover landed three feet away and rolled to a stop. Serene dropped down into the hole.

The drug urged him to follow, but he wasn't in his right mind and this could be a trap. Then again, she had freed him from prison. She was protecting him from himself as much as he wanted to protect her so he followed her down the ladder.

The light from above disappeared after two steps. A metallic thump and the small amount of light from above cut off.

He shivered and stretched his hands out and took another step. She was gone. Why did he have to be human? If he was an Other, he might be able to see in the dark. He could use the Soul Wisp, but he'd already had two people die because of his powers, he didn't want Serene to be his next victim.

He needed to find her. He fought the urge to run, calling her name. There could be anything ahead. A pit. A monster. Serene.

The darkness didn't change. Thick and black, it surrounded him. Mouth opened, he took in the darkness in long shallow drags. Musty and wet was all he could smell. He strained to hear anything. Footfalls, water droplets. Anything he could orient on. His hands swept the empty air.

He felt she was near, but that could just be a trick. If he gave into his primitive self, he would die. That primitive bastard hammered his self-control. He twitched and flailed his arms.

The darkness unmoved by his efforts, and might even have crept closer.

A sigh. "Take my hand."

He jerked back. She was so close. He hadn't known she was there.

Her cool, soft hand slid into his. Relief flushed through his system. He wasn't alone. She tugged gently.

"Why are we down here?" His voice echoed ahead.

"Shhhh. It's easier this way." She whispered back.

How did being down here make it easier? Easier on whom? They wandered through the twisted, dark underground. His only lifeline was her hand. If she released his hand, he would be alone in the dark. And worse, alone without her. He shook his head. The drug was getting to him.

"Wait here." The life line released. The dark was still, deep, and unending. His senses had nothing to work with. They could be anywhere in the city.

If she left him here, his only option would be to blindly grope his way around and pray he found another human accessible exit before falling or being ambushed by something that he couldn't see. Fear swept down his spine, but he held himself still. She'd had plenty of chances to harm him.

The same metallic sound and faint light filtered from above. A ladder. She hadn't left him or betrayed him. Something warm settled in his chest.

He climbed up the ladder into an alley with a wrought iron fence and concrete sidewalks. They were on his side of town.

She put the cover back on the manhole and turned toward him. "Lead the way."

He took her hand and they walked down the block. They were almost safe. His building was two blocks up. Flickering fireflies were their only company.

"Is that Kraft Tower?" Serene pointed to the lone building that stood amid the rubble. A single light shone from the top.

"Yes."

They walked a few more paces. She grabbed his arm and Joshua's teeth rattled with the force she had used to stop him. "Why are we heading there?"

"You wanted somewhere safe," Joshua said.

"What do those signs say?" She pointed to signs on barbed a wire fence.

Joshua pointed at each sign in turn "Danger. Keep Out. Death to trespassers. Haunted. Cursed." Cursed was his favorite.

"That tower has the worst reputation. No one goes–" She stopped mid-thought and turned her gaze on Joshua. "You read Jinn, Pack, and Aero?"

"No."

"Then how do you know what those signs say?"

He triggered a switch that opened the gate. "I had the signs made."

She stared at him, brows drawn and then her mouth made a little 'o' followed by a squeak. "You're the mad wizard?"

He chuckled softly. "I guess. He's made up. I just live there."

She released his hand and took a small step back. "Do you know how bad the reputation of this place is?"

"Yes." He'd worked hard to create it. Its reputation was his best defense. The outside traps were meant to catch and scare. The inside ones were more deadly.

"Why would you...." Her expression cleared. "You really like your privacy."

"Don't you?" He closed and locked the gate behind them and headed down the path. "Follow my steps exactly." This route was a longer path to get to the tower, but had traps that would be easier for the two of them to avoid.

In no time they would be in his room together. He could still feel the drug in his system. How would the drug affect him then? When they got up to his room, they would be alone and safe. When the drug held him the tightest, he wanted nothing more than to seduce her. When the drug was at its lightest, he still found her incredibly attractive. Neither was wise for him.

"You don't get much privacy in a Pack." Her voice sounded close behind him. "Is that a pit trap?"

"Yes, that one lets them go with a good scare after a couple hours." He led to the south to dead oak. The tree wasn't really dead, but it was scarred on one side from the Merge. The scar looked like a twisted skull complete with a skeletal body. Some of the 'bones' would clack in the wind, but the wind wasn't out tonight. The air felt heavy and ominous.

He showed her the path through the three more capture traps and four tripwire pits.

They reached the side of the building. He walked to the south-side and tapped a code on a board on the wall. The hidden door shimmered into existence and opened. He'd never brought anyone home. Not Bob or Rose. No one. He knew he was drugged, but bringing her up didn't seem wrong, it seemed necessary.

He led her up the ten flights of creaky stairs to the single door that opened at the top. His room.

Another code in a different keyboard and the door beeped and slid open. The lights clicked on and lit up the room.

The door locked and engaged all its defenses. He sagged back against the door. Safe.

Serene stood in the center of his space and turned to survey what she could see. She sniffed the air. "You are always here alone."

He was always alone. No one came to his room. No one came to his building. And yet here she was. An Other he hardly knew, that he was attracted to both from the drug interaction and the book's interference.

She had both arms wrapped around her own middle, nails dug into her arms. His chest squeezed. She looked lost, uncertain, and alone. Just like him.

Her gaze paused at the framed Spiderman comic and then landed on the Mona Lisa.

He looked around his space as if seeing it for the first time. Perhaps he could set her at ease.

"I-I collect pre-merge art."

"Why?"

"It makes me feel like I'm back home."

She tilted her head to the side and pursed her lips. "Aren't we in your home?"

He had no answer for that. He'd never quite felt at home after the Merge. So he shrugged and looked at his favorite piece, A Norman Rockwell. The young boy in a diner sitting on a stool next to a cop, also on a stool. All the boy's possessions were tied on a handkerchief on a stick on the floor. "It's the hardest thing to find."

"Home." She nodded as if in understanding and then her smile came out. A smile he'd never seen before. Equal parts sad and happy, but directed fully at him.

One stride and he was across the room. His rational side screamed out all the reasons that she was wrong for him. But her scent of lavender and peppermint taunted him and drew him to her.

He brushed his hands along her shoulder and when she didn't bolt, he put his hand on the small of her back and drew her in. She tilted her head, closed her eyes, and parted her lips. Their lips met for the second time.

It didn't last long. Serene whipped him around and grabbed

his arms using her strength to pin him on the nearby bed. His cheek pressed into the pillow.

Still, the overwhelming feeling of the rightness of the kiss had hit him in the gut and had pummeled his doubts into submission. Was this attraction real? Was this the drug? Was this the book's fault? There could be no harm in believing this was real, for just a little while.

Maybe they were meant to be. Maybe all his issues being with an Other were just confetti that blew away in the wind. Everything faded until it was just Serene. She was his world.

"Please. We should be together." He struggled, but he was caught. Part of him was glad she was so strong. It evened the field and protected them both.

"There would be no choice, there must be choice." She said it fiercely. Her voice intense, rough, passionate.

"I would love you." It was true. This moment in time he couldn't believe that it would fade, this strange fluttery feeling in his chest every time he looked at her. Could a drug make him feel this way? Could the book?

"And tomorrow when the drug has cleared, you wouldn't." The words were a murmur, almost as if she was saying them to herself just as much as to him.

"I care for you." The truth of those words burned him. He was lost to her. His obsession focused on the physical now.

"You are my enemy." Each word was a soft pop of air, her arms tightened.

He flinched. They were enemies. They didn't have to be. He could help her.

"Think of the changes we could bring about if we were on the same team." He felt wild like a whole herd of mustangs tromped through him. They knocked over fences, galloping from his heart to his loins.

She laughed, a soft, sad sound that clenched his stomach.

"You wouldn't be willing to help an Other." It stung. Was it true? He was part of an organization that was meant to help. Humans, true, but did it really matter as long as they helped those who needed it? The whole train of thought left him feeling smaller.

"I will help." He turned his head, so his other cheek pressed against the bed. He could see her no better.

"Help me find out who murdered my pack." Direct and challenging. Just like she was.

The shock of her words stilled the drug in his veins.

"I have to make sure I've caught the last killer I was tracking. The victims were children." His voice cracked. "If Stregs are cooperating and being controlled, then I've not stopped them. I can't do both." He couldn't stop until he was sure that there would be no more victims.

She stilled, seeming surprised by what he'd said. "What if we traded?"

"Traded?"

"I would have more luck finding out about Stregs than you. And you would have more luck finding out who killed my Pack at the HPA research facility."

His chest constricted. Could her pack have been murdered? She was number one on the list because she'd destroyed an HPA research lab. But speaking to her now, she didn't seem like the type of person who would do such a thing. Her actions didn't match the monster she was painted to be. But was this assessment the drug clouding his senses, or his true judgement?

"You are not the monster they say." She murmured it distractedly as if her own thoughts had run parallel to his own.

He could still feel the drug thrum through his system. It ebbed and flowed. "I have two conditions."

"What?"

"We have a truce and have to share information."

"Acceptable. And the second?"

"Stay here until I sleep."

She chuckled. "Still hoping for us to be together?"

"The drug comes and goes. Right now I'm in my right mind. I don't wish to be out of control with someone who couldn't...." He stopped unsure how to say the next part.

"You don't want to take choice away."

He nodded. "Will you stay?"

"Tell me about the attacks."

"Someone is after young human girls and taking their blood."

"It's probably a spell component."

He stilled. That made so much sense. Innocent blood was something used in spells with an evil intent. That connection made the whole scenario more probable. If it were true, then more children would die.

"I...." He had to decide right now how much to trust her. She would have access to things he wouldn't. If she didn't know everything she wouldn't be able to truly help. But if he told her, then an Other, one of the beings he protected humans from and who had reason to hate him, would know his secrets. Everything in him said that if he didn't solve this case, something terrible would happen. He had no idea which part of himself knew that. What was he willing to risk to save lives?

"Can you let me turn over?" She released her hold and he turned over. She was above him now. Her arms were crossed and her expression uncertain. As if she was not quite sure what to make of him. She was known as a champion for Others. No one was willing to give intel on her location. That implied she was trustworthy.

"I need you to know something." He watched her face trying to see if he could tell if she could be trusted.

"Do I need to swear to secrecy?" Her voice was sarcastic.

He took a deep breath. "My job is to protect those that can't protect themselves. I know if you don't have all the information you may not be able to truly help."

Her arms uncrossed. She frowned, but gazed at him seeming to try to judge the truth of his words.

"When I was a kid, I was caught in the Merge. I was on the Earth from before and was kicked forward in time."

She looked skeptical. "That's not possible."

"Where do they say I got these scars from?" His finger brushed past the scar on his arms and pointed to his neck.

"There are many theories."

"It was from the forces that crushed everything around me." Could he say the next part? He took another deep breath. He'd never told a living soul about his powers. But he had to do it to save children. "The Merge changed me. I got p-powers from it."

"Why tell me this?" She wore a puzzled frown.

"I've been tracking a killer who not only has killed children, but two full teams of HPA agents. I finally got a lead and was able to catch the creature before it killed again. The killer was a team of Stregs being controlled by another. I only know this because of those powers."

She tilted her head. She didn't seem to care about his revelation. There was no judgement, but rather a distracted air. "There's more. Something you don't want to believe."

He blinked and he would have pulled away, but there wasn't anywhere to go. "No."

"You certain?"

Was he? Could the book be involved somehow? "The Book of Secrets had your image in it."

She stiffened. "That book was lost ages ago."

"A couple of boys found it. I've been its keeper. There may be a connection between the book and the killings."

"You expect me to believe that?"

"Yes. And maybe even a connection to the death of your pack."

"To what end?"

"I don't know. It's just a feeling." Any HPA agent he would've told would've scoffed. Maybe not Rose, but any other agent. They did police work the best they could and looked for proof, not just feelings.

She nodded. "Then you should know that all I know about the night my pack was murdered was we were held in the HPA laboratory."

"You didn't see anything?"

"Each person in a pack is connected by a web of energy. We can feel what the others in the pack feel and share some thoughts. We know where everyone in the pack is." She paused to meet his gaze. Her eyes seemed haunted.

What had it been like to feel her family die? He put his hand over hers. "What happened?"

"Death shook that network, the death of so many members and the leader, it was like repeated lightning strikes."

She didn't say she should have died too, but the way she closed her eyes held her body, like she wanted to rock in the corner, said that she thought she should've died too.

"I have no real memory of what happened. Just...." She shook her head. "The HPA should have records. You can find out why my pack was targeted."

What she'd said made some sense. They could each find leads better within their own worlds. And yet he hesitated to trade investigations. Did she have the skills it took to investigate? Could he trust her?

12

SERENE

<u>Dawn, Luminous thirtieth, 299 years post-Merge</u>

Serene stood at the foot of Joshua's bed. His musk colored everything in his room, and his scent was no longer tainted with the drug. His head was thrown back. Loud snores sawed from his open mouth.

His face, slack in sleep, sent a tremor to her gut. She'd decided to help him in exchange for his help. Had she been a fool to trust him? He was the head of the HPA. The same organization that had her on the top of their most wanted list and that owned the location where her pack had been murdered. If she was wrong about him, she could end up dead, or worse captured again. She might even be putting everyone who had protected her at risk. Alesia and her son could be trapped and jailed.

She backed away and ran her hand along the picture of the little human boy. Smooth glass slid under her fingertips. The art on the walls seemed at odds with his reputation outside of these walls. Even so, his art had reawakened the wisp of hope.

For one glorious moment she'd let herself feel the urge his presence awoke. She'd imagined letting him seduce her, sweeping them to their natural ending. It would give her the belonging she craved and ease her loneliness. Her and Joshua together would be so good. And because of the magic still within her veins, she'd convert him to Pack. She'd have her pack back.

A pack that she created by taking his choices away, just as hers had been taken away so long ago. Everything in her rebelled. Her heart picked up speed and chills raced down her back. No.

She backed away a step at a time. Until the cold door pushed against her back.

She had to believe that he would take finding her Pack's killer seriously. His face had said that he truly believed that it was important to find the truth. Still, there was a small part of her that wondered if it had been the drugs he'd been given driving his actions and whether when he woke up, he'd revert to the monster everyone thought he was.

No. She could tell when the drugs had taken hold. He'd wanted to touch her. Her cheeks heated.

She had to believe that he would make good on his promise and she would do the same. Now that she was on the case, she needed a plan. She knew nothing about Stregs, but Walter knew something about everything. She'd start there.

She closed the door which locked behind her and followed the trail they'd taken in. Once she was off the Kraft Tower grounds, she changed form and crept along the walls.

She made her way through dark streets. The streets hadn't always seemed so dark.

It *was* dark out, since the sun hadn't yet risen, but it was more than that type of dark. This early hour had more sounds. More scents. The air was full. The city was on the move.

Her perspective had changed. Every footfall was now a

potential enemy, every whisper of sound was a potential stalker. They were all looking for her. Or maybe for Joshua. She had no idea who had captured and drugged him. Or what had made that stink when she'd been tracking him.

She jumped from one building to the next and walked along the rooftop, sniffing every so often. Walter had a series of burrows on the north side of town. No river crossing this time.

She got off the rooftops when the Lizardfolk's homes were close. Broken houses teetered on either side. The shifting sand made a bad foundation. Spring storms washed out supports and tipped them over. The path soon became more wild.

Over the next rise, jagged house fragments, boulders, and holes pockmarked the land. Some of the holes were entrances to traps. Some led to dead ends. Some led deeper into the warden of chambers and tunnels that the Lizardfolk lived in.

She went to the edge and waved at the sentry post. If Walter was willing to talk, the guard would lead her to their leader.

A head poked out of a hole to her right and waved for her to approach. She scrambled over the sand and followed the guard into the complex.

The thick smell of healthy earth, moisture, dirt, and a small touch of decay filled the tunnel. Serene breathed with her mouth open so she could taste the air. This was her wine. The subtle hint of clover. Natural real. Alive. She strolled down the tunnel and ran her hand along the wall. Small stones and roots jutted out at odd intervals.

At each intersection guards stood. They nodded; a short quick jerk of their chin.

She rolled the sleeves of her shirt. Sweat trickled down her back. The air turned more sultry with each step forward. She turned a corner.

Walter lounged on his rock under a heat lamp. His rainbow

scales glimmering in the light. His eyes closed and his breath even.

"I wassss not expecting you." His eyes remained closed, but he rolled to expose his pastel colored belly to the light.

"I need your expertise." She rubbed the back of her neck. This was going to cost plenty. Walter was a friend, but he was Lizardfolk first and with Lizardfolk it was business above anything else.

"Yesss?"

"I need some answers on Stregs and how they can be controlled."

"Such an odd request. I exssspected you to ask about your pack"

She grabbed his arm. "Do you know something?"

"No."

She examined his face, looking for some clue that he was lying. His face betrayed nothing. It could be a negotiation tactic. It was possible Walter wouldn't be interested in looking into Stregs unless it seemed reasonable for her to be interested.

"There've been Streg killings."

"Pack?"

"Humans."

"What do you care about humanssss?"

"The killings may be linked to the death of my pack." This was a reason he would understand.

"Who ssssaysss thisssss?"

Her heart stopped. She'd walked right into his trap. "Does it matter where I heard this if I believe it?"

Walter's head came up and his tongue flicked out. He chuckled, the grinding of stones. "You believe thissss?"

Practically even if she didn't think the actual events were linked, the fact that she and Joshua had traded made everything linked. "Yes."

He opened his eyes and his gaze started at her feet and moved to her eyes. "I will help if I can. But I need your help firssst."

"What do you need?" Damn, what would he ask for? She was unsure how much information on Streg was worth.

He made a slow arm movement. "You will not like it."

"Tell me."

"I need you to deliver a messssssage."

It made no sense that he would need a message delivered. He had plenty of men who could deliver his messages. He had no need of her help. "To whom?"

"Alesssia." He spoke her name like a caress. Walter found Alesia attractive. Even if she was attracted in return, the relationship could go nowhere. She was a princess. Her life was not her own. All this attention could do was hurt her and possibly start a war. Her being a Seer added a whole layer of complication that Walter wouldn't have information about.

"You will hurt her." She softened her voice. If he cared about her at all, maybe that reminder would change his course.

"Ssshe is not asss fragile asss you think."

"If her brother finds out that you're sniffing after his little sister there will be war."

Wren seemed the more easy going of the two friends, but when it came to protecting his sister, he was ruthless. She shivered remembering the guard who'd pinned Alesia for a kiss. Wren had walked in and challenged the guard to a duel. The duel had lasted less than a minute. Wren had uncoiled like a snake and lopped off the head of the guard and had mounted it on a pike for three days as a warning to others.

"Thisssss isss the only thing you can do for your anssssswer." He sounded like he didn't care, but the stirring of red at his throat betrayed him.

She closed her eyes. Could she get the information

anywhere else? Probably not, or he wouldn't have demanded such a price. If she couldn't break the case, could Joshua use that as an excuse not to hold up his end. But if she did Walter's favor and Wren ever found out, she might insight a war between the Lizardfolk and the Aeros. Wren killing Walter or Walter killing Wren would bring both factions to war.

"I need to be able to read it and decide. If there's anything that will hurt her, no deal."

Walter lidded his eyes. The red on his throat swelled and then faded.

"No. It is sssealed on the Desssk."

More sweat dripped down her back. The guards fidgeted. Probably wishing they'd no idea what was going on. She wished she were that lucky. She couldn't start a war between the factions. The world seemed too fragile. "You will owe me."

For a long moment he stared at her and then nodded.

"I will deliver it to her hands." What she didn't say was that she had no intention of letting Alesia keep it. That letter would be burned soon after touching Alesia's hands.

Walter nodded. "Very well. I will find you an anssswer."

Serene followed the guard out of Walter's lair. All she had to do was figure out how to have it touch Alesia's hand without Alesia ever finding out the contents of the letter.

13

JOSHUA

Joshua knew that he dreamt by the dirty hay smell, the pattern in the thatched roof above his head, and the faint buzzing of flies circling. So achingly familiar from so long ago. This was where he'd hidden with Delilah when he'd first landed in this new world.

Delilah had been kind. She'd shared her food from the little village and showed him how to survive. The rest of the village had thought the weak new boy, unrelated to anyone in the village, would make the perfect sacrifice to their Other keepers.

And now, like he'd been then, he was helpless to stop what he knew was coming. His body pressed into the floor unresponsive to his commands. Hay prickled his back and legs.

On cue, Delilah's scream echoed from the doorway. A young girl's voice raised in terror.

His throat closed and his heart, a wild thing, tried to flee his chest. His whole body fought the extra gravity holding him down. Just as it had that night. Even if he broke free in the dream, nothing he did could change the past.

Delilah's straw doll stood up on his chest and pointed to the door. A door that shrank and got farther and farther away, moving in dream-space. Even if he were able to rise, the door was too far away to stop what was going to happen next. His stomach twisted.

She screamed again, and then the scream cut off mid-note. Silence followed.

His harsh pants broke the silence.

It was his fault. He was responsible for her death.

Joshua gasped and for a moment the silence of her scream echoed in his mind. He focused on the rough sheets between his fingers, and his deep breaths in and out until he could once again bury the images from the past.

He released the sheet and rubbed his face and just missed sticking his finger in his eye. His tongue stuck to the roof of his mouth. His body ached as if his muscles had been replaced with taffy. He hurt worse than the day after he'd fought Big Benny. Joshua hadn't thought of that fight in years. He'd proved, despite his young age, that he had what it took to be an HPA trainee.

He leaned over to look at his floor. For the first time since starting his training regimen the idea of getting down on the floor made him feel nauseated. He stood up slowly, the cold floor grounding him.

How had he gotten home from the party? No image came to him. His stomach tightened and the hairs raised on his arms. It was important that he remembered.

His last memory was talking to Elder Martin at the party. He must've had too much to drink. He remembered drinking something musty, but he'd not drunk enough to account for how disconnected and fuzzy he felt let alone having no recollection of how he'd gotten home. Something was wrong.

Lavender and peppermint hung in the air. It tightened his stomach and brought a myriad of feelings, including hope. That in itself was strange.

He walked into his washroom and dunked his head in the wash bin. The cold water cracked against his skin, sending ice dripping down his neck and back. He slurped the water, but no amount of water would clear out the strange taste. One last spit and he wiped his face.

A battered poster of a puppy hung above his wash bin. He'd been looking at his art with someone. No one ever came to his home, so maybe he'd dreamed the person.

He walked through his room, trying to figure out what was going on, but the memory stayed stubbornly away and the restlessness that said he was needed somewhere else grew.

Maybe if he started at his office, he'd be able to piece his memories back together. He'd start there and retrace his steps if he had to. Worry made his head throb. He'd never lost a chunk of time before. Could this be related to the book and his powers being back or was it related to something else entirely?

He needed to go to his office. He had the strange feeling that he'd promised someone he'd help with something. There was the sensation that there was something important he must do. And he was running out of time to do whatever it was. Frustration with his vague recollection had him slamming the door. He took a deep breath and set the locks.

With each step toward the office, unease rippled through him. It felt as if he neared an electrical fence. The dark haired man with the large nose standing on the corner looked familiar. Had he been down the block when Joshua'd left the Kraft tower? The unease grew.

Joshua switched directions and took a slightly longer route. A red headed woman crossed the alley ahead of him. He hadn't seen the woman before, but it struck him as odd that she didn't even glance down the alley. It was like she knew he was there, but didn't want to look.

He was being followed.

A little, dark haired girl stuck her thumb in her mouth and watched from a stairway. A large woman sat sorting beads. Joshua met her gaze, and her eyes widened. She grabbed the girl by the arm, pulling her inside. The beads scattered on the stairs and rolled toward the HPA tower. His unease grew. The humans around the HPA either ignored the agents or were glad to see them. He'd never had a human who knew he was HPA flee before.

Joshua walked through the front doors of the office and whispers hissed around him. His co-workers from ten years of working at Human protection agency stepped out of his way and avoided eye contact leaving a trail of aftershave and spilt black coffee. Even Bob dodged into the bathroom. Could they know about his powers? Had something happened that he didn't remember that had caused the HPA to reject him?

Joshua approached the line to the scanner. As if he were some force of nature, the line parted and he stood first, and only, in line.

Paula and Angelique, the floor secretaries, stood near the scanner. Backs against the hallway wall, they watched with gleaming eyes. Paula pulled out some candy and popped one in her mouth. She chewed and leaned forward, eyes glued as if waiting for a show.

The burly blond cop and his skinny buddy stood as Joshua approached the gray box. The door slid open. Joshua stepped into the Detector and placed both hands on the sensor. The light turned blue.

The murmur of the crowd stopped as if they all held their collective breath to see what would happen.

The light turned green. A bell chimed. The door slid open.

The bigger cop pointed his gun at Joshua. Sweat beaded on the cop's face. His hand trembled. The machine had said he was human, but the cop acted as if he'd expected a different answer.

Joshua's heart sped, but he straightened his back and met the cop's gaze. He was too far into the building to turn back. Maybe now that he'd passed this test, whatever was going on would dissipate.

His skinny buddy pulled the gun down. "The light is green."

Garlic heavy breath hit Joshua.

"You know garlic doesn't work on vampires?" Joshua gave voice to the novice's common misconception.

The skinny guard paled and made the sign of the cross with his finger and scrambled away from Joshua. That was odd. It was almost as if the guard thought Joshua was a vampire. Something could've happened last night that would account for this odd behavior. He'd know if he'd been converted or infected by something, wouldn't he? Unease trickled down his spine.

The watching crowd whispered, but when he glanced at them, they silenced. Passing the detector hadn't changed anything. He was still in trouble. They must think he wasn't human and the detector had missed it.

Joshua took his time walking towards the elevators. If he ran, they would chase him. If he didn't already have the crowd behind him, he would have fled.

Joshua waited for the elevator, legs braced apart, hands at his sides so he'd be able to grab a weapon more quickly.

No one else crossed through the detector. There should've been a steady pinging, but an uneasy silence hung behind him. He entered the elevator and turned to see the whole room staring back. Looking at him as if he were different.

He felt different. Still human, but his reactions were slower than normal, his thoughts were sluggish. He hadn't noticed anything odd at the Gala. He did remember talking to Elder

Martin, and feeling frustrated, but normal. Something after that moment must have changed everything.

The door closed and he slumped against the wall. Every person in the HPA thought he was a monster.

The elevator door slid open on his floor. Most of his men sat at their desks with weapons out. Never a good sign. They were getting ready for a hunt. And Joshua seemed to be positioned as the prey. The sense of foreboding deepened. If it had spread to the hunters, then he was in desperate trouble. The first flush of fear hit his chest.

Thomas sharpened his favorite knife. The shing shing sound echoed eerily through the mostly silent office. The back of Joshua's neck tightened and his heart thumped a panicked beat against his chest. He felt like he had just entered a lion's den naked. What could've changed in the last day? Something must've happened after the Gala to account for his team's response. He needed to act as normal as he could until he could figure it out.

Hugo stared at Joshua as Joshua poured coffee. More and more gazes seemed to focus on him as he grabbed the files from the previous night. The whole roomful of people stared at him as he walked to his office.

The door latch caught behind him and he slouched against the door.

Safe. He was safe within his office. Joshua flipped the switch that turned on the sensors in the hall. Any step within five feet of the door, would cause the alarm to buzz.

Joshua sank into his chair, putting his coffee and files on the desk. The office had no windows; windows were not safe. The army cot stood in the corner with rumpled sheets from his cat nap before the Gala.

He moved a paper and saw his mirror necklace and the photo of his friends from the Archive. Surprised confusion, pushed its way through his mental fog. He touched the necklace with the tip of his finger. The glass was real. In his fatigue, had he forgotten to put the photo and necklace back in the safe? He glanced up. The safe stood an open maw of darkness. He gasped and couldn't catch his breath.

The safe was empty.

His heart thundered in his body. Everything came rushing back in a slideshow of moments. The party. Meeting Serene. The alarm. The prison. Being rescued. Serene. Switching investigations. He slumped into his chair. Everyone in the office must think he'd slept with Serene and that she'd transformed him into Pack. The skinny guard must've thought they'd said vampire.

He blew out an unsteady breath. Someone had expected him to come back from the Gala as something not human. It had to be someone with reach within the HPA. It lent support to the idea that Serene had been set-up too. It made no sense that he was the target.

Shaking his head at the unsolved questions roiling in his mind, he stood and glanced at the safe. It didn't look forced. Someone had not only gotten into his office, but had figured out how to open the safe. He got down on his hands and knees to examine the carpet. The carpet had no residue and didn't have an odor. The ball of paper was still wedged under the desk.

Unless there had been some sort of breach, odds were good that whoever had set him up was also involved with stealing the book. And that human was affiliated with the HPA and might be here in the office.

If he could figure out who had betrayed him, he might have some options to address the issue and find the book. Otherwise, he was trapped in his office until the hunters decided to kill him.

He could use his powers, however, when he used them not only did he get physically weak, but those closest to him were at risk of dying. Could he find out what was going on and still escape without killing anyone?

He wasn't willing to hide when there could be an army of Stregs. He had to take the necessary risks and do what he could to protect the people of this world.

He'd been able to create smaller spies the last time. If he could make them even smaller, he could cover more ground.

He closed his eyes. Instead of creating mental hands to make the Soul Wisp, he tried to picture a tiny scoop. He flicked it into the mud and created mosquito-sized Soul Wisps. Until a swarm circled his head. His sight dimmed as if he had a bag over his head. His breathing became a slow, raspy gasp. He was empty of all but one small piece of his essence.

The flocks of Soul Wisps swirled off to each floor and then fractured to touch people. The crash of emotions and thoughts buzzed into his mind. Their expectations beat like thousands of moths' wings against a light until all he could feel was what the people in the building thought. He pulled the Soul Wisps from those that had no clue about what was going on and focused on the ones that did. Or thought they did.

Anyone who'd thought of him, secretaries, the lab folks, the guards at the front desk had all expected he'd be shot after passing the machine. They had expected him to transform into a raving werewolf or a vampire. They weren't sure of what exactly, only that he was no longer human.

Joshua sent a Soul Wisp to Thomas. He was deeply troubled by the thought of Joshua being executed in his office. Thomas knew that something was going on in the HPA, but he needed to protect his wife and child. Thomas believed if he went against the rumor, he and his family would be next. Joshua agreed. They needed all the protection they could get.

Others had concerns, but something drove them. They each thought someone had told them about Joshua no longer being human. But tracing back led to a crisscross pattern with no one person having started the lie.

He found a trail of rage and fear that led to a partially shielded mind that fled out of his range. A Soul Wisp followed, hovering close hoping to pick up something. The mind was at the edge of his range, when knowledge slipped out. This person from the HPA had been the one who'd orchestrated his kidnapping, stolen the book, and started the HPA rumor that Joshua was no longer human. The word UnMerge echoed in the man's mind.

The shock knocked the last Soul Wisp out of Joshua's body. Left him drifting aimlessly in the sea of other people's emotions and the space between. Gradually, Joshua's essence drew back together and formed a ghost that floated above his own body attached by a silver chord.

The perpetrator's mind slipped out of range before he could figure out who it was. With him gone, Joshua would have no way of proving his innocence. The hunters would soon be brave enough to breach his office and execute him.

Joshua returned to his body with a shudder. The room shook as he convulsed. He focused on one spot at the northwestern corner of the ceiling. A tiny black spider weaved and bobbed across the ceiling. The back of the chair dug into his neck. He rubbed his arms and goosebumps rose under his fingers

He swept his internal space looking for Riders.

Clean.

He reached for his coffee, but his hand thumped the cup sending droplets scattering across the desk. Everything felt heavy. His eyes ached. There was no way he'd be able to leave. Maybe if he stood and packed a quick satchel to replace the one he'd left at the Gala he'd get his second wind.

He grabbed his spare satchel and added in holy water, his special mixture, salt, a stake. The items on the shelf blurred.

Saints, he was tired. He slowly sat behind his desk. The glass necklace and the picture were still on his desk. He'd take them with him. If he left anything in his office, it would likely be destroyed. He put the picture in his bag and put the necklace on. The cold chunk of glass was cold against his chest.

In his desk were the files of the top 10 most wanted. He pulled out the file on Serene. He'd not looked very closely at it. There was no way he could now. That also went into his bag.

Serene had saved him from literally fucking his life away. Why had she done that? A human, someone in the HPA had betrayed him yet one that he had hunted had not. It made no sense.

He'd agreed to find out what had happened to her Pack. Find the killer. Everything in him said that this was all connected. The Stregs, the pack killing, the book, and even his betrayal were all pieces in a bigger plan. And somehow it all added up to UnMerging the world. He shuddered. The world might not survive. If this whole plot was about the UnMerge he had one day to figure out what was happening.

The alarm buzzed. Pounding on his door sent his stomach tumbling to the floor.

14

SERENE

Morning, Luminous thirtieth, 299 years post-Merge

Serene wished she could lay on the cool stone of the stair and pant in her furry form. Instead, in her human form, she sat on a stone bench halfway up the stairs non-Aeros used to access the Rookery. Her leadened legs reminded her that she'd already climbed fifty flights and still had fifty more to go. Alesia would be in her brother's room at the top.

Getting across the city had been easier this time. It had been as if someone was aware of her movements and helping her. It could be Walter, or the Hive, or her imagination.

The Aeros had let her into the Rookery with no questions. If Wren as their leader had given his blessing to her being a member of the flight, then she was. No matter what she looked like.

She still hadn't figured out how to get Alesia to touch the letter without her knowing the contents. Walter would know if she was lying and wouldn't give her the information she needed.

So she had to do exactly what she'd told Walter. The words, not the intent.

The stairs wouldn't walk themselves. She stood and resumed her climb, tracing her fingers along the sparkling stone. Aero builders loved playing with sunlight. It distracted her from the ache in her legs.

Alesia stood by the window, looking out. Her hand ran up and down her arm in long slow strokes.

"Alesia."

Alesia jumped and spun. Her face brightened and she raced across the room, embracing Serene. "You're alive."

Affection warmed Serene. She hugged Alesia back. "Yes."

"Wren said he saw you at the party." Alesia said it like she couldn't wait to find out what had happened.

"He told you that?" Word had traveled fast. She hadn't been aware anyone had noticed her. She guessed going to the party naked had drawn attention.

"And that you were talking to Joshua Lighthouse. And that you both left the party around the same time." Alesia took her hand and leaned in like she was sharing a secret.

"Indeed."

Alesia blinked and then stamped her foot. "That's it? That's all I get?"

Serene laughed at Alesia's expression. "What your brother said was true." She'd never felt uneasy talking to Alesia before. But the idea of discussing her plans to seduce Joshua and her confused response to him just seemed wrong.

"Were you really trying to seduce him?"

Serene jerked back and focused on Alesia's face. "What?"

"You go naked to a Gala and happen to converse with the man who is the head of the HPA...."

Serene could see the interest in Alesia's face. She'd been protected and sheltered in the Rookery. The conversation and her own impressions of Joshua had called into question so many things. Could Serene talk to Alesia?

Alesia reached out her hand. "What is it my sister?"

It was more than Joshua, what bothered her was deeper. Seeing Joshua struggle against the drug and try to make the choices he could had warmed her to him. It'd reminded her of her own past. "All my choices have been taken from me." Her stomach plummeted.

Alesia wrapped her long fingers around Serene's wrist. "You never made any choices?"

The soft question made her think of that night years ago that she had taken the dare and trespassed on the Pack's land. The Pack had been outside of the city and unbeknownst to her had been struggling under a curse that had made them desperate. Desperate enough to chance converting a human girl.

"I guess I decided to expose the legend." Serene's laugh sounded unsteady in her own ears. "One bad choice started this whole thing."

"And that is how you became pack." Not a question but a statement.

Serene nodded. "After that there were no choices." She'd been lost and trapped all of those years.

"Didn't you leave the pack?" Alesia pursed her lips and looked at Serene out of the corner of her eye.

"Yes, but–" She'd left the pack when her son had been born. When her son hadn't been bonded to the pack, she'd had no choice. It was leave or give him up. She couldn't give up her son. So she'd resisted the bond and left the pack to raise her son.

"Didn't you raise your son on your own with no pack to protect you?"

"I did, but–" What choice did a mother have other than to raise her child as best she could? To do what it took to keep her child safe.

"Didn't you choose to go back to the pack instead of having your son fight the pack leader, your mate, to the death as a way to join the Pack?"

"Those were not choices." Serene scoffed. In each case she'd taken the only option available to her.

Alesia shook her head slowly and met her gaze solemnly. "They were choices. They were big hard choices with tough consequences. The community got a healer. You held that pack together."

She'd never thought about it that way. She'd known what she'd had to do and she'd done it. If she hadn't loved the people involved maybe she could have let her son die or the pack wither. "But it was all for naught." Her voice was small.

"Because they died?"

Serene nodded. Grief and regret brought heat to her eyes. She blinked a few too many times. "Not quite a happy ending."

"The pack had children which formed other packs which survived. Maybe your pack was not meant to live." Alesia said it slowly as if tasting the words to see if they fit.

Serene looked up and examined Alesia's face. The seer peered back. A look of compassion warmed her face. It was a look that few could master. A look of truth. Serene's heart throbbed and her skin chilled.

"Perhaps you are meant to hold something else together."

"What?" Serene held her breath to see if the Seer would answer.

"Something bigger is happening."

"Everything is linked."

The Seer nodded. "Your human friend has caught the tail."

She meant Joshua and his idea that everything they were investigating were linked to something bigger. She must pay Walter's price. She wished she knew if she was dooming her friend in the process. "Will I start a war if I give Alesia Walter's letter?"

"Perhaps." Alesia smiled a warm soft smile a fond remembrance of something once held.

"And if I don't?"

"Then many will die. You spoke of choices. Do not forget others should have choices as well." Then Alesia blinked and the otherworldly presence left the room. All the ideas on how Serene might trick Alesia into touching the letter, but not knowing it was from Walter faded. The Seer was right, Serene couldn't take her friend's choice away. It was possible the letter could do more good than harm.

"Alesia, I have something for you from Walter."

Alesia's face flushed and she glanced away. "Yes?" Her hold became timid on Serene's arm, a feather touch.

Serene pulled out the letter. She held it out to Alesia, who seemed very hesitant to reach for it.

"Why would you bring this to me?" Alesia reached out and touched the edge of the letter and then tucked her hand under her arm.

"I had to."

"Had to?" Alesia raised an eyebrow.

"No, I chose to. Please wait to read it for a few days."

Alesia nodded and then took the letter. "For you, anything."

"I'm not sure it would be wise for Wren to see it." Alesia had to know how dangerous this would be for Walter and her people.

Alesia glanced away. "Wren doesn't know everything."

Serene grinned. "Good. You need a secret or two to keep him on his toes."

Alesia looked away. "You will have to leave again."

"Yes." She looked at Alesia's sad face and realized she was making another choice. "I tried to seduce Joshua, but it didn't go well. He was drugged and taken after the party and I rescued him from jail. They let us go for some reason and I took him to his home."

"Egads. Did he give you what you needed?"

Serene shook her head. "He seemed completely unaware of what had happened. But...."

"Yes?"

"He thinks a Streg killing human children and my pack's death may be linked. The Seer agrees. There's something big going on." Serene shook her head. The idea that these things were linked still surprised her.

"Wren has said that the world is more fragile on the Merge anniversary."

"You think someone is trying to UnMerge the world? I can't imagine someone figuring out how to UnMerge the worlds."

"Someone figured out how to merge them together." Alesia shrugged.

The words felt heavy in the room. Alesia was right. Someone had figured that out hundreds of years ago and had wrought catastrophic changes to the worlds. Or so the stories said.

"It's more likely to be some sort of power struggle between the factions."

"Perhaps." Alesia popped her lips together, a sure sign she had an idea she was working through. "Stay here tonight and rest. You look like you could use it. I'll get you transport to Walter in the morning."

Serene stifled a yawn. Alesia was right, she needed sleep and the Rookery was an excellent place to get some.

The next morning, Alesia arranged a ride on a giant eagle, one of the working animals that the Aero's kept. The bird was bigger than Serene and cocked its head in her direction. Alesia stroked the feathers along its head.

"How do I hold on?" Serene approached slowly.

"You can ride in her claws or on her back."

The thought of having foot long daggers wrapped around Serene's body made her shiver. "Back."

Alesia helped her onto a small flat pad on the bird's back. She gripped with her legs.

"Not that tight, or she'll drop you."

Serene jerked to look at Alesia's face to see if she was kidding. She looked serious. "Can't I hitch a ride with you?"

Alesia grinned. "It would be unseemly for a princess to carry you."

That was not the real reason. Alesia seemed nervous. Her feathers more puffed than normal. "You have other plans?"

Alesia nodded and handed Serene a bag. "Give her this treat when you get off of her. It will make it easier to ride her the next time."

"Why would I need another ride?" Serene loosened her grip.

Alesia just grinned and whistled.

The thrust of her wings sent them shooting into the sky. Serene kept her eyes closed so she wouldn't accidentally strangle the bird and end up dead. Her stomach rolled with each twist and turn of flight. Then the blasted bird dove what felt to be straight down.

She was going to die. She was going to die. Don't squeeze the bird.

The bird stopped with a little hop. When she opened her eyes, she saw a large rock formation to her left. It must be the guard post.

Serene slid off the bird onto shaking legs. The bird cocked it head at her, reminding Serene of the treat. She opened the satchel, expecting a wafer, but saw a dead mouse. She grabbed it by the tail and tossed it into the air. The bird snatched the treat and then hopped away, jumping back into the air.

A single Lizardfolk poked his head out and escorted her to Walter.

This time when Serene entered, Walter was pacing back and forth, his tail whipping behind him. "You delivered the letter?"

"Yes." That seemed to calm him. He stopped pacing and came to her side.

"Ssshe read it?"

Walter was above all else a businessman, she needed to make sure she didn't give away too much for free. It would make him respect her less. The last thing she needed was for him to think she was not worthy of helping. "That was not a condition."

"True."

The silence lengthened and she wondered if she had made a mistake. "What do you know about Stregs?"

"Evil creaturesssss. A mix of living, dead, magic, and something the Merge brought from the human world that createsss them."

His words brought to mind the smell of the person carrying Joshua the night she'd rescued him. Could that smell be a clue? Perhaps, but Joshua seemed to be the most worried about who might control them. "Can they be controlled?"

Walter's flap moved showing a quick flash of red. "If they could be, the controller would have an army of hard to kill, blood thirsssssty killerssss."

She tried to imagine such creatures and failed. It made no sense that someone would create such a creature, but maybe if she knew how she'd have another clue about where to look. "How would someone create a Streg?"

"With a living target and many dead."

"And then what?"

"None of my sssourcesss have sssuch knowledge."

Something about the way he held himself made her believe him. He truly didn't know how to create Stregs. It could be he never really tried to get that information. Once information was learned, it could never be unlearned. She really didn't need to know how to create them, just maybe who might be able to. She needed some angle to investigate that might lead to an actual person. "What else?"

"That issss what I know." He gave a shrug and a small smile.

"I thought you would gather information for my question?"

"That was not a condition of our deal."

She puffed out a laugh. Walter was tricky. Where could she go next to get information? She couldn't go back to Joshua and say Walter had tricked her. And even if he hadn't tricked her, how much could he truly find out about Stregs in such a short period of time? "You still owe me."

"I would try the graveyard."

She shuddered. Graveyards were no place for the living. "Why's that?"

"It issss a placcce with many dead."

15

JOSHUA

Joshua was trapped in his office. There was one door and no other exits. Exits could be used as entrances. He'd never thought his organization would come after him. They'd been unified in the protection of humans. That was what he stood for, so the idea that they could be at odds and that the HPA could've been breached, hadn't seemed possible.

Now there was no choice but to fight his way out.

"Damn it, open the door." Rose didn't shout, but her voice penetrated his door. Relief flowed through him. Rose could be trusted.

Joshua opened the door and saw her pale face and the red ponytail she always wore. Her chest rose in short quick breaths. The hallway was dark behind her. She pulled him out of his office, shut his door and tugged him into the office two doors down.

"They are coming. We still have a chance to get out. Ready to run for it?"

His heart sank, the hunters had not given him much time before pouncing. "I can't." He would have to figure out a way out of this mess without getting Rose in trouble.

"You can't take on the whole HPA by yourself. Even with my help." She sounded exasperated.

Maybe if he could show her the physical impossibility of it, she would leave. "No, I am physically not able to run. I've been drained."

"Saints." She closed her eyes and tapped her head. "Okay new plan–"

"Listen. You have to help Serene." He knew how he sounded, sending an HPA agent to help their number one most wanted. He touched her shoulder and held her gaze. Helping others was the one thing she might leave him for. He had to get her out of here.

"Have you been controlled? Blink twice if you are being controlled." She said it dryly, but was watching his reaction.

"I know this sounds crazy. She was set-up by the same person who set me up. A Conduit is involved." When he'd sent out the Soul Wisps while trapped in the office, the person who'd known the most had had the word UnMerge blazing in his thoughts.

Surely that was not what all these things had in common. "It may have to do with a plot to UnMerge."

He had never seen her look so shocked. Her eyes wide, and mouth opened.

"Serene is looking for leads on what was controlling the Stregs. I'm trying to get answers on what happened the night the HPA research lab burned. I'm hoping it will lead us to what is really going on."

"I can help you."

He gazed into her face. She looked as if she'd braced for him to say no. But he did need help. He needed Rose to help Serene. Then even if something happened to him, there would still be a chance to save children and stop an UnMerge plot. "Yes."

She stood up straight and stared at him. He'd never asked for help before.

"I need help getting out of this building. Then you have got to help Serene. Please."

"You went to ask the book. Is this the book talking?"

"No. Maybe. I don't know." He slumped back. Gods, he was so tired. The dead weight he used to call his arms shifted up to rub the grit in his eyes. "I just know you helping me directly will have the HPA after you. If you can't help Serene, then I need you to be free to find out what's really going on."

"There is a Healer in Shifterville, Master Phil. He might be able to help." She touched his arm. "I will find Serene and help her."

Relief loosened his legs.

She pulled out a twine and bone bracelet. "Use this to escape. I got it from a bust a few weeks ago." She didn't look at him, but he knew there hadn't been a bust a few weeks ago. At least nothing on record.

Joshua shivered, but took the bracelet. "What does it do?"

"It will make you look like whatever the person who sees you fears the most. The magic won't last very long, but long enough to get you out of the HPA building." Her head cocked and she flicked her gaze to the door.

He slipped it in his pocket. "Thank you. I-"

Her hand slapped over his mouth and gripped his cheeks like some senile auntie. Joshua pulled away.

She made a shushing motion, held his hand, cutting the circulation off in his fingers, and peered out the door crack. A fine tremor raced up her arm. A bead of sweat trickled down her neck.

<u>Boomp-ba-boom</u>.

Joshua's stomach dropped. The sounds came from the direction of his office. They'd used a rune, a focused blast of power, to break into his office.

She yanked him out the door and pulled him down the hallway away from his office. His heart sped, but his body still felt heavy.

He stumbled and she steadied him. He leaned heavily into her as they ran. Over his shoulder, a cloud of debris and smoke filled the hall.

Down the corridor and to the left, she opened the stairwell door and glanced inside. They'd have to get past the guards at the bottom. How was she going to get out without being seen with him?

Once the door was shut behind them, she shoved his arm, stamped a foot and pointed down the stairs. Her face was fierce and pinched, but her eyes were wild. She was going to act as a distraction so he could escape.

Rose stomped up the stairs making enough noise for a whole herd of dragons.

He stumbled down the stairs. Even with the adrenaline racing through his system, he was running out of energy fast. He had to get out. He sent one Soul Wisp ahead and took the stairs down two at a time.

A door above him clicked open. The murmur of voices receded following the upward stomping. He kept going down. Rose was smart, she'd have a plan.

Two more floors down. The stomping and voices no longer echoed in the stairwell.

<u>Clang-Crunch</u>.

The stairwell shook. A whoomp of heated air pushed Joshua. His feet slid down a stair and he scrambled to catch his balance. Chills raked up his back.

Had the blast they'd used gotten Rose? She'd led them up the stairs. Hopefully she'd gotten away, but what if she hadn't. If she was hurt, it was his fault. His intestines twisted around like mating snakes.

There was nothing he could do to help her. If she was still alive, they would kill her if they thought she was helping him. Rose was smart. She'd have a plan and if she got caught, she'd make them believe she was on their side.

One last floor. His Soul Wisp found the two guards from earlier on the other side of the door. They blocked his escape. Their fear of vampires should make the bracelet Rose had given him more effective on the guards.

He put on the bracelet and stepped out.

"V-vampire." the skinny cop pointed a shaky finger.

"Get the stakes."

"You get the stakes." The skinny cop looked at the fat cop, then turned and ran. The skinny guard banged the stairwell open and raced up the stairs.

Joshua leapt at the fat guard, teeth bared. The fat cop reared back and let out a squeal. "Wait for me!"

They were gone. One obstacle cleared. He was one step closer to leaving the building. He locked the stairwell door with a flip of a switch. That would delay them a few more moments.

He stalked out the door, and people scattered, screaming. The bracelet must be making him look terrifying.

Soon the front lobby was clear.

He ran out and once he was around the corner, he took off the bracelet. It disintegrated in his hand. He was on his own.

Joshua leaned against the alley wall and caught his breath. His arms and legs felt like lead. He closed his eyes. It would be so easy to give in and sleep. But he couldn't. He had to keep going for as long as he could. The HPA would have agents on the streets looking for him.

He needed a place to hide out until he got his strength back. His tower would be guarded now. He had few friends and none he could go to for help.

If Rose survived, he wouldn't be able to approach her directly. It would be too dangerous for her. He needed to focus on Serene and tracking down what was going on.

Rose had never steered him wrong before so he headed southwest. Maybe he'd survive long enough to find Master Phil, the healer in Shifterville.

16

SERENE

Mid-morning, Luminous thirty-first, 299 years post-Merge

Walter's guards led Serene out of the complex to a ridge overlooking the city. It sparkled in the daylight. There was just one place to bury the dead in New Nadezhda, Malani Necropolis in the southeast part of town. She wouldn't have far to go to get there. She could be in her wolf form until she reached the cemetery, but she wanted to be human to breach those walls.

She'd walked a block before the normal daytime noises stopped abruptly.

A footstep echoed behind her. It was purposefully done. The person wanted to be heard.

Serene lifted her nose and smelled a human female. The way the human walked screamed HPA. She switched form and slid through the shadows, using every trick she remembered about losing humans. It took longer, but she finally made it to the entrance of the cemetery. It was a long shot, but maybe she'd be able to find something related to Streg at this place filled with the dead. If someone were creating Streg, this would be an ideal place. Most people didn't go into the cemetery except for funeral days.

Serene changed to her human form and put on the clothing from her backpack.

She ran her hand along the iron spikes set in the ground. The cold iron made a barrier between the walkway and the graveyard. Someone had piled rocks and debris between the spikes. The spikes were close enough together that even a small person or her wolf form would have trouble getting through.

A pale mist hung in the air growing thicker toward the center of the graveyard. Chills swept her body. Hundreds of years ago the makers of the Malani Necropolis had added a spell within the walls which would keep it daylight within the boundaries. It'd been intended to keep the dead at rest. The spell must've broken, because the shroud of fog reminded her of twilight. Twilight was when the undead would start to move. Unease lifted the hairs on her arms.

The gate that blocked this entrance had cold iron spikes and scarred burnt wood. It towered above her.

This was it. Once she entered the cemetery she would be unable to use her wolf form. Something about the ground at the cemetery prevented transformations, but encouraged restless undead.

The gate would close at dusk and if she were still here, she'd be trapped all night. No one had survived being trapped in the cemetery. But it was only mid-morning, nightfall was hours away. She should have plenty of time to get in and get out before the gate closed for the night.

She slipped through the gate and opened her senses. A sickly sweet smell of rotten meat and decay was to be expected, but she caught just a trace of the strange smell from when

Joshua had been kidnapped. Elation bounced her steps. The cemetery would have clues.

Small digging sounds and clicks came from the shadowy areas between the leaning headstones and trees. Even the trees didn't seem right. They looked like skeletal hands reaching from the ground. She swallowed.

She followed the hint of scent that had been near Joshua when he'd been kidnapped, trying to stay to the main paths. Ahead the path ended at a large statue of a man astride a horse. Both he and the horse had the same twisted expression of fear and rage. The smell continued stronger beyond the statue. She'd be a fool to get off the path. At least on the path she would be able to find her way out.

The mist and shadows filled the space between the statue and the leaning gravestones on either side. She could go back and try another turn, but she'd have no way to know if that was the right way. The Cemetery was built to confuse the dead and keep them in. She glanced toward the shadows near her and noted the quiet. There was a scratching sound. Whether that was good or bad was debatable.

Time was running out, the last thing she wanted was to be here when the dead awoke. She'd have to chance getting off the main path.

She took a deep breath and walked between the statue and the gravestone.

The mist thickened and muted the noises around her. After two steps, everything felt different. The air seemed heavier. The shadows moved. Were they the dead or just a trick?

The smell intensified and she followed it.

A snap sounded ahead and she froze, holding her breath. The sound could be a foot fall. She bit down the urge to call out. If it was the dead, she didn't want to announce her presence.

She took two more steps, before something knocked her to the ground. She grunted and her heart pounded.

She bucked up and rolled to the right striking out, a thunk and loosening of pressure behind her told her she'd hit it. She pushed off the ground throwing what had been on her back to the side. She stood and tried to summon her claws, but nothing happened. A bubble of panic made it hard to breathe, she was almost defenseless in this form.

She shot to her feet. A large wolven creature with glowing red eyes stared back. The stench of decay pummeled her. It rolled to its side and leapt back up. White bone gleamed from its chest and back leg where the meat looked gnawed off.

She backed away a step at a time until cold stone touched her back.

She was trapped.

17

JOSHUA

<u>Mid-morning, Luminous thirty-first, 299 years post-Merge</u>

Joshua stumbled to the east away from the HPA building. Shifterville wasn't very far away.

He plodded a few blocks further. He couldn't hurry. It was all he could do to keep his legs moving. He wished he could curl up somewhere and sleep, but if he did that, he wouldn't wake up. There were too many predators out in the world, even in the daylight. No, he had to keep his legs moving.

He rubbed his eyes, but couldn't get the grit out.

He tripped and fell against a building. He blinked and looked up. He was no longer in the human part of town. Even his laughable human senses could tell he was in Shifterville. Layered, lush greens covered stone work. Deep gashes marred some of the tree trunks that lined the path. This part of town looked like some forgotten stone-village overrun by the jungle.

A dark spot on the crumbling walls could have been a door or just a shadow. He had files on each of the species. The HPA's intel on this area said the houses were low to the ground and defensible. A community dug into their lair was almost impossible to dig out. Not that they would give anyone the time. Mutual aid pacts and alliances would give an enemy five minutes tops before a counter assault happened. All controlled by scent, howls, and tree markings.

Dirt paths between stone walls crossed and meandered into the quiet woods. Only the occasional lamp post flickering into view showed he was still in town.

He would never find the healer let alone a safe place to rest in this maze.

The sound of metal rattling on stone and a strange call echoed down the alley. Joshua rounded the next corner and stopped mid-step. A boy with wild, red hair stood before a small fox that struggled to free a leg caught in a trap.

An HPA Trap.

"Lissa, you have to stop struggling." The boy's voice broke at the end. Then he tipped his head back and howled. The howl was a call to his pack. Joshua waited a heartbeat, there was no response.

Joshua knew he should pretend that he hadn't seen them and walk on by. He was weakened by the use of his power and running out of steam fast, but how could he leave a boy in trouble? Even if there was a chance this was a trick. The trapped fox's eyes were wide, ears flat, its tail thrashed like a possessed snake. Joshua couldn't leave the boy—or the fox. Both were young enough to be innocent and didn't deserve to be caught in HPA traps.

"Can I help?" Joshua pitched his voice to be soothing and walked closer. The boy might attack if Joshua wasn't careful. In his current state, he might not be able to defend himself, but he had to take that chance.

At the sound, the boy whipped around. His fangs grew and he snarled, "Go. Away."

Joshua crouched down to the boy's level, and lowered his head a few degrees, to act like a beta, this was standard training an agent received. "I can help."

The fox whimpered. The boy wilted at the sound. He glanced at the fox and back at Joshua. His eyes glistened. "The trap gets tighter if you touch it."

Joshua inched closer. He knew this trap. Knew its cruelty to those that struggled or tried to escape. It shouldn't have been left out to trap the innocent. It was only supposed to be used under dire circumstances. "Who is Lissa?"

"My little sister. I-I was supposed to keep her safe."

"Let me see." Joshua crawled forward and put one hand near where the trap held her leg. The other hand slid carefully along the cool metal and found the hidden release. He triggered it. The trap snapped open and dissipated in a cloud of ash and sulfur smell. He sagged. The trap was disarmed, so it wouldn't continue to hurt her.

"Is Lissa hurt?" The boy was on his knees next to him with one hand on Joshua's leg. His voice caught.

Joshua stroked her fur, moving his hand closer to where the trap had been. The fur parted on her back legs and revealed a deep red gash.

He picked her up and her little tongue left a warm trail on his forearm.

The boy gnawed his lip and stroked Lissa's fur. "Looks deep."

"We need a doctor." Now that she was free, he needed to disengage. Someone would recognize him.

"What doctor will see us? We have to take her to a healer. Come on." The boy tugged Joshua toward the alley. This was good. Maybe whatever healer the boy took him to would know the one he wanted to find. The boy's hand was firm and his step never hesitated as he walked through what appeared to be a solid wall. Joshua closed his eyes and felt an odd ripple, like he'd jumped into a pool.

Joshua blinked, hoping his eyes would adjust to the sudden dark. The boy must've pulled him through the wall. Nothing the HPA had gathered about Shifterville mentioned fake walls.

The boy tugged him and when Joshua stepped again, it was light again. The buildings squeezed in on each side of him. He was in a narrow gap with rubble nearly blocking the street.

The boy led him through another wall below a window. Joshua ducked and his hair brushed the ceiling.

Joshua lost track of how many walls and alleys they walked through. The fox was getting heavier with each step. The HPA would never find him here, but his energy would be gone before too long.

The last secret tunnel sloped down into a cellar. The steady drip of water echoed. The smell of decay was so strong, Joshua tasted mushrooms.

"Master Phil?" The boy scratched on the door and it opened. Flickering candles struggled against the darkness from the far side of the room. A wet snuffling sound came from the corner. The deeper into the room they went, the darker the room became. There was magic here. Something that cloaked the room.

"Michael, why did you bring him here?" The low voice echoed off the walls. A long ivory claw glowed faintly from the corner and pointed at Joshua.

Joshua turned to shelter Lissa.

"He saved Lissa from an HPA trap."

"Whatever you may think of me, please help Lissa first," Joshua said. The girl shouldn't suffer because he'd been the one to carry her here.

A long curl of black smoke snaked out of the darkness and grabbed Joshua's waist, dragging him closer to the dark corner.

"Please don't hurt her." Michael's voice sounded young in the dark.

Something snatched the pup from his arms and then tossed him back toward the door. Joshua landed on his butt and slid back to the wall next to the door.

He heard a few muttered words he couldn't make out and then a golden glow emanated from the corner and silhouetted the pup who floated in mid-air. The pup whimpered and then yelped. The glow intensified. The pup stood in the air and leaped into the darkness. Slobbering noises and squeaks filled the darkness.

The low voice chuckled.

Lissa appeared whole, healed, and her body moved with the force of her tail wag. Her head came up and then she leapt up onto Joshua's lap. She put her paws on his chest and proceeded to clean his chin. Joshua nuzzled her back and ran a hand down her leg. It was fully healed. Blood rushed to his heart, filling him with amazement. This was a true and powerful healer.

"Michael, take your sister and go." It was a deep command that thrummed through the room. Joshua flinched. He wasn't sure he could get off the floor, let alone take on a true healer.

Michael scooped up his sister, hugged her in his arms and left with a sideways glance at Joshua. "Good luck".

"So Joshua Lighthouse," the deep voice thrummed once more. "Why shouldn't I kill you where you stand for your crimes against us?

18

SERENE

<u>Noon, Luminous thirty-first, 299 years post-Merge</u>

Serene's gaze darted around the mist filled hollow. On one end, the undead wolf stalked closer. A low hissing growl echoed in the space.

She spotted a metal pipe in the weeds to the left. The pipe could be used as a weapon.

The wolf lifted its muzzle and moaned. The hairs on the back of her neck rose. The creature was calling its pack. Using a weapon, she might've won a battle against one, but if a whole pack got involved, she'd be dead. And then undead.

A woman in black with a red ponytail stepped from the shadow. The way she moved and the leather she wore identified her as an HPA agent. She threw a globe that spread what looked like silver goop on the undead wolf.

The woman grabbed Serene's arm. "Run."

Serene flinched from the contact. Her heart sped. This

would be her one chance to figure out what had made that stench. The woman headed toward the cemetery entrance.

Serene grabbed the pipe and veered away, following the scent.

The woman was next to her. "What are you doing? The closest exit is that way." She jabbed her finger behind them.

"The scent is that way." Serene pointed ahead. The scent was getting stronger, but a distant moan sounded ahead.

"Heavens to Betsy," the woman said.

Serene jumped over a skeleton that seemed to be putting itself back together. What had she gotten herself into? If they didn't find the source of the scent and get the hell out, they would be trapped here all night. Which meant they'd be dead.

The human chucked something to the side and pulled Serene into the shadow next to another statue. She motioned for silence.

Serene tried to breathe as quietly as she could. She took huge silent gulps of air to get her body under control. The air chilled the sweat from her run and her heart raged in her chest.

The wind shifted and she could smell the wolf. She held her breath. It trotted into the clearing and lifted its head seeming to sniff the air. Some of the silver goop still stuck to the wolf's back making it easier to see.

It trotted to the object the human had thrown and disappeared. Serene glanced at the human. She wore no badge or insignia. This was the female human she'd thought she'd lost before getting to the cemetery.

By unspoken agreement, they kept to the shadows. As they walked, the freshly cut graves and leaning headstones gave way to small buildings for the dead. Dragging footprints crossed the path and claw marks decorated the edges of nearby stones.

The deeper she went the heavier the air felt. A touch on her shoulder and a hand closing over her mouth set her heart racing. Warm air feathered against her ear. "You need to calm down." The words a soft hiss.

Serene closed her eyes and worked to calm her breathing. Worst case she could climb to the highest building and hide on the top. She was going to be fine. She could trust this human. At least for a bit. They had to find the source of the smell. She couldn't let Joshua down. She couldn't let her Pack down. She had to figure out what was going on. Pushing down the fear, she took a deep breath.

She opened her eyes and nodded to the human. The scent was stronger and led even deeper.

In the middle of the cemetery, the gravestone fell away and a large building stood in the clearing. The scent came from that building.

"Tell me what you're seeking is not in that building," Rose said.

Serene couldn't admit to Rose that she wasn't sure what she was looking for. She was following the scent from the night Joshua had been kidnapped. The scent wasn't fresh. Whatever it was had spent time in this building, but didn't seem to be there any longer. She hoped there'd be clues inside. "Maybe. Let's go in."

The human woman got closer. "Is this wise?"

She smelled like smoke and faintly like Joshua. Warmth trickled to her chest at the thought of Joshua. This woman was a part of the HPA, and she might be Joshua's friend. But she could also be his enemy. If Serene asked bluntly, perhaps Rose'd give herself away. "How do you know Joshua?"

An odd expression crossed Rose's face, but she looked away before Serene could read it. "Joshua –asked me to help you." She paused after Joshua's name, as if she was just as surprised as Serene was that Joshua had asked.

Serene looked closely at Rose. At first glance, she looked like a pale, dark haired human, but there was something about her that seemed off. She'd tracked Serene with more ease than most humans could have. She looked fully human, but she moved too quickly, too quietly. Her nose flared almost as if she had keener senses than a human should. Added all together Rose was like her. No longer human. Did Joshua know this woman wasn't human?

A moan from the east made her decision if she should trust Rose more urgent. She had a limited amount of time and really could use an ally. Even if she didn't know who else had wanted Rose to help her, did it matter? Serene would trust Rose.

Serene crept to the door of the lone building. It opened with a touch. The smell was stronger here and there was something else. The acid smell of fear.

The torch light flickered, illuminating the short stone hall and the opening into a larger room. The center of the room was dominated by a large slab of white stone. Straps crisscrossed the slab and as she stepped closer she saw a body covered with pasty, white skin with the blacks and greens of new bruises. She couldn't see his face from this angle, but she'd guess he was a full adult. Human. Dead.

As she moved closer, he turned his face toward her. His eyes opened and he flexed his arms but, even with flexed muscles, the bonds, didn't move. A tube of black and green went into his arm.

Serene jumped back. He must be an undead now.

"Help me." His voice was cracked and hoarse.

Serene shivered. Most undead couldn't speak. Only ghosts and intelligent undead like vampires could still use language.

Rose checked his eyes and pulled his mouth open, revealing no fangs. "He's alive."

Why would Rose care? The HPA was notorious for despising humans who were changed. "He smells dead." Serene said.

"That's this junk." Rose pulled out the tube and flung it across the room. "We need to save him."

"He's dead." Or as good as dead. She could smell the taint oozing from his pores. That gunk was part of the smell she'd been following.

"Do you think this is his choice?" Rose's face was gray and she looked as if she wanted to be sick.

The question slapped Serene across the face. The transformation wasn't complete. They still might have a chance to save him. Not only could he tell them who had done this to him, it was the right thing to do. She would've wanted someone to save her or at least give her a choice in her transformation to Pack. "I know a healer."

Rose nodded, ripping off his ties. The man shut his eyes and shuddered.

A candle sputtered, drawing Serene's gaze. On the table against the back wall sat a book. She climbed the dais to the book. On the pages of the opened book was a careful sketch of the human from the table's face with notes.

It wasn't what she'd expected to see. She'd expected to see crazy rantings not precise notes. She flipped earlier in the book to see if it said anything else about the man, like how he'd been captured. Instead she saw the face of another man with his skin stretched over bones, and elongated incisors. He was labeled as dead. She flipped back and he got healthier looking, until he looked like a normal human.

She paged back to a previous sickened version and the word Streg jumped out from the page. Her heart stuttered. She'd found the process to create Stregs. Disgust twisted in her gut. Someone had been in the process of creating a Streg." This might help her son cure him. She tucked the small black book into her bag.

A noise from outside brought her to the door. She glanced at

Rose still bent over the man on the slab and then she peered outside. Had that shadow moved? Something lurched in the mist. The more she looked the more movement there seemed to be. The wolf wasn't back, but other undead were rousing.

"Rose we have to leave now." Serene kept her voice soft and level which was at odds with how she felt.

"We still have time until the gate closes," Rose said without looking up from the man on the slab. She seemed to be checking him for wounds.

"Yes, but the horde of undead are starting to rise."

Rose's head snapped up. "Shit." She lifted the human over her shoulder with ease. "Let's get out of here."

"We need a plan," Serene said softly. Anything loud would draw attention to them.

"I don't suppose you can change?"

"No." A skitter of fear raced up her spine.

Rose nodded. "We need to move fast. They'll be waiting for us the way we came in."

"Have any more of those charms?"

Rose shook her head. "They won't attack me."

Serene glanced back at Rose's face. Her face was scrunched as if she'd eaten something rotten, but like she didn't want to spit it out. "Is that what happened? You're an undead?" She made sure to keep her tone even and judgement free.

Rose's eyes widened and she took a step back. "How did you know?"

"You smell human, but you're too strong, too fast, and have too good of senses."

Rose huffed a laugh. "Is that all?"

"I was human at one point, before I became Pack so I recognize it sooner. I won't betray your secret." She glanced away and back to the rising dead. How were they going to get through that horde?

"You're strong?" Rose asked.

"Yes." Seemed like an odd thing to ask, but maybe Rose had a plan.

"Climb up this building to buy me some time. I saw a broken flagpole as I was running here. I'm going to grab it and have you hold onto the top."

"You can do that?" Serene's chest tingled. If Rose could do that, she was stronger than the strongest pack member had been. Maybe even stronger than two.

Rose bit her lip, and nodded. She wasn't visibly straining under the weight of the man over her shoulder. In fact, she may have forgotten he was there. Maybe she really could lift Serene, the man, and the pole Serene would ride on.

"I'll start climbing." Serene left the front door and darted up the wall. Groans rose around her. They could probably smell her now.

She climbed to the roof above the door. Zombies scrambled at the walls on either side, but weren't coordinated enough to make any progress. The skeletons also seemed unable to get a hold to pull themselves up. Undead were tenacious, it would only be a matter of time before they figured out how to scale the wall.

Rose walked out the door between a zombie and skeleton and headed back the way they'd come. Serene held her breath and watched to see if the undead would ignore Rose. The undead didn't seem to notice Rose. They still scrabbled at the wall, trying to climb it.

Rose disappeared into the mist. Serene's stomach twisted. Rose could leave her here and then Rose's secret would remain safe. She'd seemed shocked and afraid when Serene had guessed her secret. Maybe afraid enough to sacrifice Serene in favor of keeping her own secret safe. Serene needed a backup plan in case Rose didn't come back.

From where Serene roosted, she could see a dozen graves shifting. Hands poked out of the stirring dirt and grabbed the gravestones or other nearby objects and pulled the undead up. She wondered how many graves there were in the cemetery and how many contained restless dead. One skeleton grabbed ahold of a zombie and pulled it into the grave.

Even with them being mindless, they would overwhelm her with numbers. There were no nearby roofs to jump to. If Rose left her here, she'd be dead. She would let so many people down. Her pack would never get justice. Her son would never know what had happened to her. And if Joshua was right, the one lead she'd found to the bigger mystery would be lost. She shivered as a skeleton climbed on top of another skeleton, scaling higher on the wall.

Her hand brushed a loose tile. She pulled it off the roof and hefted it. It was the size of her hand and heavy. Maybe she could throw the tile at a skeleton and make it fall away from the wall. She stood and then chucked the tile as hard as she could at the skeleton that had found another to stand on. The tile thwacked of its head with no effect. The sour taste of dread coated the back of her throat. That had been the perfect shot, tiles were useless against them. So far she had nothing that could stop the tide of undead.

She walked the perimeter of the roof. There had to be something else she could do. A layer of undead three deep surrounded the building. At this point, getting down without help would be suicide. She stepped away from the edge. A skeletal hand reached up and dragged its nails across the tiles with a screech.

She covered her ears.

The skeletal hand slipped off.

Another screech and then a third from a different part of the roof sounded. Her throat ached.

If Rose didn't come soon, the undead would breach the roof line and she'd have nowhere to go. A screech behind her and a new noise. The claws caught.

She swung back and saw the skeleton starting to pull itself onto the roof. Her heart stopped. Rose needed more time. She ran at the skeleton and kicked it in the head. Pain shot up her foot, but the claws dislodged and the skeleton fell back with a crunch.

Where are you Rose? The fog thickened, closing her view.

Something white fluttered out of the mist almost at her height. She stumbled back. Could it be a ghost? Her heart thundered and she pressed her lips together to keep from screaming.

A scree and catch behind her. She turned, fists clenched. Another skeleton was about to make the rooftop.

"Jump on," Rose's voice called from the ground.

Serene jerked. "Gods, you scared me." She let out a shaky breath and grabbed hold of the pole. She wrapped her arms and legs around it. If Rose wasn't as strong as she thought, Serene would be dropped in the middle of the undead. She glanced back. The skeleton had pulled itself most of the way on the roof.

"Ready?"

Serene's heart fluttered again. "Go. Go. Go."

The pole moved away from the building, just as the first skeleton stood. The skeleton followed after her and fell on the undead below, knocking them over.

Serene held on tighter. That was close. If Rose hadn't come back, she'd be dead now. All of her hopes for getting justice for the pack would be dead too and she'd never see her son again. "Thanks."

"Yeah." Rose's voice sounded strained. This must be a tough load even for her.

"Just bring me to the nearest fence, I can jump off the top."

"Go-Good idea." Rose panted.

Suddenly the bar tipped and Serene yelped as metal clanged on metal. It was the fence. Serene scrambled over the top and dropped down on the other side. Rose followed quickly after. The shadows on the cemetery side of the fence boiled. They had to get the pole off the fence or a host of undead would pour onto the streets.

Serene jumped back to the top of the fence and pulled. The pole wouldn't budge. "It's too heavy for me." Rose must be even stronger than Serene had thought.

"Get down." Rose pulled her off the fence. She landed in a bush a few feet away. When she looked up Rose had knocked the pole back into the graveyard.

A zombie reached through the fence toward Serene. The fence still held. If Rose hadn't come back for her, that could've been Serene mindlessly trying to escape.

"Thanks." Serene grinned and stood.

Rose nodded, but she looked strained, breathing too hard. Sweat sparkled on her face.

"Need me to carry him?" Serene offered.

"I've got him." Something that almost looked protective flickered across Rose's face. Whether the protectiveness was toward Serene or the man she carried, Serene had no clue.

Now all they had to do was get to her son's house and see if he'd be able to save the man and find out who was making Stregs.

19

JOSHUA

Joshua held his breath, the threat hung between him and Master Phil. It filled the small, dark chamber. Healers made powerful enemies, but even better friends. Joshua wasn't sure which way this one would go. His stomach knotted, but he took one calming breath. "Wouldn't that bring you down to my level? A healer becomes a murderer?"

No response. Joshua counted each slow breath that echoed in his ears. At twenty, sweat trickled down his back. Had he gone too far?

"Why did you save her?" The healer said finally, his voice calm and even. "The HPA and you in particular dislike non-humans."

She was too young to be truly evil. He'd had no hesitation in believing in her innocence, unlike the Streg from earlier. "Lissa was innocent."

The words rang in the room. Perhaps Joshua's conviction

made them louder, or maybe it was speaking the truth that strengthened the volume. Either way, a moment later, everything changed.

The darkness melted away, leaving a simple stone room. A shaggy shifter sat half turned away at a small table laden with bowls of vegetables. The shifter was one of the pack. It was odd he was alone. Packs were notorious for being aloof and clannish. They wouldn't share their healer. Master Phil must be truly powerful. Speckled grey and white hair shifted with his movement as he picked up a knife and began chopping garlic.

"Why are you here?" His voice no longer echoed with power. A whiff of garlic and onions set Joshua's stomach rumbling.

He bit his lip to keep the truth in while he thought of the lie, but stopped. He'd been given a chance. The healer could've done him harm, but so far he hadn't. Serene had been willing to help him. Maybe Others weren't all evil creatures. If the healer wasn't evil, the truth would be better. "Rose said you might be able to help with the drain."

"How did it happen?" There was no pause in the knife's rhythm, no sense that the healer had recognized Rose's name.

"I-I." Joshua cleared his throat. "I used powers I have, but it drained me of energy."

The cleaver stopped and he wiped his hands. "May I touch you?" His face, as he turned to gaze at Joshua, said he was looking for a reason to say no. Or maybe he thought Joshua was lying.

"Yes."

Master Phil stood, placed his hand on Joshua's heart and his other hand on Joshua's forehead. He sniffed and drew back sharply. "I will help with your drained energy, but you must tell me what happened before you ventured to my door."

Joshua met his gaze, but Master Phil's face was a mask. Nothing flickered beneath the surface. He'd been telling the truth, there was no point in lying now. Someone in the HPA had betrayed him. He had no one left on his side besides Serene, Bob, and maybe Rose, if she'd survived. He needed allies. He had nothing left to lose at this point by telling the whole story.

"I've joined forces with Serene of the Pack. She's investigating the Streg attacks. I'm investigating the murder of her pack. Or I was, until I was betrayed by someone in the HPA."

The healer's eyes widened just slightly which made Joshua want to tell him more.

"Both events are somehow linked to someone wanting to UnMerge the world." Joshua had no idea if the Packs knew each other and knew when one was decimated.

"So quiet evening at home." The healer's voice sounded distracted and sarcastic.

The healer couldn't have known how Joshua had spent the night. Joshua thought about Serene in his home and how she had saved him. How that event had planted the seed for seeing things differently. "This investigation is stickier than normal."

"Why?"

Joshua rubbed his eyes and slumped into the chair. If he couldn't crack this case, not only would he die, but the UnMerge would kill Serene, Rose, Bob, and everyone else he knew. "The pattern is bigger than normal and I just can't figure out who could be behind it. Or why."

The healer nodded. "The trick is to use some of the energy in the world, not just your personal pool."

Joshua pulled his lip, had he ever heard about a personal pool of energy? The concept sounded vaguely familiar, but he couldn't find the reference in his head.

"I can refill the pool. But you would have to trust me."

The way Joshua was feeling he could sleep for a week and still not feel better. If everything was linked the way he believed, he didn't have a week. He had a day. Could he trust this Other healer?

There weren't many he trusted. But did he have a choice? He did trust Rose and so maybe he could trust Master Phil by extension. This would be the second Other he had chosen to trust which made him feel uneasy. Had he just been meeting exceptional Others or were his feelings about them wrong?

Joshua nodded, afraid what his voice might sound like.

Master Phil gently touched Joshua's forehead. "This is a pool of magic at your center. This is where you are pulling your power. It is closed off to the world."

Warmth and energy filled Joshua. A feeling of lightness and energy filled him. "What did you do?"

"I refilled your pool with the world's energy."

"My pool?"

"Everyone has an inner pool that is their life force. If you have powers, your inner pool can be used to power them."

He'd never thought of magic needing a power source or of his weakness as a sign of a drained battery. If his magic drew upon his battery maybe he had a rechargeable source and with time, his battery filled back up. His time away from his powers might've given him a more full pool than he'd had just after the Merge. That would explain why he'd been able to use his powers more. Maybe magic was more logical than he'd thought.

"Thank you. Is that how you heal?"

"In part." Master Phil sat back at the table and chopped onions. He seemed to be in no hurry.

The room seemed brighter and sharper. Joshua shifted the chair he sat on and even that small motion felt easy. It was like waking up after a restful sleep and starting the day full of energy. Now that Joshua didn't feel rundown, he needed to decide what to do.

He'd almost forgotten that he'd stuffed Serene's file into his bag.

"May I?" Joshua gestured to the only part of the table free from vegetable debris.

Master Phil nodded. "What do you have?"

"This is the file covering the night the HPA complex burned." Joshua sat and flipped open the slim folder. There was one page. It said 'Serene of the Pack' above a grainy picture that could've been any petite female.

One line of history: Mated to Alpha of the Pack in year 279.

That was her history. She was number one on the list and that was all they could find on her. The lack of details reinforced the idea that she'd been innocent.

The next section was about the night, over a year ago, that the HPA lab had burned.

<u>Event</u>: HPA Complex burnt to the ground. No pictures.

<u>Casualties</u>: Five human guards dead, two dozen pack members dead. Including the alpha.

These facts made no sense. A whole complex didn't just burn and have so few people missing or dead. If there'd been a fire, the dead should've been spread out amongst the guards and prisoners. And it was odd to have so many of one species die. The idea that she'd been set up was beginning to look even more likely. Anger tightened his jaw. The HPA was supposed to help humans who couldn't protect themselves from the monsters of the world. It wasn't supposed to be used to murder a pack and set up one of its members to take the fall. The HPA was not supposed to be comprised of monsters.

He went back to the file.

<u>Witnesses</u>: None

<u>Evidence</u>: None

<u>Suspect</u>: Serene of the Pack

That was all that was in the folder. No other photos or

supporting documents. No interviews with the guards. No list of who was also imprisoned at the time. Nothing that actually linked Serene to the HPA Labs. Determination straightened his back. Serene was someone wronged by the system, it was his duty to make it right. Which lined up nicely with his promise.

The healer ladled out a bowl of soup and handed it to Joshua. "You'll need your strength."

Joshua wolfed down the soup and pondered Master Phil. Yet another Other being kind when he didn't have to be. The healer hadn't needed to feed him or even help him. He could've been booted out or killed for breaching the healer's territory.

Instead, the healer had healed him and fed him. Maybe he'd even help him go to the archives. He'd look at the arrest records, and maybe he would see if he could find out who else had been there.

The Archive was independent from the HPA but still affiliated. Madeline and the other people in Copy made sure that the HPA records were brought to the Archive. But it was Alex who was the master of that domain. A mix of regrets and anger still pulsed through him when he thought of Alex. Joshua may've been the cause of Marvin dying, but it was Alex's actions that had prevented a rescue attempt.

Joshua would have no problem entering the Archive. Anyone was allowed to visit. But, it'd been a long time since he'd seen Alex. Almost ten years. So much had happened last night Joshua had seen Alex.

Joshua had lost his best friends; one had died and Alex's friendship had shattered. He'd left the Archives for good and fought his way into the HPA. All while being the new guardian of the Book of Secrets. Could he face Alex and his past?

He was running out of time. The anniversary of the Merge was one day away. He had to figure out what was going on and what these two events and the Unmerging had in common.

"Master Phil, I need your help to get out of Shifterville and over to where the Archive is."

After a moment more, Master Phil loaded the veggies into the steaming pot. "What will you pay me?"

Joshua opened his mouth to offer a gold piece which was standard for top intel, but closed it just as quickly. He had nothing. Nothing on his body. Nothing he could offer from friends or connections. Nothing he could even offer as a favor. He swallowed. "What do you want?"

"You will owe me a favor."

20

———

SERENE

<u>Late afternoon, Luminous thirty-first, 299 years post-Merge</u>

Serene knocked on her son's door. After a moment it opened. Her son glanced at her questioningly. The faint scent of Joshua hung in the doorway but dissipated when she entered. Joshua had been here. Daniel had magic within his home to suppress smells so he could treat more people safely, so Joshua must have been here very recently.

Odd after so much time having never crossed paths with Joshua, she'd crossed it twice in a single night. He must've been here for a reason. Perhaps following a lead. Or perhaps he'd discovered that Daniel was her son. It was pointless to speculate.

She shook her head to focus on the more critical issue. "We need your help."

He glanced at Rose and the man slung over her shoulder. He nodded. "Place him on the table."

Serene held the door as Rose entered and placed the man

gently on the table. Rose had her lip in her teeth and looked worried.

"Tell me what happened." Her son's voice was even and calm.

Rose took out a vial. "This is what they were pumping into him to transform him into some kind of undead."

Her son frowned and sniffed the contents of the vial. "I don't recognize it."

The quick shake of his head gave Serene the first flash of worry. Perhaps this was going to be far harder than she'd thought. "I also found a journal." Serene held up the book she'd found.

"Let me see what I can do to stabilize him." Daniel went to the wall and picked out several different jars, sniffed them and then added some of each jar's contents to a pot he moved more directly over the fire.

Serene watched her son move around his home. He looked confident that he could save the man lying unconscious on the table. If her son could save him, not only would Serene have helped save the man, but she would've found a huge clue to what was going on with the Stregs. This man might be able to provide a vital clue to who was behind the killings. If so, she would be holding up her end of her bargain with Joshua.

"How long ago did you find him?" He checked the man's eyes, pulling the lid up. He tried to open the man's mouth, but it resisted.

"Maybe an hour." Serene said. It'd taken them awhile to get out of the cemetery.

"Open his mouth." Could Daniel know Rose? Had they interacted before? That would explain how he knew Rose was strong enough to open the man's jaw.

Rose stepped closer and pulled down on his chin and pushed on his forehead until his jaw opened.

Daniel looked down his throat and felt his neck. Then grunted. He grabbed his herb bag and placed candles in the holders on the floor around the table. The candles made a star. Taking another bag from the counter, he dumped the contents, drawing lines between and around the candles. The scent of salt and something else, maybe Rosemary, drifted to her. She rarely got to see her son do magic.

"What are you doing?" Rose wrinkled her nose as if the smell irritated her.

"Stand at the edge." He waved to one end that had a loop on the floor. Rose stepped inside. Her hands fisted at her side and she looked at the ground.

"Serene, stand in that loop." He indicated a loop on the far side. "Bring the book."

She stepped into the spot.

Daniel stepped into the last loop and stood. He took a deep breath and all emotion vanished from his face. "Bí an draíocht fhuar seo," He muttered in a language Serene didn't know.

The circle glowed a sickly green around Rose, her son, and the man on the table. Daniel gazed at the man, starting at his feet and working his way to his head. He also glanced at Serene and Rose. His face didn't change as he examined them. A small trickle of sweat streaked past his ear.

Serene hadn't watched her son work. Even though the situation was serious, she couldn't help the warmth of maternal pride. She could see how hard his work was and how much he cared.

"Téigh i síocháin." He raised the bag and a bright light flashed inside the circle. "Check the book. This isn't something I've seen before. See if anything in the journal looks like it could help."

Serene stepped out of the circle and went to sit at the dining table. She brought out the journal. It had the name Andre and then the Creator on the front. She had a flash of memory at the name. When she'd been pulled out of the cage the night the Pack had died, someone had said Andre. Excitement shot through her. He'd been there the night her pack was murdered.

Rose looked stunned and dismayed. "Can we save him?"

Daniel's expression hardened. "I don't know. This is both magical and biological."

"How do you know?" Rose asked.

"The spell circle I did looks for things of science. I can see the magic in the goop they used."

Serene glanced down at the book. The answer had to be in these pages, but there were literally hundreds of pages of notes. She flipped to the beginning of the entry on this man. There had to be a clue about what they'd injected into him.

"Did either of you touch him?" He rummaged in a chest he had at the side of the room.

His voice was off and a chill of fear swept up her back. Serene thought back. No she hadn't actually touched him. "No."

"You saw me carry him in and force his jaw open for you."

Her son nodded and pulled out a big black flag. When he shook it out, a large skull with crossbones covered the flag. Anything with bones on it had to be bad. He caught Serene's gaze. "That green glow meant that he is contagious."

Serene froze. "What did you say?"

"This man was contagious. That means that Rose and I caught whatever they were trying to pump into him."

Serene's mind went blank. Then roared. Her son was going to die. No worse, turn into an undead because she'd involved him with this investigation. "What can I do?"

"I can work on the magical component, but I need you to find something for the biological one."

Biological one. Where would she even begin? Serene gazed at Rose. "Can the HPA help?"

Rose bit her lip and shook her head. She looked as if she might say something, but instead she paled and kept quiet.

"What does biological component even mean?" Serene asked. If it was up to her to find an answer, she needed as much information as possible.

"We live in a merged world. My mentor in healing taught me that the humans brought things called viruses with them when the worlds Merged. They affect the body itself but with a different mechanism than magic. Over the generations people lost the science that protected against viruses. Only a few healers had this knowledge." Her son opened his door and draped the flag over the door.

Serene shook her head. "We're wasting time. That journal said that we only have a day until it becomes permanent."

"With what was done to me, maybe there is something in my blood which can hold off the infection." Rose was not quite looking at either of them. Her shoulders were stiff and her face blank as if bracing herself for their rejection.

"It's worth a try. Thank you." Daniel touched Rose's arm gently. "Mom, you need to leave. Take that vial on the shelf in case you find something that can help. Get us what help you can."

"Mom?" Rose's eyes went wide.

Daniel nodded. "We all have secrets."

Where should she go? She'd go to every person she knew if she had to find some way of helping her son and Rose.

There weren't many true healers. Wren was out because he was a politician not a magician. Walter might be able to help, but she had nothing more to trade with him. There was Joe and the Hive that he led. They did have eyes everywhere, but it was hard to say if they'd be able to help her with tracking down knowledge on a biological component. Joshua'd said he came from before the Merge. Did everyone from his time know about science? Alesia would be a good choice if the Seer were to appear. The Seer had shown up every time Serene'd visited, but would the Seer come this time?

Serene wanted to hug her son, but knew that would spread whatever they had caught. He would die without her ever being able to hug him again if she couldn't find the biological component. She grabbed the vial and tucked it into her bag and backed toward the door. The fear congealed into resolution. She had to find a cure.

21

JOSHUA

Late afternoon, Luminous thirty-first, 299 years post-Merge

Joshua licked his lips, but it felt like sand had invaded his mouth. The Archive looked the same after all his years of avoiding it. The stocky grey building hunched on the street like a rundown animal shelter. The back was layered in chain link fences, and splotchy yellow grass.

What choice did he have but to face his past? Everything in him knew the events that had happened since the Streg attacks fit together. If it all did fit, then he had until just before the anniversary of the Merge to put the clues together. That's when a plot to UnMerge the worlds would attack.

Which meant he had to face Alex.

Joshua shoved his hands in his pockets, left the alley, crossed the street, and pushed the door open.

A small reception area with bright orange carpet, a handful of mismatched chairs and a desk greeted him. A gray haired woman with deep creases on her face sat at the wooden desk. The smell of mothballs and dust hung in the air.

The old woman at the desk squinted at him over her knitting. She looked the same now as she had the first time he'd entered the archive fifteen years ago right after being rescued. Her eyes still glinted red in the light.

"Do I know you?" Her voice, a throaty purr, was at odds with the gray bun.

"I'm here to see Alex." He knew better than to lie to a guardian of the Archive, but that didn't mean he had to answer her questions.

"Hmm. Alex is in the rotunda." She tilted her head, then smiled a smile that said I remember you, which made him uneasy and drudged up memories from the day Marvin had died.

The scene around him disappeared as he remembered that day. He'd passed the Guardian on the way into the Archives. The wizened old lady who could move like a panther, but looked like she'd be more comfortable petting her ten cats than being the oldest and wisest and touchiest being in the Archives. On that day, the toothy grin of the Guardian had caught Joshua by surprise.

"Happy Birthday." her voice, a throaty purr, enhanced his impression of her cat-like traits.

Joshua hesitated. He'd forgotten about his birthday. He'd turned fifteen this morning. "Thank you."

"That which is broken can be fixed." She looked back down at her knitting.

Joshua grimaced. Now he would have her words echoing in his head as he tried to unravel the puzzle. Worse, the words could be for now or at some point in the future. They might not even be directly related to him. He sighed.

Fifteen was the earliest age he might be able to get into the

HPA. He'd have to physically defeat their champion as the first test to get in. Most started later, in their 20's. He didn't want to wait that long, but if he lost the fight he'd be barred from trying to join again. He just didn't feel ready.

Raised voices echoed down the hall. It sounded like his two best friends were at it again. Lately, they fought constantly about the mirror. He paused when he entered the rotunda.

"Just because you are too chicken, doesn't mean it can't be done." Dark haired Marvin had the haughty expression only he seemed to be able to produce.

It was directed fully on Alex. Despite his frail appearance, Alex didn't wilt under the assault. "We were told not to." Alex crossed his arms.

"No, we were told that unless we were ready to confront our destinies we shouldn't," Marvin shot back.

"Does it matter? No one knows how to open the mirror." That statement usually stopped the argument, but this time, Marvin smiled and gestured to Joshua.

"Actually, I found out that Josh here can open the mirror."

Joshua's stomach dropped. The last thing he wanted was to have to choose between his friends. That's what it would come to, if he opened the mirror. Alex would never forgive him, and if he didn't try Marvin would storm off. The last time Joshua had made him mad it had been almost six months before he'd seen his friend again.

"Who told you that?" Alex huffed and flags of color reddened his cheeks.

"The guardian." Marvin smirked at Alex. He knew that the Guardian was the only source that Alex would trust.

"The Guardian should not be disturbed unless it is important." Alex muttered.

"It is important."

"Is not"

"Why do they get to decide what's important?" Marvin leaned into Alex's space with his hand fisted and rising.

"Guys. Listen. I still don't know how to open the mirror. So it doesn't matter," Joshua said. Maybe there was still a chance to stop the fight.

Marvin sighed and rubbed his eyes. "The guardian said that summoning that which you got in transition would allow us to go down the path of our fates."

"That could mean anything," Alex muttered.

Joshua tried to keep all expression off his face. Marvin was watching him closely. The Guardian might be referring to the powers he'd gotten when he'd lived through the Merge. He hadn't mentioned them to anyone besides Delilah. He'd even purposely failed a test that was supposed to tell if he had powers. More than just humans used the archive. If he was anything other than human, the HPA wouldn't let him be an agent.

Marvin put his hand on Joshua's shoulder. "Please. You know what my Father was like before he died. I've got to find something else, or I am going to be trapped following in his shoes. I just can't." Marvin's voice wavered at the end.

Joshua had only seen Marvin's father thundering and shouting like some evangelist minister. The man had been obsessed with the fate of his family. Joshua had once asked why Marvin's father had been so angry. Marvin had said that something had happened years ago and it had cursed the family. He wouldn't say what had happened, only that his father was obsessed with breaking the curse. Marvin didn't want to be like his father or have the same obsession that had ruined his father's life.

"How will this help?"

"I will be able to prove that my Father was wrong, that the family is not cursed."

If he even tried to open the mirror not only would his secret be at risk of getting out, but Alex would think Joshua was choosing Marvin over him. Alex had issues with being left behind. It had to do with his mother and how he'd become an orphan. But if Joshua didn't even try, Marvin wouldn't forgive him. Marvin had been searching for a way to prove his father wrong since his father's death. If Joshua didn't even try to help him, it would end their friendship. There'd be no middle ground.

Marvin had been his friend since they met. He'd helped Joshua adjust to the world. Had shown him around the city and had even helped him come up with a plan for how to join the HPA. Without Marvin, he'd be huddled in the Archive like Alex.

Though it felt like he would be betraying Alex he decided he would try to help and hope that his effort came to nothing. That would be the best for both of his friends.

"What did you need me to do?"

"Open that mirror." Marvin pointed to the mirror.

"Smart ass." Joshua stepped toward the mirror. He could at least try and then when it didn't work, they could go back to normal. He rubbed his hands down his pants.

Alex blocked his way. "You know this is wrong."

"Is it? Or will it help Marvin?"

"We would be breaking the rules." Alex said in a fierce whisper. "Bad things happen when you break the rules. Especially here."

Joshua's unease twisted his stomach. Alex was right, this would break the rules of the Archive where they'd been living. Alex and Joshua full time and Marvin whenever he'd been able to get away from his father. This was their place of refuge. They had the run of the place, but the one thing they had been told that they must never do until they were older, was to mess with the artifacts. The Archive had many of them scattered throughout its labyrinth of tunnels. The Mirror was the only one that had called to them. Specifically Marvin.

"Maybe we're old enough now. I just turned fifteen."

"If we do this as a team we'll be fine." Marvin held out his hand to Alex.

Alex sighed and shook his hand. "Do you really think this is a good idea?"

"I probably won't be able to open it, no matter what the Guardian says." That was his hope. That the mirror would stay shut and everything would return to normal.

Alex shook his head and backed away. "I have a bad feeling about this."

"It'll be fine. You'll see," Marvin said.

Alex and Marvin both backed up and Joshua stood in front of the mirror. He took a breath and closed his eyes. For the first time since Delilah, he created a tiny soul wisp and sent it to touch the mirror. With any luck, nothing would happen. He could stand here for a couple minutes and it would be all over.

"You are a guardian, you may enter," a voice inside his head said.

A crack sounded in his head and a line formed in the mirror. It thickened, becoming a door within the glass.

"You did it." Even hushed, Marvin's voice communicated how excited he was. "What now?"

Joshua shrugged.

Marvin ran his hand along the mirror and then drew back with a hiss. "It bit me."

"Mirrors can't bite," Alex chided.

Joshua stepped between them before the fight escalated. "Let me." He felt the edge of the door and grabbed it and pulled, opening the glass and revealing a dark void.

Joshua glanced at Alex who shivered and stepped away.

"Last one in is a rotten dragon egg," Marvin said.

"Wait!" Joshua called, but it was too late, Marvin had leapt through the door.

"I'm afraid." Alex was much paler than normal. "What if it...."

Alex was terrified of large spaces. "Stay here and guard the door?"

He gulped, but nodded.

Joshua squeezed Alex's shoulder, feeling how thin his friend had become. "I'll be right back."

Joshua turned toward the mirror again.

"Wait. You might need this." Alex handed him a ball of twine. He wrapped the end around a post nearby. "So you can find your way back out."

Joshua took the twine and let it spool out behind him when he entered. Once he stepped into the darkness, the inside of the mirror was like walking into an opal. Shimmers of blue, pink and white surrounded him. He put his hand out and felt nothing. He took step after step, the line playing out behind him. He had to find Marvin, who would be lost in this place with no way of getting out.

"Marvin?" Joshua's voice echoed oddly. "Can anyone hear me?"

He cocked his head, but the silence felt like a heavy blanket. Even the beating of his heart seemed muffled. He thought he heard a scuff ahead, so he walked hands outstretched trying to feel his way.

Then his footsteps tapped and the swirling colors morphed into a stone passageway which opened up to a room. A gray stone pedestal stood in the middle of the room and open on the top was a book. Light flickered making the ink on the pages look as if it were moving.

Marvin stood next to the book. His face was pale and drawn.

"Marvin?"

Marvin didn't move, but did begin to pant and twitch as if he were experiencing a nightmare.

Joshua took a step closer. The slap of pages moving, drew his gaze. The book had opened to a page that had a beautiful rendering of a woman. Color filtered over the page as if the artist were invisibly adding color. She had deep green eyes and wavy dark hair. Something in the picture caught him and made his heart beat harder. She was captivating and seemed to gaze at him with a look of compassion and admiration. His body reacted. His hormones sizzled.

"J-Josh?" Marvin was pale and sweating. He licked his lips. "I can't get past the shield. Can you?"

Everything in Joshua said that they needed to leave or things were going to get worse. Marvin needed help. "We need to get out of here."

"No. Please." Marvin's face twisted as if this were the only way he would live.

What could it hurt to take down the shield? Marvin looked like anything could set him over the edge, as if he was holding onto his sanity by a spider's thread.

Joshua sent the soul wisp to the book. A shimmer glowed around the book and then popped, leaving the book free.

Marvin's hands clenched. "You're the book's guardian. You need to take the book and protect it."

Uneasiness skittered across his back. The feeling that he was missing something scratched between his shoulders. When he'd first entered the mirror, the voice in his head had said he was a guardian. Perhaps he was meant to take the book and be its guardian. He picked up the book, closing it and tucking it into his battered backpack.

"Joshua!" Marvin screamed. Shadows swirled around him like living entities. Everywhere they touched Marvin wrinkled and shrank.

Adrenaline raced his heart. "No." Joshua ran closer, but the shadows pulled Marvin farther into the mirror.

Marvin screamed and then it stopped mid note. Just like Delilah's had when she'd been murdered.

Joshua fell to his knees. It was his fault. Twice he had used his powers and twice people had died. He couldn't catch his breath. He was evil, just like the Others in this world. The upwelling of grief, fear, and regret boiled within him making his guts heave and his throat close.

Finally the heave of emotions loosened its grip. Sitting on the floor in a mirror was not going to help the situation. What could he do to make amends? The HPA. He would join the HPA and spend his life working to save as many people as he could.

The twine was gone, but he could sense the way out. He walked, grief making his legs heavy. What would he tell Alex? Alex had been right to try and stop them. Maybe there'd be a way to mount a rescue and still save Marvin from the shadows. Maybe in this case the Guardian would help.

He stumbled out of the mirror and fell to the ground.

"Praise be." Alex stepped over him and swung at the mirror with a candelabra. The mirror smashed into thousands of pieces.

"Nooo." Joshua scrambled forward. Now there was no hope of saving Marvin. A sharp sting on Joshua's hand, brought his head up. A piece of the mirror had wedged into his palm. Blood welled around the dark glass.

"It needed to be destroyed since...." Alex started.

Joshua stopped listening. He knew that Alex had been trying to do the right thing, but Joshua couldn't look at him. Guilt and anger stabbed sharp edges into his throat, closing it. He held back the tears for his fallen friend. He closed his hand on the glass and relished the pain. It was what he deserved.

That had been the last time he'd seen Alex.

The slide of the ridged pattern of the hallway walls across his fingers brought him back to himself. The wallpaper overlapped like dragonfly wings. His stomach felt as if a swarm maybe of dragonflies fought to escape and join their brethren on the walls. There was no telling what he'd find in his ex-friend's face. Would he see forgiveness or condemnation?

22

JOSHUA

<u>Early evening, Luminous thirty-first, 299 years post-Merge</u>

Joshua pressed his hand against the cold wood of the closed door of the Rotunda. This was his last chance to back out. Alex would hate Joshua for abandoning him. The only way to the stacks was through Alex and since Joshua's magical access had probably been pulled years ago, he needed permission. Or he would be fried by Archive defenses.

Joshua took a deep breath and opened the door.

On the other side of the rotunda, Alex stood before an empty canvas with a brush in his hand. He was a collection of sinew and sticks under his white Archive robe. There was no burst of anger within Joshua, just regret.

"Joshua, you are just the person I need. I am trying a free painting experiment." Alex's smile stopped short of his eyes. It was the polite smile of someone needing to be nice to the boss's son.

Fear stepped up his heart and wet his palms. This was a test.

He could see it in the way Alex held the silver paint brush in his hand. This brush might even be an artifact from the Archive the same way that the book had been. Joshua stepped forward and Alex handed him the brush. A tingle zinged from his fingers to his chest.

The brush pulled him toward the canvas and he seemed to go through. He held on and closed his eyes against the swirling colors that consumed his vision.

The feeling of motion stopped. He opened his eyes.

Dark slick walls and black sand beach surrounded a still pool of water. The sand squished between his toes. The breeze raised the hairs on his bare legs. The brush was still gripped in his hand. Something about the way the water and walls looked seemed fake as if this was not a real place. The way the mirror had looked when they'd gone in.

"What am I supposed to do?" Joshua called out hoping that somehow Alex might hear him.

"This pool has many names. Only at pivotal moments in one's life will the surface reflect back an image." Alex's voice rang in his ears, seeming to be both nearby and very far away.

Alex's words didn't help him at all. The wind seemed colder. Master Phil had mentioned Joshua's pool. The brush must've brought him inside himself to his own pool. Hopefully the pool didn't reflect the owner. Or else his life, it seemed, was bleak and empty except for the distant echo of dripping water.

Maybe he was meant to stir the pool.

He squatted near the pool and extended the brush to the water's surface, and gently stirred the surface. The tip slid just beneath the surface.

The scent of Lavender and Peppermint filled the room. And there, shimmering just beneath the surface was an image of Serene.

He pulled the brush out and moved it on the top of the water, not touching it, but moving the brush as if he were really painting. Once he brought her image more fully to the surface he stepped back. She smiled back at him for a moment then her image rippled gently away, returning the pond to its mirror state. Confusion swept through him. What did it mean that he'd seen Serene?

"Joshua?" Alex's voice echoed down from the dark behind him.

Reality snapped and Joshua staggered. He was back with Alex, but now Serene's image stood in sharp detail on the canvas before him. Long dark hair covered one eye and fell in long waves past her shoulder. She smiled like she knew a secret, but would never tell.

"So what they say is true." Alex moved to his side to look at the painting.

"What do they say?" Joshua could not move his eyes from the canvas, more specifically from Serene's eyes. He could no longer blame the drug for his attraction to her, but it could still be the book.

"That you are no longer human and have turned against your own kind." Alex said calmly and with no judgement as if the answer to the question didn't matter or interest Alex.

Joshua snorted. Whoever had set him up had been thorough. He was still human and hadn't betrayed anyone. "More like someone in the HPA betrayed me."

"And you seek vengeance?"

Joshua tilted his head and reached out a finger to hover over Serene's cheek. "Perhaps I seek justice."

Then with an audible snap, the magic released him. Joshua shook himself like a gremlin taking a dust bath. "Did I pass?" Joshua turned toward Alex and crossed his arms.

Alex smiled that you-will-have-to-wait-and-see smile. "What is it that brings you back here?"

Joshua waited for the 'after all this time', or for Alex to ask why Joshua had left. What could he say, he'd been young and dumb and had been afraid for his friend? That he'd been angry that Alex had taken any hope of saving Marvin?

But Alex didn't ask. He just waited with his arms crossed. The pang of disappointment surprised Joshua. They needed to move forward, not rehash the same things, but he wanted to make amends. At least apologize.

"I need records for the night Serene became the most wanted. I need a list of people who were incarcerated at the Lab."

Alex blinked for so long Joshua wondered if he'd fallen asleep. Then he opened his eyes and tilted his head. "Why?"

Joshua really had to think about what to say. He wanted to gloss over the details, but Alex had always known when Joshua wasn't telling the whole truth. "I think it's related to a case I'm working on." Joshua shook himself.

Alex pursed his lips and then glanced at the painting Joshua had made. "What about this picture?"

Joshua had to look away from Alex. "We all have secrets, weaknesses."

"Secrets." As if that were some magic phrase, the next words tumbled out from Alex. "I know this woman."

Joshua's head snapped up and for the first time since coming into the room, he really looked at Alex. The network of veins and arteries crisscrossed under his pale skin; the throb of his pulse was a beacon of his distress. Dark purple bruises under his eyes showed how many of his nights were sleepless. A bubble of sympathy went through Joshua.

"I had a dream of her. Only she was pregnant." Alex paced the room. His hand trailed on the wall. The dust drifting toward him, forming mounds on the wall where his fingers touched.

When they'd been kids, Alex had done that when he was nervous. The earth had responded to him.

"What happened in your dream?" Joshua made his vice calm and even. Whatever the dream had been, it affected Alex deeply. Knowing Alex was the most stable person he'd met, and that he'd been affected so deeply made Joshua nervous.

"A Bender was set loose on the Pack."

Fear raised the hairs on Joshua's arms. A Bender was a strong psychic who could bend a person to his or her will. There were a few documented in the archive. Odd that a Bender would come to Alex's dream.

"Each member of the pack protected her until they broke and then it was just her and her unborn child."

Shock and dismay buzzed through Joshua's system, causing sickness to well in his stomach. The HPA had imprisoned a pregnant woman and murdered her pack.

Alex wrung his hands. "I felt it all." His voice cracked at the end.

Reluctant sympathy toward his friend opened Joshua's heart toward him, but Joshua hesitated to reach out. Touching Alex might not bring him comfort. This dream could explain why he wasn't sleeping. He'd always cared too much. Seeing those deaths, even in a dream, must've been very hard on him.

"And?" Joshua asked as the silence stretched on too long. Alex's face said there was more and that he hadn't even gotten to the worst part. Joshua waited, knowing that if he asked anything more or drew attention to himself, Alex would close up.

"He made her turn. There was backlash and I passed out." Alex fidgeted and shifted from foot to foot as if standing on hot coals.

The sick feeling expanded. Joshua had to help Serene. He needed to get Alex out of his emotion and focused on facts. It'd always been facts that anchored Alex. "Bending is a rare talent. Isn't it?"

"None have made it past puberty without being killed or locked up in a long time." Dust and dirt kicked up around Alex and formed four small vortexes on the floor.

Joshua felt the first stirrings of unease on the skin at the back of his neck. If Alex's talent was being triggered without him knowing, Alex was very upset. Would a dream really upset him this much? Maybe it hadn't been a dream. "Are you sure it was a dream?" Joshua said it slowly with long pauses.

Alex's eyes skittered between Joshua's shoulder and the canvas like a hyperactive mosquito. "I woke up in the woods near the burnt husk of the research facility. I had to w-walk back. I think they may still have a hook in me." He licked his lips and his hands shook until he clasped them.

Sympathy and an urge to protect his friend gripped Joshua. Alex was agoraphobic. This chamber was the biggest room he could be in without panicking and passing out. How long had it taken him to return to the Archives? How had he made it back in one piece?

Joshua put his hand on Alex's shoulder. Alex had never liked being close to others, but this felt right.

Alex sighed and closed his eyes and hung his head. "A Conduit controlled me and the Bender."

Joshua gasped and fear raised every hair on his body. A Conduit was something whispered about or used as a scare tactic between factions. A Conduit had a level of psychic control that allowed them to control people as a Bender did, but a Conduit wasn't limited to one at a time. A Conduit could also read minds while controlling many, acting like a puppet master, or just planting the seed of an obsession.

"Conduits are theoretical. A myth or a Rider deeply embedded in its victim." There hadn't been a recorded Conduit.

Any person who had been able to control more than one person had always been taken over by a Rider. That dark force could invade a body and take over. A rider could be dealt with by removing the hook it had into its host, but a person born with such power would be unstoppable.

"And I knew the person's signature." Alex gnawed his lip. "I think."

Joshua shivered. If a conduit was controlling Alex, who had been trained in logic and observation, they were looking for something specific or using Alex's senses. Or maybe they wanted access to the Archive. But since Alex never left the Archive, how had they gotten access to him. This place had more protections than anywhere else in town.

Could someone have gotten into the Archive? If they had, they would have access to centuries of accumulated knowledge from the city. And perhaps even worse, to the Artifacts hidden within. "What was the last thing you remembered before the dream?" Joshua had to know.

"I was here in the office."

Someone had breached the Archive. Someone had stolen Alex away from inside the Archive.

Joshua jerked his head back as the wave of shock hit him and his body stiffened like a dragon stunned mid-flight. The surreal sensation of the slow motion fall, as wings stopped flapping, spread through him. It made no sense that not only one, but two of the rarest and most powerful psychics existed and were interested in Serene and Alex.

Joshua couldn't leave Alex vulnerable.

"I-I can help remove the hook."

"You have to have powers to do that." Alex bit his lip and shook his head. A fifth vortex formed above him.

If he confessed to having powers Alex would know that Joshua had lied all those years ago. He might never forgive him, but if he didn't say anything he would leave Alex to be used by these seemingly evil forces. Forces who could use Alex's knowledge of the Archive to unearth other artifacts.

"I." Joshua cleared his throat as the truth lodged there for a moment. "I do, actually."

Alex sat down on the bench, the vortexes trailing behind him. "You have powers? This whole time?" The hurt in his tone sliced through Joshua's gut.

"Yes."

"Did I ever really know you?" Alex slouched forward and stared at his hands.

Regret clogged the back of Joshua's throat. "It was not a part of myself I shared. It was easy to fail the test."

Alex shook himself and then straightened his back. "I need you to touch my hand and close your eyes. I can show you how to remove the hook." Alex's tone was one a teacher used for a pupil.

Joshua did what he was told.

"Focus your talent on seeing me."

Joshua focused his mind and tried to use his Soul Wisp, to look at Alex. Alex was a grey and black shadow. "I see grey and black shadows."

"I see. Is there an edge? Something not cloud like?"

Joshua saw what looked like a J hook on a fishline caught in Alex's heart. "Yes, in your heart."

A fine tremor raced up Alex's hand. "Reach in with your mental hand and tug gently"

Joshua tugged gently at the line. It was caught with a literal hook that pulled at Alex's heart. He pretended he was removing a real hook from a fish. He gently worked it out, taking his time so as to do as little damage as possible.

The hook slid out. But as it was sliding away, the barb transformed into a snake. It hissed and struck out. Joshua pulled himself and Alex out of the way.

"Mine." The snake hissed, circling them.

Alex seemed comatose, not able to move. It would be up to Joshua to protect him.

The snake faked a strike. Joshua pulled Alex out of the way. They landed in a heap. Joshua on top. A hissing laugh from behind was the only warning of the next strike.

Joshua wished he had a shield on his back. The tough one that would repel a blade or snake bite.

The snake struck his back and landed on the ground next to them, reverting back into a simple hook. Then the hook itself disappeared.

Joshua's heart thundered in his ears. He'd expected to die or at least feel the bite of the snake, but instead he'd imagined a shield strong enough to protect against the snake. Perhaps this was another aspect of his powers.

Alex was free, but whoever put the hook in him knew it. And would be back.

23

JOSHUA

<u>Early Evening, Luminous thirty-first, 299 years post-Merge</u>

Joshua opened his eyes. The Rotunda still looked the same. Alex still stood near him. The only differences in the picture were the changes to Alex's face. The strain had vanished from his face. Color flushed his cheeks, making him look more alive. The hook had been draining him for who knows how long. "The hook said 'mine'."

Alex's lips pulled into a thin line. "Don't worry about that."

Joshua had never witnessed Alex doing anything but what he thought was the right thing to do, even if it had been hard. He couldn't leave Alex vulnerable. "No." Joshua caught Alex's gaze. "You are far too important to be put at risk."

Alex swallowed, then reluctantly nodded. "I can put the Archive in lockdown. No one can get to me or the Archive then." Alex stared at his feet. In a soft voice, with the same hesitance as a rabbit testing the air before coming out to eat, he said, "Stay here with me where it's safe."

Warmth loosened Joshua's chest. For one moment he thought about doing just that. They could stay enclosed in the archive defenses until they shriveled up into husks surrounded by the accumulated knowledge of the world. He could spend his days with Alex again. He could have the friendship he missed and he could keep Alex safe.

But it would all be ripped away if the UnMerge was successful.

He had to leave and face the world filled with beings that hated him at the moment. He needed to find out who wanted him dead, who wanted to UnMerge the worlds, and perhaps along the way, find out more about Serene and the slight sliver of color that had worked its way into his mind like a splinter.

"I can't."

Alex's shoulders slumped even farther forward, but he nodded.

"I can't just hide here. I need to see this to the end. No matter what the cost." Joshua nodded once and shook Alex's hand.

"If someone has been using me to see, then you can't go out the front."

Joshua nodded. "Give me five minutes to get out the back before you lock down." The knowledge he might never see Alex again grew in his mind. He needed to take responsibility for his past actions. "I'm sorry," he said before he could lose his nerve.

Joshua didn't want to be distracted. This was important. "I'm sorry for leaving you. Back when everything went so crazy. It was because of me, not you that I left. I was afraid that my powers would hurt you." He'd been afraid they'd kill him, just like they had the others. His heart stuttered and then took off running, he didn't want any more lives on his head. That was most of the reason he'd left.

Alex looked away. "Crazy things happen. Only by not

standing by your friends and supporting them did you cause the hurt."

"My powers caused the death of two people." The guilt still hung on his shoulders pulling him forward.

"How? Did your power reach out and stop their hearts or directly kill them? Did they fry nervous systems like the Bender did?" Alex's tone was tart.

"No," he admitted hesitantly. But he'd been there for each death. He'd used his powers just moments before each death. There was a connection between those events. Wasn't there? Doubt crept in. Perhaps he was not fully at fault.

"Then get over it." Alex nodded.

Joshua laughed in disbelief. Alex was very wise, could he be right about Joshua not being responsible?

Maybe. Which was better than the hell-no Joshua'd had believed earlier. Maybe someday he'd really believe those deaths were not his fault.

Alex opened a panel in the wall and pulled out another folder. "This is what the Archive had about who was in the HPA labs the night it burned. I pulled the records trying to make sense of that night." Alex held out the folder. "You'd better go now before I lock down."

"I'll come back to visit when this is over." Joshua took the folder and put it in his backpack. He sprinted down the hall.

The door at the end stood ajar. A soft light filtered out of the room and so did the smell of chocolate cookies. Joshua had never understood why an archive would smell like cookies. The scent now, like it had all those years ago, made him feel at home. He slipped through the door and closed it behind him with a soft thump.

The shelves extended for as far as he could see, a ladder attached to each section. Each shelf was 30 feet wide and just as tall. Everything looked exactly the same as the last time he'd been here. Maybe the space between the first two shelves seemed a little smaller. The green light still winked at each intersection. The lights had always been for status, he'd never seen them anything but green. Then again he'd never been here during a lockdown.

The light turned yellow. In thirty seconds it would turn red and disintegrate anything not registered to the archive. That meant Joshua and anything on him would be obliterated. Fear scratched at his spine. He shook it off and started running.

The door was in the far corner of the south wing. He counted each intersection until he hit twenty and turned right and went to thirty and then left and went ten.

The exit should be ahead, but the shield was expanding faster. Blast it. The lights were red one intersection away. He ran, arms pumping and legs moving. The air cooled behind him as the ward extended shelf by shelf. Just ten more and he would hit an exit shaft.

The shaft appeared and he pushed hard, four more steps. Three. Two.

The door slid shut behind him and with a red glow disappeared into the wall.

"What do we have here?"

Joshua turned to see Thomas leaning casually against the wall. The pistol in his hand gleamed in the dim light and pointed directly at his center body mass. The way they taught all HPA operatives.

24

SERENE

<u>Evening, Luminous thirty-first, 299 years post-Merge</u>

When Serene entered the Rookery, there seemed to be half the number of guards and the hallway to the stairs echoed hollowly. She trekked up the stairs and found Alesia sitting in the hard backed chair Wren sometimes made guests sit in when he didn't like them. Unease flicked down her spine. It didn't make any sense for Alesia to sit there.

"You are here." The Seer was already present. She sat straight backed and severe. The frown thunderous. Why would the Seer be in control? Could there be something wrong? Was Alesia in trouble?

Serene had no way of knowing when the Seer would leave. This might be her one question. Her son was in mortal peril, but there may be more ways to save him. This might be Alesia's only chance.

"Lady Seer, what must I do to help Alesia?"

The Seer blinked. The frown fading from her face and

easing into a neutral expression. Neither smiling nor frowning. "Why would you ask about your friend when your son's life balances on a knife's edge?"

How could she explain the agony of this choice? She'd be devastated if her son died. "I love them both. Alesia may not have any other chances, but my son does." What she wanted was for both of them to live and be happy.

"This is unexpected." The Seer's voice was a distracted mutter.

If the Seer hadn't expected Serene to ask that question, could Seers be as all powerful as they seemed? Or were the events they were trying to prevent big enough to upset even a Seer. "Lady, can't Seers see the future?"

"The future is hanging on the balance. The path is not clear."

Serene pressed her hand to her chest to try and remove the ache. If a Seer had no knowledge of how to proceed, there wasn't much hope. "What must I do?"

The Seer seemed to consider as if weighing the different options. "Bring Alesia with you to find your son's cure."

Serene's heart thumped in joy. Until that moment, she hadn't believed there was anything she could do to save her son. Not really. "Where is the cure?"

"Seek your answers where the sand meets the air."

Serene bit her lip, the whole northern district beyond the Pyramid was sand and air was everywhere. That made no sense. Air was above the full dessert which extended leagues. How would she be able to find the right place? She slumped. It was hopeless.

"When did you get here?" Alesia's soft voice broke into her thoughts. Her friend looked around the room puzzled. She looked so dazed and confused. Had the Seer taken over for a long time?

"What's the last thing you remember?"

Alesia blinked her eyes and licked her lips. Not seeming to be able to answer. She shivered and blinked.

Sympathy warmed Serene, and she wrapped her arms around Alesia. Serene felt how fragile her friend was. Hosting the Seer seemed to be taking a toll on Alesia. Serene needed the help and her friend needed the distraction. Perhaps it would be wise to invite Alesia to help. "You know what you need?"

"What?" Alesia's voice was faint.

"An adventure. Come with me? I need your help."

"You do?" Serene's heart broke just a little at how surprised Alesia sounded. Like she'd never felt needed before.

The Seer had been so wise. No matter what happened, this would help her friend. "Yes. You've already helped me so much. Will you help me more?"

Alesia looked uncertain for a moment, and then nodded. "Where must we go?"

Serene repeated the puzzle the Seer had said. "Seek your answers where the sand meets the air. But I have no idea where that is. Maybe we can fly over a large area and see it."

Alesia laughed softly. "We won't need to do that. I know where we must go."

Relief coursed through Serene. She nodded, grateful Alesia was on her side. "Good. Lead the way."

Alesia hesitated. "We need to take the secret exit."

"You have a secret exit?" A small pop of surprise teased her. The idea of her timid friend having a secret made her grin.

"No, but Wren does. He uses it to have private meetings with Walter." Alesia walked ahead at a leisurely pace. She nodded at a guard as if she were out for nothing more than an afternoon stroll.

The feeling that if they were caught and stopped, both of their worlds would be shattered sat on Serene's chest. The weight made it hard to smile, at the guards and hard to focus on where they were going. The guards must be used to her being awkward as they didn't seem to notice.

Alesia headed in first and pulled Serene in behind her. The door closed with a soft click.

"This is Wren's office," Alesia whispered.

Serene hadn't been in his office. Few had. Her first impression was of the room being over stuffed with books. On almost every surface perched little books and large tomes that looked as if three men might be needed to lift them. Since most of the books were brown or tan in color, orange, purple and red drew her eyes. She'd no idea this many books existed.

A large, black cauldron squatted in the corner of the room. There was no laundry hung around it nor did it smell like cooking. It made no sense for Wren to have such a cauldron.

The only surface not smothered with books was a desk with a shelf behind it. Instead of books, glass vials glittered on the shelf. She stepped closer and realized that different things filled each bottle. One glowed purple, and another seemed to have worms, the next had fur. How odd. They all had neatly written labels across the front. Eye of Newt and fairy dust were just a few of the labels. Her son had bottles of many things he'd used in his healing. She'd seen his collection of ingredients, even if she hadn't seen him heal. These bottles were different.

A large crystal glittered from the ceiling in the sunlight. The crystal hadn't been there when she'd first stepped into the room. It must've been hidden by magic. She shivered. If Wren were a wizard, that would explain everything in this room and his cold and detached manner. Wizards were known for being controlled. They had to be or spells would go awry and kill the spell caster. Strange how Serene had never noticed any signs Wren was a wizard outside of his office. Could it be a secret?

"Is Wren a wizard?"

Alesia nodded. "We must hurry. I am not sure when Wren will be back."

Serene's sense of urgency increased as the chills did. Wizards were known to be fiercely protective of their secrets. What would Wren do if he found them in his office?

Alesia led her around a book shelf which jutted into the room. On the far side in a corner, was a globe. Alesia spun it and clicking filled the room. Each click raised the hairs on her body as if something were building.

Serene shifted her gaze to the door. Now that she was deep in the room, it felt even more dangerous.

Then in a swift motion, Alesia stopped the globe. A final click and the bookshelf opened.

Serene held her breath and waited for an alarm, but nothing happened.

"Come." Alesia stepped inside. A torch lit and light flared, revealing a small room bisected by an intricate silver line which glowed faintly. The room was empty of anything else.

The feeling of danger and Serene's urge to flee rose, but she gulped air. Alesia wouldn't knowingly put her in danger. She was safe. She just needed to trust her.

Serene stepped in and stood next to Alesia. The door shut behind them. "Once we cross the threshold, I have no idea how to get back."

Serene shivered and reached for Alesia's hand. Alesia's cool hand in her own steadied her. The line was probably a magical portal which could bring them almost anywhere in the city. Serene either needed to trust her friend or run now. There was a chance that while Alesia thought it was safe, that she was unaware of the danger they were in. Serene knew that Wren wouldn't put Alesia in danger. He'd never been anything but protective of his sister. But there was a chance that he hadn't expected her to traipse through his office and enter this secret room. Serene realized she either needed to take that chance or come up with another plan.

She'd have to take the chance, not only did she have to trust her friend, but hope that the Seer's view of the future saw this path and wouldn't let them die pointlessly.

If they could make it back out to the surface, Serene would be able to get them back to the Rookery. But first they would have to figure out the Seer's puzzle. "I can get us back. Lead the way."

Alesia stepped forward and tugged Serene across the line. A thickness in the air and slight chill folded over her as she breached the line. Once the feeling faded, a second torch lit, revealing a long hallway.

When Serene looked back, there was nothing but a dirt wall behind her. This was powerful magic and she had no idea where this would lead, but she trusted Alesia. The fear that had been plaguing her lessened, leaving her cold. With luck this would lead to Walter and unravel the Seer's clue.

Serene kept Alesia's hand and together they walked down the tunnel. Every few feet a torch would flare ahead and the one behind them would extinguish.

They walked in silence until a torch lit and revealed a wooden door with a brass handle. This door could lead anywhere, but it was their only option.

The door was hot to the touch. A good sign it led directly to Walter's heated den. Serene opened the door, letting in a surge of heat.

Walter looked up from his work bench, his throat went red. "Alesssia?"

25

———

JOSHUA

Joshua raised his hands slowly spreading his fingers, to give Thomas all the signs that Joshua wasn't a threat. Thomas hadn't shot him, when Joshua had first left the Archive. Maybe there was still a chance to reach him.

He watched Thomas' left shoulder for a hint of how he felt. The shoulder would tighten if he was going to shoot. His shoulder stayed steady and the gun's sights stayed locked on Joshua's chest.

When Joshua had been trapped in his office, he'd used his Soul Wisps and had seen that Thomas had been reluctant to follow the HPA agents into Joshua's office. He'd seemed strangely sympathetic to Others and not outraged at Joshua's defection.

Joshua worked to keep his face open and friendly. They stood there facing each other long enough that a fly landed on

Joshua's shoulder. He didn't even want to twitch. What could he do or say that would help Thomas see that he wasn't the enemy?

"Why are you trying to UnMerge the worlds?" Equal parts disbelief and outrage colored Thomas' words, but the gun didn't waver.

Joshua blinked. A mix of surprise and anger rolled through him. He'd lived through the Merge, there was no way he'd want to live through that again. Where had Thomas gotten this misinformation? This was different from the misinformation earlier. Someone was still actively trying to turn people against him. But why this story? "I'm not. I don't want to UnMerge the worlds." Joshua's words came out clipped and forceful.

Thomas tugged his ear and then tapped two fingers against his bottom lip. The gun wavered and then dropped. He tucked it back in his holster. "What the hell's going on?"

Joshua took a deep breath, his arms and shoulders relaxing. He wasn't out of trouble yet. The gun could come out just as quickly as it'd been tucked away, but he had a chance. "You need to be more specific."

Thomas laughed on an outward breath. "Why are you being accused as the head of a secret faction that wants the world to UnMerge?"

This was new. What would someone gain by spreading that particular rumor? They must have a different endgame in mind. "I have no idea. Someone has done a great job trying to discredit me."

"They want you more than discredited, they want you dead."

Joshua flinched. Hearing the words from Thomas's mouth made them much worse. It meant his enemy was actively encouraging the spread of the rumor that he wanted to UnMerge the worlds. "How did you find me?"

Thomas shrugged. "An assignment to grab you here came moments ago. I grabbed the assignment."

Joshua nodded, his mind spinning. If it was just moments ago, that supported the idea that there was a link between the hook and the HPA. It indicated that everything really was connected. Which meant that the Conduit that had been using Alex was also using the HPA and was also connected to the Streg killings. If this was a big conspiracy, then a different set of Stregs might have gotten another victim.

"Have there been more Streg attacks?"

Thomas gave a solemn nod. "Family of four and took out another team." A strange expression flickered across his face, but was gone before Joshua could read it. It left him wondering why Thomas had taken the assignment and how it related to whatever Thomas was hiding.

Joshua slumped. All his effort and risk and still more people had died. "Damn." The Conduit controlled people. Maybe if he could figure out how the HPA had found the kill site, it could give him a lead. "How did the HPA find the site?"

The question appeared to give Thomas pause. He rubbed his chin and really seemed to think about it. "Not sure."

Was it Thomas who was controlled? But if he was being controlled, wouldn't Thomas just kill Joshua instead of exchanging information? "What's the rumor on the street?"

"We cut off communication to the other factions and the moles and spies. We aren't supposed to talk to anyone not human."

Something was off. The way he shuttered the emotion in his eyes and twisted his fingers made Joshua think that this last directive might be why Thomas had grabbed the assignment.

The news wasn't good. If the humans had cut off all communication, it was a prelude to war. All of the factions would know it and would be at high alert. In fact, one of them might think bringing Joshua in might ease tensions. "So we are running around like some blindfolded cyclops?"

"Since you are a traitor working for the Others, we can trust no one." Thomas sounded uncertain and maybe something more.

"The HPA will do anything to prevent the UnMerge." Thomas didn't sound convinced, and he wilted under Joshua's gaze and looked away.

"What if they're wrong? What if Walter is just another victim in a bigger plot?"

Thomas stared at Joshua. "I never thought I would hear those words from you."

"What?"

"That an Other might be innocent."

Joshua closed his mouth. He'd seen plenty of innocent Others. Plenty of people who were non-human who had given him a chance when they hadn't had to. When it would've been easier not to give him a chance. Not all non-humans were evil. For all their differences, Walter hadn't ever been stupid. He'd always looked out for his people and his friends. "Walter being behind the UnMerge makes no sense. We can't let Walter and his people die."

Thomas nodded as if Joshua's words resonated with him. "I can help."

For one moment Joshua wondered if Thomas was part of some elaborate hoax to make an example of him. But Joshua's gut said Thomas's willingness to help save Walter had to do with Thomas's secret. "What's the plan?"

Thomas blinked and a look of profound relief softened his features. "I know a shortcut."

Joshua pushed down thoughts of being led into a trap and followed Thomas south through the back alleys and quiet streets in the same ward as the Archive and in the complete opposite direction of where they needed to go. At least they were heading away from downtown and the HPA headquarters where HPA agents were sure to be on the lookout for Joshua.

Behind one of the shacks, Thomas touched a panel and whispered something. The words didn't sound human. Another clue? The wall shimmered away, revealing stairs heading down into a cool dark tunnel. Moss on the ceiling cast a soft green glow.

"Just keep going straight, this will lead you to Walter." Thomas stood aside to let Joshua enter.

Joshua gazed up at Thomas's face. "What will you do?"

"See if I can delay the HPA to give the LizardFolk time to evacuate."

Thomas going back to the HPA and quietly sowing distractions made sense. Especially with his sympathy for Others. "I'll hurry to give them as much warning as I can."

Thomas hesitated, seeming to search Joshua's face for something. A look of grim determination hardened his jaw. "If Walter won't believe you, tell him I sent you."

Joshua nodded. Thomas had just admitted that not only did Walter know him, but trusted him. When Joshua had come back to the HPA after defeating the Stregs, Thomas had acted oddly at the mention of his family. Perhaps the two were related. Perhaps Thomas knew Walter would trust him because Thomas was a part of his clan. If Thomas was a part of the LizardFolk, that relationship would be enough to get him brought up on charges at the HPA.

Joshua nodded. "Be careful. The HPA may have someone who can read thoughts trying to UnMerge the worlds. They will kill you if they find out."

Thomas gave one stiff nod and closed the door, leaving Joshua in the tunnel alone.

Joshua waited for his eyes to adjust and then ran as fast as he dared down the tunnel. He had no idea what direction it led. If he was right about Thomas, then this wouldn't be a trap. Every moment he wasted brought the Crylons that much closer.

He wiped the sweat that trickled down his face. The air was sultry and dried out his throat with each gasp. He must be getting close.

Around the next corner, a closed door marked the end of the tunnel. Without even stopping to catch his breath, he pushed the door open.

Walter stood at a big stone table, looking at a map. Next to him stood an Aero female and Serene. Warmth unfurled in his chest at the sight of her. Her face seemed tired and maybe puzzled, with a slight pinch above her nose and a hint of dark circles under her eyes.

Had something about the Streg investigation led her to Walter? Serene shook her head at something Walter said. The fact that neither looked up, made him think this wasn't a trap. Which meant he needed to get them out of here as soon as he could.

"You need to get out," Joshua said.

Walter turned and jerked the Aero female behind him. She looked familiar, like someone he should know and yet he couldn't place her.

The guard near the far door raised a spear, but froze at a gesture from Walter. "Why are you here?" Walter's tone demanded answers.

Joshua lifted his chin and squared his shoulders. "The HPA thinks you're behind the UnMerge."

"That'sssss asssssssinine."

Joshua sighed and rubbed his eyes. Walter would think this was a trick. They needed to move on and start getting his people evacuated. "That doesn't stop them from thinking it. They are coming here to destroy your home."

Walter hissed. "Let them try."

Joshua understood his reluctance. This complex was almost indestructible, but even this short exchange could mean the difference in how many people Walter could save. Except for one thing. "The HPA is bringing Crylons."

Walter gaped at Joshua. Eyes wide, mouth open, his tongue flicking in the air, face a study of surprise. "Crylonsssss?"

The guards drew back as if Joshua had the plague. A current of cold air swirled into the super-heated room.

Walter's eyes narrowed, looking like suspicion was winning. "How do you know thissss? You are an outcassssst. Maybe this is a plot to get ussss out of a fortified location."

Walter would be left with a tough decision. Would he trust Joshua? If he did, he and his people would have to flee their homes. If it was an HPA trap it would flush them out and eliminate them. Now was the time to test whether Thomas's name held any power. "Thomas told me."

"Lava spurssss. It'ssssss true then." Colors flooded Walter's skin. Yellows, Pinks, blues, and reds until his skin swirled with various shades of red. "We need to get out now."

Walter's response confirmed the connection between them. Despite their differences in species, Walter trusted Thomas and had a reason to believe that Joshua wouldn't know to use Thomas's name without Thomas's prompting him.

Walter pushed Serene toward Joshua. "Get him out. Alessssia ssstayssss with me."

Joshua twisted to get a better look at the Aero female. Alesia was the name of Wren's sister. Could Wren's sister be here?

"Stay safe." Serene hugged Alesia and grabbed Joshua's hand.

The touch of her hand caused an answering warmth in his chest. He was glad to see her. Not only for the information she might have, but because he was glad to see her.

The back wall slid open to reveal a dark hole with a ladder

going down. The last time he'd gone down a dark hole with Serene he'd been drugged, this time he knew he could trust her.

Joshua hesitated at the top of the ladder. There were thousands of families. The young and the old. There were food supplies and even locations to flee to that needed to be arranged. He couldn't imagine moving all of the families who lived within these tunnels. Every able body might be the difference between an elder or child surviving. "Should we stay and help them?"

"You'd scare them. Come." She headed down the ladder.

Was he really that big a bad guy? Was his name really used to scare little kids? That was one of the many things wrong with how the HPA had conducted itself. Joshua glanced back and saw the way Walter's arm went around Alesia. When Walter caught Joshua staring, Walter narrowed his eyes at him.

Joshua nodded back. Now that he thought of non-humans as people it was both easier and harder to read them, but he thought Walter looked territorial as if Alesia was his.

Joshua went down the ladder, finding Serene waiting for him at the bottom. "Was that Alesia, Wren's sister?"

Serene nodded warily leading him down the tunnel. "Say nothing."

After the hug Serene had given Alesia and the look they'd exchanged, he gathered that Alesia was her friend. It was obvious that Walter cared about Alesia as well. There would be trouble between the factions if the relationship was not sanctioned and Wren was surprised by it. "I won't."

She searched his face and then smiled at him, a smile that was part surprise and part happiness.

The warmth returned to his chest at the thought he'd pleased her. The light faded with each step until he wasn't able to see the way ahead. "We seem to always be meeting in dark tunnels."

She chuckled and her warm hand slipped into his. "How is your investigation going?" Her tone was light, but something about the way she said the word made him think her mouth was pulled tight. If that were true, he could guess her thoughts. Since Joshua was tracking down her pack's murders, what did Walter have to do with the Pack's murders?

"I have the HPA records from that night and know more about what happened, but not about who is behind it. Stopping at Walter's is unrelated."

She didn't respond, but tugged him down the tunnel. Perhaps her visit to Walter was a part of her investigation. Should he ask? They needed to get as far away as they could from the compound. He decided he'd ask her later after they were out of danger.

The sound of their footfalls echoed in the long tunnel ahead.

A distant rumble sounded, sending a trail of dust from the ceiling. The Crylons had breached the compound. It had happened far faster than he'd hoped. Had he given Walter's people enough time to escape? "Think they got out?"

He must have sounded worried because she squeezed his hand. "They have a plan."

Having a plan was one thing. Having it stand up to Crylons was a different thing. But there was nothing he could do now. He'd done all he could. Joshua looked down the tunnel, spotting a glimmer of light ahead. If they were almost out of the tunnel, perhaps he could ask about the investigation now. "Why were you at Walter's?"

"I found out how they created Streg, but it infected my son and Rose. I came looking for a bio-log-i-cal cure."

Relief that Rose hadn't died at the HPA building collided with worry in his chest. Rose hadn't died at the HPA building, but she was in danger from infection. Serene had done it. Not only had she found a lead, but it was a big one. If she'd really found out how they were creating Streg, that was an incredible break in the case. "Tell me everything you can."

Serene told him about Walter, and finding the man and the journal at the Cemetery and what her son had said about the magic and biological component being mixed. He wasn't sure how to connect this information with the bigger plot. "They are making Streg. Damn. Any idea who?" It was another confirmation of a much bigger plan. "What sort of biological thing are they using?"

"The Journal said Andre the Creator. I don't know what the biological component is." She sounded worried.

He was worried too. It was his fault that Rose was caught up in this mess. They had to work with the clues they had and find a biological cure or Rose and Serene's son would end up Stregs. He squeezed her hand. "What next?"

"Walter seemed to think I'd need more information before I could find anything. He said there were many biological components the humans brought with them."

Joshua thought of the plagues and diseases that had been in his world. Without knowing what it was, there would be no way for him to have a chance at helping. He didn't know of any stores of biological weapons that had survived.

"What about you?" She asked.

Tracking down the biological component was tempting to save his friend, but if this was a plot to UnMerge the worlds then everyone would die. The pack murders were connected to this mess somehow. He still had the file from Alex on who had been at the HPA lab when it burned. But the HPA was on a rampage. The HPA would use his name combined with anyone else's as an excuse to demolish that faction. The Conduit would take down the HPA and quite possibly the whole world. There was only one choice that made sense. He took a shaky breath. "We need to get the word out that the HPA has been compromised. A Conduit is controlling someone high in the ranks."

The darkness was still too thick for him to tell what Serene thought about his words, but the twitch of her hand and the way she gasped made him think he had surprised her.

"I can get the word out if I go to Joe's."

The Silverfolk had mentioned Joe's to him at the Gala. They had said that it was a place to help with secrets. Joshua hadn't been to Joe's for a few weeks now. There was something about that place he'd found soothing. It was the only place he'd found that would make a burger and fries just like he'd had before the Merge. She'd be safe there. He'd have to trust she could get the word out. "You can read the journal there."

"What will you do?" She asked.

"I don't know."

26

SERENE

<u>Evening, Luminous thirty-first, 299 years post-Merge</u>

The bell rang as Serene walked into Joe's. She didn't remember exactly how she'd gotten there. She'd taken Joshua as close to the HPA labs as she could stand and then she'd bolted.

"I didn't expect you so soon." Joe grabbed her favorite snack from behind the counter.

Serene took a steadying breath to try and control the riot of feelings and thoughts that ricocheted through her head. Alesia was with Walter without Wren's knowledge. That could easily cause a war. The HPA had just demolished the Lizardfolk's stronghold. Joshua had insisted the HPA was being controlled by what amounted to the one thing universally feared: A Conduit. Her son and Rose would die and turn into Stregs if she couldn't figure out the biological component in the Streg conversion process. And Joshua was at the HPA labs. Which at the surface seemed the least of her worries, but the closer she'd taken Joshua to the labs, the worse her mind had scattered. The worse the need to flee had been, leaving her sweating and aching. Joshua had noticed and sent her back to Joe's.

"What's wrong?" It was Joe's tone of compassion that undid her.

She told him everything. With each sentence she uttered and each set of supporting details she put on the top layer of her mind for Joe to see, the more grim Joe looked.

"I can pass the word." He took her to a booth and set tea in front of her. "The best thing you can do is read. The key to saving those infected is in that book."

She had no idea what she was looking for and her son's life depended on her. It would be so easy to fail. To miss a clue and have to kill her son so he wouldn't spend eternity a mindless undead.

Joe crossed back to the counter. When he sat back down in his chair, she felt utterly alone, but then she realized that even though he wasn't moving, the energy around him seemed frantic. He was probably in contact with every member of the Hive, passing along the information she'd given him. He glanced her way and nodded toward the book that lay unopened before her.

Yes, she needed to focus.

She opened the small black book and started to read. If she got lucky, she'd figure out the biological component before her son died and turned. Anguish tightened her hands on the book. It crackled in response. If things went really badly, none of them would see the next sunrise.

27

JOSHUA

Joshua walked until he hit the edge of the great preserve and found a trail head. Signs marked the path. 'Danger, unregulated area', 'Trespass at your own risk', 'Not monitored by HPA'.

He'd used the same trick to secure his home as the HPA did to discourage humans from entering the preserve. They could enter if they wanted to, but many of the residents hated humans. The preserve was the one place where human law didn't extend. That was the theory anyway, a theory that HPA had encouraged. Just as he had encouraged the myth of the mad wizard of the tower.

The trail wound between lush green trees. He ducked under branches and dodged past overgrown bushes. The sweet scent of wild flowers and something musky hung heavy in the air. Nothing felt malevolent to his senses. He startled a Death Kitty that crashed through the foliage.

The path grew steeper and when he reached the top, he could see a valley and beyond to the wilds.

Even though he'd not gone to all the HPA properties, he'd made sure he knew where they all were. Every HPA agent studied the maps of important HPA buildings. The research facility should be in this valley.

He walked down the path that twisted into the valley. The trees that lined the path crowded out the feeble sunlight and darkened the path. Weeds and sticker bushes crowded between almost as if encouraged to grow. There were no game trails or open spaces. Just this narrow trail that the forest leaned into. The trail once wide enough for three across now barely let him pass without thorns tugging on his shirt.

The thorns on the bushes dripped foul smelling goop. The underbrush crackled as if talking about him. The rest of the normal bird noises and wind faded, leaving only the rustling and creaking of the plants.

He sent a Soul Wisp into the brush. A non-animal awareness and intelligence that was like nothing he had ever touched filled the woods. It was the forest itself that seemed to have an intelligence. The trees in the city were no more like this forest than a guinea pig was like a dragon.

The closer to where the complex had been, the deeper and darker the trees became until he had to pause and put his hand on one. The bark was rough beneath his fingers, yet cold. The tree radiated rage. It was palpable, throbbing through the air, a shimmering of cold green. What had happened here that had caused the very forest to respond?

He rounded the next corner into what looked like a forest graveyard. Sharp sticks with no leaves poked up from the ground, the grass lay in twisted, brown strands as if the water had been cooked out. It was as if there was an invisible line between the rage filled forest and the forest graveyard. One tree had a branch that extended beyond the invisible line. It changed from lush growth to a nude branch at the demarcation.

Before the fire the HPA tower would have been in the center of the clearing, but the clearing was empty now. Burnt to the ground wasn't a vivid enough description for what was left. Not even a shell of a building remained, just a thirty foot wide hole in the ground.

Joshua walked closer and could see the prints in the soil surrounding the hole's center. Impressions where prisoners had fallen, bare clawed-feet, hand prints and knee prints trapped in the mud where they'd crawled. Deeper indentions gave mute testimony to those that had lifted them. There were even some booted tracks probably from the human guards.

He circled the site. The survivors had fled in all directions. Some of the tracks just ended. No bodies, the impressions just stopped.

It didn't make any sense for tracks to have survived this long. Surely the elements should have washed them away a year later. He reached down to feel one. It felt like clay that has been baked in a vast amount of energy, leaving the print hardened. He shivered and glanced around again.

Nothing moved within his vision. No birds or squirrels or pixies. Just heavy air and the rage of the forest behind him.

The hole seemed to swallow the light as he walked nearer. It was just a trick of the light, but it made him think of black holes and other vortexes which wouldn't release you if you were foolish enough to get caught. The hole he'd jumped through during the Merge was much smaller and he'd had to go in fast. At least now he had a way of checking it out without going in. He sent a Soul Wisp down.

Level after level of blackened dripping walls plunged into the earth. Nothing moved. He sensed no magic, no electricity.

On the bottom level, the floors rippled away as if something had sent a wave through them. The deeper he went, the larger and more blackened the ripples became. It seemed to be some sort of backlash, but the feel of it was dulled and faded. It was more than the passage of time. Something had wiped away the feeling. A Conduit would have that power. A conduit would be able to clean the area of psychic echoes, probably pulling the energy from the surrounding vegetation as a power source.

Another dead end.

The urge to leave fought with the urge to do a thorough job. He should climb in and investigate with his own eyes. See if he could spot a clue. This was too important to give into his fear.

The sky's color had faded to the point everything seemed surreal. He probably had an hour before it would be full dark. Hopefully, that would be enough time to go in and get out of what was left of the HPA labs.

He climbed down.

Some time later, he lay on the floor catching his breath and staring up at the sliver of sky. His arms and legs ached and twitched. He stretched his hands out and then made fists to get the blood flowing. He caught his breath and then stood and walked in the direction where the record room would have been.

The Soul Wisp glowed a soft blue in the dark hall. It should be twenty paces and then a left turn. The blackened stone walls leaned in. His passage stirred the air enough that the wall trembled. One false move might send them tumbling.

He turned and saw a wall where one shouldn't have been. He touched it and the wall quivered, raining dust and soot down on him.

This section didn't match the plans of this building. Someone had changed the building or the plans had been wrong. He walked along the wall until he came to an opening. The wall looked wounded. The space where the door had once been, had been replaced with crumbling bricks and twisted metal. The door itself had been twisted off of its hinges and embedded in the wall ten feet from this entrance.

This was the room they'd added. The walls were thicker than normal. It seemed odd that they would need another room.

He entered, sending the Soul Wisp high in the middle to cast as much light as possible. Two dozen cages lined the back wall and in the center a set of chains lay twisted on the floor. He hadn't expected cages. The HPA did use cages sometimes for a creature who went feral, but to have a dozen of them was wrong. It was as if this room had been used for something worse.

He turned to survey the room and noticed the small desk slumped against the wall. The legs had collapsed on one side. Papers cascaded from the top to the floor in a precarious water-fall. The ones on the ground and most of the ones on the desk were blackened and illegible.

One folder had survived with only singed edges. He grabbed the folder and tucked it in his backpack. The walls looked cracked as if a tornado and rockslide had mated and produced offspring here. This is where the backlash had happened.

Someone had wiped out the mental echo, but they couldn't wipe out the smell of fear and death, even after all this time. This was where the Pack had died.

A shiver crawled up his spine. The room felt colder than it had just a moment before. Uneasiness persisted. If the Pack had died as Alex had implied, they very easily could be ghosts. They'd be trapped where they had died, in this room, until released. Based on how they'd died, they might even be polter-geists, a type of ghost who could affect the material world. Which meant they could fling matter and stop hearts.

He eased back toward the door. Maybe he could escape before they fully manifested. A ghost was almost invulnerable to attack. He had none of the weapons or charms that could affect them. They were still locked in the chest at Elder Martin's house where he'd left them at the Gala.

The edges of the desk frosted. When he gasped, so did his breath.

The Pack was about to manifest.

They flitted at the edge of his vision. His heart spiked in his chest. Glancing back, at the door, he hoped maybe he could make it out of the room where they wouldn't be able to follow.

Before he even took a step, a dozen faint wolves lined up blocking the door. The room pulsed with anger and anguish. The biggest wolf lifted its head and howled.

Fear and sympathy raged within Joshua's chest. He covered his ears, but it did no good against the noise in his head. The Soul Wisp in the room vibrated apart and its light faded, leaving the room in inky darkness.

He was alone in the dark with a couple dozen pissed off murdered pack members, who could kill his soul.

The energy of the ghosts flickered and swirled around him, a pack of wolves circling dinner. A sweep of cold air, and something pushed his shoulder, jerking him to the side.

His presence must have triggered them. Maybe if he could hide, they would go away and he could get out before they appeared again. It was worth a try.

He pulled his essence inward toward his pool. He felt a strange stretching that sucked his extra senses inward. He couldn't see a difference, but yet somehow it was different. It was like touching through a blanket with gloves on or walking on a sunny day with squinted eyes.

Once everything was pulled in, he waited. Almost meditating, his breathing slow and even, his body still he focused on the here and now in this room at this second.

Time passed and he sat in the dark. He felt like a kid with the belief that if he couldn't see them, they couldn't see him.

Then the hairs raised on his arms, and deep in his bones he felt the energy in the room stir.

Gradually he peeped just a small bit of himself out to read the room, like a snail raising just the tip of an antenna.

The wolves struggled in cages. One by one as if the doors were opened and they were dragged out, they would step forward. Each time they hit the center of the room, they convulsed and twisted as if a strong current had struck them. Until at last the Alpha stepped forward. He lasted longer than the rest jerking and contorting longer than the others. His low, anguished howl ripped through the room shaking the walls as he collapsed.

The room went dark of all energy. He'd heard of this before, but had never thought to see it. The ghosts were trapped replaying their last moments. Because they'd been a pack, the moment was the full collection of their deaths. He shivered and took a step to the door, but the echo of that last howl and the agony on the wolf's face stopped him. There had to be a way to release them. Leaving them trapped here wasn't right. He had to figure out a way to help them.

A pool of energy formed and reformed the pack members in their cages.

The same scene replayed over and over. They died one after another protecting something. They must be protecting Serene.

Then the loop would start over with the same terror, determination, death.

Poor bastards. They'd been in the loop so long that nothing but rage and grief survived. They would be down here forever. He probably could escape if he ran when their energy was at the low point. But he couldn't do it. He needed to at least try to rescue them. Serene had to be the key. Maybe if he showed them that she was safe, they would be able to leave.

Joshua carefully shaped his inner world and created Serene.

Projected her image before them just as the cycle ended and would have started again.

"I need your help." Joshua mimicked Serene's voice.

The energy in the room quivered, creating a small earthquake. Tiny lightning bolts sparked from the cages and gathered into a ball where they had all died. A rotating storm of electricity hovered in the air.

"This man will be the one to save me. Protect him," the fake Serene said.

Zzzzpt.

The ball crashed into the ground. The shockwave knocked Joshua off his feet. He gasped for breath. Dust from the ceiling scattered down. The floor and walls groaned. A distant crash sounded.

The edges of the room faded and a tinny whine sounded deep in Joshua's ears. He focused on his breathing. The gasping slowed to a steady rhythm. The room now quiet except for his breathing. Not a flicker of activity. Elation filled him. He'd done it, he'd freed the Pack.

He generated a Soul Wisp and it lit up the room.

Inches away, the Alpha's human form glared at Joshua. Joshua fell back. He hadn't freed the Pack, but they seemed to be aware now.

The Alpha's eyes filled with what must be hatred. Canines stabbed out from beneath his curled lip. The low growl menaced Joshua, promising a slow death.

Joshua's gut twisted at the hatred in the Alpha's gaze. What had it felt like to watch his family die? Joshua had been head of the agency. He should have known about this and stopped it. But he'd been too absorbed in his own pain to notice or care what a mess the HPA was making of the world. Regret clogged his throat. It was his fault.

The Alpha picked Joshua up and pushed him back into the wall.

Joshua froze, but his heart raced. This proved the Alpha was a poltergeist. Only poltergeists could touch the real world. Joshua swung on the ghost, but his arm slid through, hitting the wall behind.

The Alpha smiled, a primitive sign of aggression made up of sharp teeth. His other hand glowed red and he slapped it against the side of Joshua's head.

Air whistled by, blocking out all other sound and chilling the sweat on his body. Swirling colors consumed his vision just as they had when Alex had brought him to his inner pool. He landed in a pile on the sand next to his pool. The Alpha had brought him here for a reason.

The Alpha stood over Joshua in human form. The rest of the pack lined up against the wall. The Alpha stepped forward and knelt before the pool. "Let's see how the pool judges you."

The Alpha dipped his hand into the pool and stirred. The pack howled a long calling howl meant to reunite the pack.

The Alpha stood and stepped back, smirking. The ripples stilled and an image floated to the surface.

Serene reflected on the pool's surface.

The Alpha laughed. A long laughing howl. "So you think Serene will love you? She only loved me as a pack member and not with her whole heart."

"We are working together to save the world." As Joshua said it he wondered if it was accurate. He did find her attractive and if it turned out not to be a product of the Book of Secrets, he'd be interested in.... What? A relationship? A chance? Perhaps, but they had to save the world first. That was far more important than any attraction he might feel toward Serene.

The Alpha tilted his head. "What is wrong with the world that you must save it?"

There was an underlying sarcasm to the Alpha's words which annoyed Joshua. But he pushed it down. "A Conduit and Bender have a plot to rip the world apart."

A secretive grin lit the Alpha's face. "Once you save the world. Remember choice was taken from her once." He bent and stirred the pool once more and a scene appeared in the water.

A younger version of the Alpha stood before a younger version of Serene.

She stood protectively in front of someone. Her brows were drawn and her whole body looked poised to fight.

The pack lined up behind the Alpha. They seemed worried. Swift glances passed between members. The Alpha had his hands out in supplication.

Words that Joshua couldn't hear were exchanged.

Serene drooped and covered her face and then stood tall.

"My son stays free and protected from the Pack and I will go with you. I will love you the best I am able."

Serene turned and hugged the boy she'd been protecting and then left with the Pack.

The son in the pool turned toward Joshua and Joshua recognized him as a teenaged version of Master Phil.

Dragon balls. Serene wasn't the spoiled Other he'd thought. She had been thrown many tough breaks, just as he had and she still had the strength to continue.

When the image of Master Phil faded, the pack was gone and Joshua was in a pitch black room.

He'd have only the feeble light of his Soul Wisps to find his way back to town.

28

———

SERENE

<u>Past sunset, Luminous thirty-first, 299 years post-Merge</u>

Serene closed the journal she'd been reading and rubbed her eyes. The sun had set, leaving the interior of Joe's darker. She'd read the whole journal twice. The second time reading, she'd decided to copy the words she didn't understand.

> *Rubella*
> *inoculation*
> *antibiotic*
> *culture*

Maybe one of these words would make sense to Joshua and would give her the key. Even if Joshua knew something, the odds seemed low she could get whatever she needed to her son in time. She stared at the words.

230

Joe set two plates of food on the table she sat at. "Joshua is on his way." Joe answered her unasked question.

She'd started eating when the doorbell jingled.

Joshua walked in. His hair looked as if he'd been rolling in the mud. Tuffs stuck in different directions. A trail of sweat had washed away the layer of dirt by his ears. He looked tired, but not hopeful.

"Find anything?" Given his expression, she wasn't sure she wanted to know the answer.

He shook his head and ran his hand through his hair. "I have a couple of files to review, but no real leads."

Her heart sank. They could be at a dead end.

"Eat," Joe called over from his chair.

Joshua blinked and focused his gaze on the plate in front of him. He picked up the burger and took a bite.

This was the first food she'd had since before the Gala. She took a bite of her own and forced the food down. Even that small bite uncramped her stomach. How could she eat when her son's life was in danger?

"Did you find anything?" Joshua asked between bites.

He seemed truly interested. Maybe these words would make more sense to him than they did to her. "I've read the journal twice times and wrote out the words that seemed important." She passed him her notes.

He read the page. "Rubella, huh. Before the merge it was one of the sicknesses children were protected against."

Her heart started thumping. She didn't want to get her hopes up, but it seemed like Joshua might know something about this after all. "Where do I need to go to get this protection?"

"I'm sure the vaccination supply was lost in the Merge." Joshua's voice held a note of apology. There was both sympathy and anguish there.

She sank back. Another dead end. "So there's no way to get

ahold of a little bit of this protection? I don't think he needs much."

Joshua took another bite. His brow furrowed. The food went down quickly. He shook his head. "I'm not sure. The bad guys must have gotten Rubella from somewhere. But I've no idea where that might be."

"Are you sure?" She watched his face.

He frowned, bit his lip, and shook his head. "Nothing I can think of."

So close. She'd been so close to being able to save her son. Joshua looked as if he wished he knew something. Which meant he didn't. Maybe something would occur to him later, but that would be too late for her son. Serene set down the half-eaten sandwich. Her throat was too tight to let food through. She rubbed her eyes. If this was a dead-end, what could she do next? "What did you find?"

He brought out two folders and set them on the table. The faint smell of smoke made her grimace.

Joshua opened up the first one. "This is a listing of everyone the HPA thought was in the lab when it burned." He ran his finger along the list of names.

Serene didn't want to look. Glimpses of grimy faces flashed in her head. Her stomach rolled.

His finger paused on a name. "Alesia? Wasn't that who was with you at Walter's?"

Serene hesitated. Alesia had saved her life. She'd nursed Serene through her grief. She'd been an unexpected friend through the tragedy. Could she really tell Joshua about her? Even this little bit? There could be so many potential implications, most of which she'd never get. She glanced at his face. He wore an expectant look on his face. And as the silence continued between them, his expression clouded. He seemed to be searching her face.

He'd proven to be different than his reputation. He'd sent his friend to help her. He'd taken his investigation of her Pack's murders seriously. She would trust him with this.

"We are a team." She said it softly, but it caused Joshua's face to flush and a small smile to tug at his lips.

"Alesia was there that night. She rescued me."

The Seer had said to bring Alesia to Walter's. Maybe it was not to have Walter and Alesia meet, but for Joshua and Alesia to almost meet. Maybe Joshua was meant to meet the Seer and she would be able to give him the missing puzzle piece. Maybe that was one of the paths that the Seer had talked about.

He sat up straighter. "Do you think she might know something?"

Seers were not something talked about with outsiders. Her friendship to Alesia was one thing, giving away secrets of a whole race to Joshua was another thing. Joshua had been a non-human hater, at least in reputation up until she'd helped him after the Gala. If Joshua told the HPA then Alesia might find herself captured again. Could she trust him with the information? She looked at him, really looked at him. He seemed interested in what she was going to say. As if her opinion had value. He seemed like he was truly trying to figure out who had murdered her pack. If she withheld this information, would it stop him from solving it? "She may. Not only was she there, but the Seer has been using her as a vessel."

He leaned forward with raised brows. "What does that mean?"

"Seers are beings who can see the future. They take over women of certain lines at times of trouble." Alesia's grandmother had been taken over about the time the city had almost been overrun by a nearby hostile town. The two situations might be related.

"You've talked to this Seer?"

"She was the one that gave me the clue that led to you. She said 'It is the head that has the answers you seek.'"

He nodded, seemingly deep in thought.

"Let's check out the last folder." He opened it and laid it on the table between them.

It was lines and dots, arranged in a pattern she didn't understand. "What is it?"

"It's like a chart logging the stars." He pointed to a circle on the left with numbers. "This represents a time and the celestial events happening."

There was a red circle. "Is that tonight? The anniversary of the merge?"

"Yes."

"What's this?" She pointed to what looked like a bunch of small fireballs.

He leaned in and then all color left his face. "It's a meteor shower."

She was missing something. "Perseid?" She read the label penned in.

If anything Joshua looked even more stricken. "That's the meteor shower that I was watching when the Merge took place."

She wasn't sure what a meteor shower was, but it clearly worried Joshua. "Does that mean that the UnMerge may happen tonight?"

He nodded.

The idea the UnMerge could happen tonight was like the concept of the sun not rising tomorrow. It didn't make any sense. The visible worry on Joshua's face convinced her the UnMerge really could happen and it would be the end of the world. Even if Joshua was wrong about the UnMerge, her son would still die. The ball twisted making it hard to breathe.

She'd lose her only child. She'd done so much to protect him over the years. Even leaving the pack for awhile. She would do anything she could to protect him. That thought mirrored something Joshua had said.

The pain lessened. Something about protection. "Joshua did you say children were given protection against this sickness before the Merge."

"Yes." He looked puzzled and faintly alarmed.

"Does any human have this protection?"

"Only those born before the Merge got that protection."

Hope lightened her chest. Maybe Joshua was the key. "And you were born before the Merge?"

"Yes."

"And do you have this protection?"

"I was vaccinated. So I should."

Hope swelled, making her feel lighter. All she needed now was Joshua to give her something. Witches used hair, maybe this was the same thing. "Could I have your hair to give to my son?"

He shook his head. "It doesn't work that way."

She slumped, deflated.

"You misunderstand. That protection is in my blood."

Hope rose yet again. It was in his blood and he seemed willing to help. But, his blood could be used to control him or track him magically. Would her asking for blood break their developing trust?

She had to risk it. "Can I have some of your blood?" Maybe a special ceremony was required to get the protection from his blood. Her son would know since he used blood in some of his healing magic.

Joshua leaned back. "What do you have to collect blood?"

She pulled out the glass vial that Daniel had given her. "This."

He nodded, glancing around and then picked up the knife. "Let me have it."

Serene's throat went dry. It was one thing to say you wanted to help, but for Joshua to willingly give his blood was nothing short of a miracle.

He pricked his finger with the point of the knife and dripped blood into the vial. "Save your son and Rose. I need to see Alesia," he said, handing back the vial.

Serene took the bottle and screwed on the cover before tucking it into her bag. "Thank you."

Joshua nodded. pressing a napkin to the end of his finger.

Joe came to their table and grabbed the empty plates. "The HPA is assembling outside, they'll be here any moment."

Serene gripped the table to keep herself from running. The last thing they needed was for the HPA to know they'd been spotted. "What now?"

Joshua took her hand. "Go as if you are going to the bathroom and slip out the back. I'll meet you at the Rookery."

"Good idea." Joe walked back to his counter.

She smiled just in case anyone was watching. She stood slowly and ambled toward the bathroom. Instead of going inside, she slipped out the emergency exit.

She scented humans nearby, but none had breached the back alley yet. She needed to hurry or the HPA would take her one chance at saving her son. She shifted form and went as fast as she could.

Hopefully she wouldn't be too late.

29

———

JOSHUA

Night, Luminous thirty-first, 299 years post-Merge

Joshua waited for the sound of the door closing before starting to count in his head. When he got to one hundred, he slowly stood up. He moved as if he had all the time in the world, not like he knew that the organization that was out to kill him was moments away from Joe's.

"I can buy you a few moments," Joe said without looking up.

Gratitude warmed him. Joe didn't have to take this risk for him. "Thanks Joe."

Joshua went out the emergency exit, closing the door carefully behind him. If he could just get to Wren's he'd be able to see Alesia. The Seer was his best bet. If he could—

The next moment he flew through the air. He gasped and flung his arms out to break his fall. He landed in a puddle.

Hugo blocked the door back into Joe's. Big, blonde, dumb and bad, like someone had pulled all the gentle out of a giant and loaded it up with cruelty and mayhem. That mayhem was focused on Joshua now that he was an enemy of the HPA.

Joshua rolled up to his feet. Hugo was a big man. One of the toughest the HPA'd hired. Joshua was much better off talking his way out of this if he could.

Hugo cracked his knuckles first on his right hand and then on his left. He grinned like a little kid who'd caught Santa and was holding him hostage for more toys.

All it would take was one shout and the rest of the crew would be here. Joshua had to take Hugo quietly. Hugo may be far heavier than he was and taller, but he was lazy and never really trained. Joshua had to be smart. He needed to dodge and keep Hugo away with front kicks until he could get in and take Hugo down.

"Hugo-" Joshua said.

"Don't bother talking, Lighthouse. I have always wanted to kill you. Now I have my chance." Hugo circled Joshua, checking his defenses.

"Why?" Something in what Hugo said was off. Hugo had always come across as a little dumb, but dedicated to the HPA. Had something changed? Joshua jabbed with his right. "Think that will make you the big man in the organization?" Joshua goaded searching for a weakness.

"I know my place." Hugo's grin twisted into something that would make a snake duck for cover. "You know what I will enjoy the most?" He swung at Joshua who dodged easily.

"Finally getting to kill a human?" Joshua said hoping his training to protect humans would kick in and Hugo would hesitate.

"Oh, I've killed humans before. You just didn't know about it. They didn't deserve it. And I did it with my bare hands." Hugo said in a trying to be cute sing-song way that was at odds with what he was saying. The hairs on Joshua's arms rose and the chill fled to his gut. How had this monster made it into the HPA? What other damage had he done? Hugo dropped his guard. The glint in his eyes calmed some of Joshua's anger. Hugo was trying to goad Joshua into close quarter fighting where Hugo would have the advantage.

"Why would you do that?" Joshua had misjudged Hugo badly. The door behind Hugo cracked open. That could be more HPA agents coming. Joshua needed to end this.

"And don't try any of your tricks, Lighthouse. I know all about you." Hugo swung at Joshua.

Joshua ducked away and then kicked out to discourage a bullrush. Joshua needed to close in on his terms. "What do you think you know?"

"That you are nothing but–" Hugo swung again and grunted when he missed. "–an Other in human clothing."

Hugo knew.

The breath whooshed out of Joshua as if he had been sucker punched.

Joshua almost forgot to duck and dodge to the side. He hadn't known so many people knew about his powers. Marvin and Delilah had known, but they were long dead. They'd both died soon after learning of his powers, because of his powers. Serene and Master Phil knew, but none of them were connected to Hugo. How had he found out?

Hugo took a step away from the back door. "I'm going to enjoy making you pay for your deception."

Hugo led with his right this time; his huge fist shot forward.

Joshua dodged back and slipped sideways. He lashed out with a foot that connected. His heel sinking into Hugo's belly.

Hugo gasped out air, but still stepped forward and swung with his other fist.

Joshua leaned back to avoid the blow and kicked, hitting Hugo in the solar plexus. A lucky shot.

Hugo fell as if cut off at the knees. His head bounced on the ground and his eyes rolled back.

Before the last head bounce, pale blue light floated from Joe's backdoor and landed on the sprawled Hugo. He twitched and then stood and, without a backward glance, walked to the back door of Joe's and disappeared inside.

"Hive will take him." Joe leaned out of the back door and nodded. "Go stop the UnMerging."

The door closed with a snap.

Relief and surprise crested in his chest. Was no one what they seemed? Now he owed a debt to a Hive.

Joshua had to get out of here before the rest of the crew showed up. He glanced out the alley. There was no one else around so he walked to the next alley down and headed toward the Rookery. Alesia would be there and hopefully the Seer would be able to help him determine who was behind all of this before the meteor shower started and the world ended.

30

SERENE

<u>Night, Luminous thirty-first, 299 years post-Merge</u>

Serene stood in front of the door of her son's home. The black flag with skull and crossbones still stuck to the door made her rub her arms. Dread swirled through her like cold fire leaving her shivering. She hesitated just a moment before knocking. Was she too late?

She knocked and waited. No one came to the door. A slow trickle of dread shivered through her.

She knocked again, banging just a little bit louder. Still nothing.

A streak of panic connected with the dread. She pushed it away. Maybe he was busy which was a better image than the Streg process being completed. She pressed her ear to the door. She couldn't hear anything. No creaks or crashes or wild gnashing of teeth. If he was there he was just not answering the door. Dread expanded in her chest, squeezing her heart. If he was there, why wouldn't he answer?

A breeze crossed the alley way, fluttering the flag on the door. The flag. Hope lightened her. He might still be okay. She huffed out a little laugh, he had the death flag on his door, of course he wasn't answering. She took a shaky breath and then used the knock she and her son had used when it was just the two of them trying to survive. The coded knock would let him know that it was her.

She waited, heart in her throat. How long spent waiting would tell her that she was too late? Ten? Twenty?

One. She closed her eyes so she wouldn't see the flag.

Two.

Three.

Four.

The door creaked open and Rose peered out.

Serene's son hadn't opened the door. Her son was dead. Pain radiated out of her chest. A dull ache pulled from her center. Serene's heart broke. Why else would Rose answer his door?

Rose must have seen Serene's panic, because her face softened. "He's fine. He's just in the middle of something he can't stop."

Relief coursed through her, she closed her eyes for a moment and let out a shuddery breath. He was still alive. "How is he doing?"

Rose's face didn't change. "Fine." something about the lack of emotion in her face set Serene on edge. It must be bad. And there was nothing she could do to help.

That wasn't true. She lifted up the vial. "I have blood from Joshua that has something that protects against the biological component."

A flash of relief lightened Rose's features. "Good. Put it on the step and then you need to go."

Indignation flared. Who was Rose to tell her what her son needed? "I–"

"Hush." Rose glanced back into the room and then lowered her voice. "It would be better if you came back tomorrow morning. Please."

Serene said nothing, afraid if she tried to say anything, she'd start crying. It was for the best. She knew that, but she didn't like it at all. Her son didn't need her distracting him. And knowing him, the thought of Serene also getting sick would be very hard for him to take. She placed the vial on the step.

"Make sure he knows that I love him," She couldn't help the tears that welled in her eyes.

"He already knows." Rose reached for the vial and then hesitated. "Is Joshua alright?"

Serene nodded. "He's following leads. He thinks it will happen tonight."

Rose grimaced and closed the door.

Serene leaned against the door. The edge of the flag pressed into her cheek. She was trusting Rose, the not quite human friend of Joshua with her son's life. If this had happened even a day ago, she'd have knocked Rose to the floor and helped her son get better. But Rose had proven herself to be a friend.

Serene wandered through Shifterville trying to walk off her feelings. The paths between buildings looked mostly the same. She felt restless and alone and was unsure where she should go.

A pungent splash of scent marked the next building's corner as another shifters clan. They'd been on good terms with her own clan, but the idea of talking to anyone and trying to say the right things sent a wave of exhaustion through her. She turned and went back to the neutral area.

Perhaps she needed to do something useful. She could help Joshua, but he could be anywhere once he discovered that Alesia was not at the Rookery. Perhaps she could go back to Joe's and at least have the reassuring buzz of the hive communication.

She retraced her steps and found herself across from her son's door. The skull flag still barricaded the door. The urge to knock rose within her, but she pushed it down. It wouldn't help them. Joe's was the best distraction. She headed out the hidden pathways to the walkway that lead out of Shifterville.

The clump of a footfall behind her and the hint of human smell in the air had her looking up. Surprise paused her steps. Humans so rarely came to Shifterville. There was no reason for one to be here on this night unless they were up to no good. Or maybe the HPA had found her. They were too close to her son's. She'd check them out and then go to Joe's.

She snuck closer to where the sound had come from. There was a short human in the next alley, running his hands up and down the wall. He could be looking for one of the secret trails. He might even be looking for her son. He could be looking for her. Perhaps Joshua had sent another friend to help. It was possible. He was worried about Rose too.

She eased forward so that he could see her and kept her human form. She'd decide what he wanted based on his reaction.

He glanced up and spotted her.

"Serene? Joshua sent me to find you." His dark hair and beard were neatly trimmed. He was the shortest human she'd seen. He looked as if he could have been a Dwarf with his stout build.

But, something about the way he said it seemed off. She took a step back. "What did he say?"

"I'm Bob. I was Joshua's partner a long time ago." He had a smile pasted on his face but it didn't seem to reach his eyes.

Joshua hadn't mentioned Bob before, but why would he. He also hadn't mentioned Rose. She let him get a little closer. There was an alley behind her that she could go into if she needed to.

"He needs your help." His voice was soft and persuasive.

She needed some way to verify that he was a friend to Joshua. "Where did you see him?" She kept her voice friendly.

He stepped closer. A trick of the wind brought his scent fully to her. It had the overtones of Streg.

A chill crept up her back. If he had the Streg smell, he was one of them. One of the people who were trying to UnMerge the world and if Joshua was correct, one of the people involved with her Pack's murders. Her heart raced in panic. She scrambled back and then ran.

"Wait." He shouted.

She sped into the alley, but it was one of the many deadends. The walls were high and slick. But even when Bob came after her, as she had no doubt that he would, she could shift and hide to elude him. As long as her malfunctioning talent shifted her to a dark color.

One steadying breath and she shifted. Her terror made it harder to control, she wavered between forms and for one horrible moment, she wondered if she was going to be able to change at all. Then she finally achieved her furry form.

Her paws and whole body were white. A shade that almost glowed in the dark. Panicking, she raced behind a can and hunkered down. He must be looking for her for a reason. What would happen to her if she was caught? The HPA lab was burnt down. Did they have somewhere just as horrible to take her? What would happen to her son?

The smell of garbage clogged Serene's nose. She huddled as low as she could. He would see her if she wasn't small enough. Maybe she could retry the shift, but shifting was motion and created some noise.

I'm small and inconsequential.

<u>Crash</u>.

The can on the end slammed into the other wall. She flinched away from the sound. The urge to run crept up her spine. She took a deep breath and let it out slowly. Running would get her caught.

"You might as well come out." Bob's voice was low pitched and rough sounding. It reminded her of that night. Her hands slicked.

Crunch. Crash.

"There is no exit." The voice drew closer. The underlying smell of the dead and Bob's smell triggered a flash. He'd been there. She was positive. That night, in the background. He'd been there. Rage and fear twisted in her, sending her heart racing and raising the hairs on her back and arms.

Her wrist ached with the memory of being tied. In her memory she could feel the panic of her pack. Her own anxiety soared, tensing her muscles in anticipation of the next memory. The way her mate had held them together. Two other humans had been in the room. One who smelled just as scared as she, stood ridgely by the door as if unseen hands held him there. The other was human, male, and the smell of Streg shifted around him like his own personal coat. His eyes were that of a lunatic, wide and wild. She braced for the feeling of a pack member being ripped from her mind. Connelly, one of the Betas had been first.

Dread and helplessness paralyzed her, darkening her vision, sucking her in.

Crash.

"We will find you."

She shook her head in denial. Her pack was dead. She wasn't at the lab, she was in an alley and needed a way to escape. She couldn't get past Bob without a distraction. Perhaps she could make it look like she'd escaped already.

Sometimes these old alleys had places where the bricks

weren't solid. It wouldn't be big enough for her to go through, but maybe if she staged it correctly, it would look that way. She turned toward the wall and used her claws and teeth to find a loose brick. If she couldn't get one out she'd be trapped. She wiggled the brick out. The next one came out with a little effort.

She'd need four or five bricks for this to work. She attacked the next one in quiet determination. The next one and the next one until she had a small pile of bricks. The entrance wasn't big enough for her. She pulled some fur with her teeth and spit it into the hole and made a footprint that looked like it led in.

She backed up, wiping her trace with her tail until she was in the far corner. If he took the bait, she could sneak away and make a run for it.

She waited, breathing in shallow breaths.

<u>Crash</u>.

The next can collided. She twitched, but held still. The impact sent rotten vegetables around the alley.

<u>Crash</u>.

Then another can smashed into the one she'd hidden behind. Her breath hissed out. That was close. She glanced up,

"What the hell." Cans screeched across the concrete. "How the fuck did she get through there?"

Relief flashed within her causing her to shiver. She wasn't quite free yet. She had to get by him without him noticing.

More cans went flying.

With quiet smooth steps, she hugged the wall on the opposite side of the alley. She crept with slow steps, glancing back. Bob was prone, trying to look through the hole she'd made. If she could just get around the corner, she'd have a chance to run for it. She rounded the corner without him seeming to notice. Relief loosened her lungs and her heart slowed. She had escaped them. All she needs to do–

<u>Wump</u>. <u>Crack</u>.

She jumped, but a steel trap slammed down, trapping her. She pulled at the bar and snarled. The face of one of the other humans from that night stared back at her.

She was caught.

31

JOSHUA

Night, Luminous thirty-first, 299 years post-Merge

Joshua needed to talk to Alesia and hope that the Seer would make an appearance. He'd never seen a record of what a Seer actually was, just some vague rumors documented from the last time the city had been in trouble less than a hundred years ago. It'd been unclear what role the Seer had played in the city's defenses against the assault and siege from the neighboring town. The Crylons were credited with winning the war, but no one knew how they'd been engaged. Even if the Seer didn't come, Alesia was a witness he could interview.

Most Aeros lived at the highest peak of the mountain range to the southwest of town, Falcon's Ridge. Abominable snowmen, check. Year-round snow, check. Accessible only by air, check. It would make sense to hide something valuable there. Sense to everyone but Wren.

He'd been the only Aero who'd wanted to live within city walls. Since Wren lived here, Alesia should be there as well.

Joshua stared up at the Rookery which looked like a cross between a skyscraper and a cactus. The tall base had been designed to keep predators out of the 'flowers' above. Predators like Joshua.

His first circuit around the houses at the foot of the tower he focused on the neighborhood. White splotched roofs and clean streets. Humans, dwarfs, shifters mingled on the streets. None of them looked up when a dark shadow passed over the street. The residence didn't seem to be afraid of the Aeros. No one paid Joshua any attention. He was just another human on the street walking.

The next circuit he paused at a shop with the best view of the Rookery. He picked up a basket pretending to hold it up to the sun to see the weave, but he was really looking beyond. The houses stood far enough away from the tower to make it impossible to scale the homes and use them as stepping stones to the higher level of the Rookery.

How was he going to get in? The Rookery loomed over him, dark and remote, as if taunting him. Alesia was his best hope for information.

An Aero swooped above his head, plucking garbage off the street before giving one great flap and whooshing upward again. No one on the street even flinched at the Aeros swooping. The shopkeeper organized the baskets on his stoop. The children in the streets played marbles.

He watched the Aero disappear into the clouds and an idea tickled his brain. Maybe he was looking at this all wrong. Aero patrols guarded these streets, monitored every aspect of the area. While they were busy keeping the streets clean of bodies and the usual trash, maybe he could hitch a ride to the top. He put the basket back and nodded at the shopkeeper. There'd been a building taller than the others but farther back from the

Rookery walls. That would make the ideal spot to attract attention.

He had to get to Wren and Alesia as soon as he could. The UnMerge spell would be cast tonight and he was running out of time. But if the Aero patrols had orders to dispose of him, then he'd never get an audience with Wren. He'd end up dead or turned over to the HPA which would mean he'd eventually be dead. His one shot was that Wren would want to talk to Joshua before any punishment. All he had to do was call attention to himself. Not the brightest plan, but he had limited options.

He blew out a breath and walked back to that tall building and climbed to the roof. His heart hammered in his chest. He was either going to get taken to Wren or become lunch for one of the birds.

In the middle of the roof, he dropped his hood and looked up at the side of the building Wren should be in.

He waited for one of the shadows to near and then waved his hands and shouted, "hey birdbrain. You looking for me?"

The rush of wind, a dark shadow, and he was surrounded by bird claws and plucked off the roof. This was not an Aero, but some bigger bird.

The wind whistled around him and got colder. He was cupped by the toes. The talons crossed beneath him. Perhaps it was a good sign that the bird hadn't impaled him in its talons.

The bird released him mid-air and he rolled onto a stone floor. When the world stopped spinning, six Aero guards stood in the room. Each with a light spear out, but not pointed at him.

He could've tried to roll up right away, but got the sense that the guards wouldn't be happy. So he got up slowly.

The bird that had brought him settled in its nest in the room. Its feathers raised. A young Aero brought it a treat and soothed its feathers.

"Come with me." One guard led the way to an inner staircase. Either his idea had worked or he was being led to a cell. A wide well-lit staircase ascended around the outside of the tower. Large windows allowed a view of the town sprawled out below. Every couple of turns a floor opened up revealing white robed people clustered together talking. A dark haired human female who reminded him of Rose, stood in the middle of one such group. He realized that the rest of the people were actually kids. Human, Aero, and many other children watched the woman who seemed to be giving a lesson.

He kept walking up. As he got higher and higher in the tower, the number of people dwindled until the stairs ended in a large door flanked by two massive and scarred Aeros. They hissed and stared at Joshua.

He flinched and then schooled his features to depict calm, despite his rocketing heart.

"Come in. Lighthouse." Wren's voice said from behind the door.

A guard opened the doors. Inside a huge airy library occupied the floor.

Wren, wearing white, stood by a shelf with hundreds of books. He plucked one from the case.

Huge windows that held perches surrounded the room. Each had gouge marks the size of Joshua's thigh. The bird who'd picked him up had smaller talons, which left him wondering how big the bird that had made the marks had been. Or perhaps it hadn't been a bird. Joshua realized how much he didn't know about Wren and his people.

Wren turned a page and walked to his desk. "Give me one good reason I should not feed you to the birds or turn you over to the HPA for a significant reward?"

Joshua clenched his fists behind his back to hide his nerves. Wren hadn't been mercenary before. Hopefully, he was bluffing.

"I need to talk to Alesia about events linked to a plot to UnMerge the worlds."

Wren's gaze lifted to Joshua and his crest and the feathers of his neck and shoulders rose. "Alesia has nothing to do with it."

Joshua considered this. He'd never seen Wren this worked up about anything.

"She is not a part of the plot, but has information I need to find out who's behind the plot."

Wrens's eyes narrowed. "The humans closed off all communications."

It wasn't a question, but Joshua felt he needed to answer it anyway. "The HPA leadership has been breached. Many within are ignorant of what is truly going on. Just as I was." Joshua met Wren's gaze.

Wren snapped the book shut. "Indeed. What is your intention?"

"Stop the UnMerge." Whatever it took.

Wren chuckled, a warbling sound that filled the room. "How?"

They were still at odds. Joshua needed a way to get Wren to listen and believe him. Joshua gestured towards a chair.

After a long pause, Wren nodded.

Joshua waited for Wren to sit and then sat. He had no good answer for Wren's question. "I don't know, but I have to try."

"How is Alesia involved with this?"

"She was there the night the HPA lab burnt to the ground. She was there when Serene's pack was murdered. And she's had a Seer visit her."

Wren froze and his face settled into grim lines. Based on the wild array his feathers were in, some up and some down, some puffed and some sleek, his thoughts were as chaotic as Joshua's.

"Follow me." Wren stood up and went out the door. It

slammed with the force of his exit. The guard stood still with wide eyes that never left Wren.

Joshua jogged after Wren and followed him down the stairs to a nondescript door. Wren knocked. There was no answer. As the moments ticked by the feathers on his crest rose.

Wren opened the door and stormed into a large room with a wall full of windows. Colored glass hung from strings and swayed and tinkled in the windows. A door led to another chamber and a white desk with a mirror sat against the inner wall. A colorful woven carpet covered the floor. The quality of the furnishings made Joshua think this was Alesia's room.

"Where is she?" Wren muttered the question to himself, but then he glared at Joshua. "Have you seen her?"

Joshua raised his hands palms up, and didn't look Wren in the eyes. Wren might take that as a sign of dominance given how riled up he was. "I saw her earlier today."

"Where?" The words snapped out. Wren's hand drew closer to his sword.

Joshua had never seen Wren this close to losing it. "She was with Serene and Walter at the Lizardfolk complex." Joshua watched Wren's face carefully, trying to glean what was going on in Wren's mind.

One thing was certain, if Joshua made one wrong move, Wren would kill him. Wren hadn't been this angry with any of the tricks played on him at parties. He was breathing heavily and his hand was white knuckled on the sword. "Why were you at the Lizardfolk complex?"

"I got intel that the HPA was bringing Crylons to destroy it."

Wren's feathers puffed, indicating the news had alarmed him. "I have to find her."

Joshua nodded. "The people who are behind the UnMerge might have her. If you have any leads at all, I'll follow them and find her."

Wren stared at the necklace laid in the center of the desk. He snatched it up and handed it to Joshua. "You see her, you put this on her." Wren showed Joshua the key in the locket. "Do this," he said, turning the key.

Joshua took the necklace and tucked it into a pocket. "What does it do?"

"It will take her back to my study."

Joshua waited, still hoping Wren knew something that might help him. Help the world.

Wren closed his eyes and let out a breath. "What do you know?"

"Stregs are getting innocent blood. A full Pack was murdered. There are monsters in town."

Wren shook his head.

If Wren didn't connect any of those things to anything useful, there was one more thing he could tell him, but it would mean revealing his own secret. "The Book of Secrets was stolen from me."

Wren blinked and tilted his head. "How did you come to have it?"

The question was soft, but Joshua could feel the significance behind it. Wren's sleeve slipped revealing a golden bracelet. His intuition told him how he answered this question was the key to something big Wren could tell him. He was now almost certain Wren had a Secret of his own. What might Wren need to hear in order to reveal his secret?

Joshua had nothing to trade. He had no credit with the HPA. Many of the factions would turn him in on sight. And yet, this was a test of some sort. Perhaps a test of trust.

All he had was the truth. Perhaps he should tell it. All of it.

"I was born before the Merge. I was caught in it and propelled forward in time. When I first landed here after the Merge, I ended up at a human village kept by Yarg. I was to be their next sacrifice, but was rescued by the HPA and became an orphan at the Archive."

Wren nodded and stroked the bracelet. "The Yarg are very primitive."

"The Archive was where I found the Book of Secrets. I realized how evil it was and locked it up for years in my safe."

"There are things you didn't tell me that bother you."

Wren was good and reading people. It didn't seem relevant, but if it would help establish trust Joshua would tell him almost anything. "A girl at the village died to save me. I was too weak from experimenting with the powers that I got from the Merge to prevent her from attacking the Yarg in order to protect me. I was with another boy when I found the book. It was my powers that opened the mirror. The other boy died." Guilt, regret, and anger stirred, but it seemed duller somehow. Like perhaps he'd partially forgiven his part.

Wren watched Joshua from the corner of his eye. "How is Alesia involved?"

Joshua realized that Wren's bracelet must tell him if the truth was being spoken. He repeated the truth about Alesia.

Wren slumped and rubbed his hand across his forehead. The silence in the room thickened. "I know where the Book of Secrets is."

For one moment Joshua thought he meant that Wren had stolen the book which would make Joshua a fool for trusting him. Joshua lined up the facts and couldn't get them to work with the idea that Wren was to blame. "How do you know?"

"I was there the night the HPA lab burned. I was outside trying to break in."

Joshua stilled. He wasn't sure how Wren knowing the location of the book and being at the HPA Lab were connected. Wren being at the HPA lab that night added a new layer to the story. Wren being there meant he'd been desperate. Which made sense if his beloved sister had been captured. Perhaps he had seen people who were not on the official list.

"I'd found no way in. No way to get past the defenses." Wren's shoulders hunched as if remembering his defeat.

The urge to apologize for that night rose, but Joshua knew he had to wait.

Wren stared at his bracelet. "Then a blast lit up the sky. I was still frozen in shock and grief thinking I'd lost my sister when the hatch opened and three men fled. A few minutes later, Serene brought up a body and laid it by the entrance. Then she came out with more people. Some were able to walk and help, others were not and she carried them. I couldn't believe it when one of the people she brought up was my sister. Alive. I revived her and would have left, but Alesia...." Wren swallowed and closed his eyes.

Perhaps the Seer had made her first appearance. When Serene had told Joshua about Alesia, he'd gotten the impression that Alesia being a Seer was a secret. Wren's expression blanked as if he didn't want to think about what had happened with Alesia that night.

After a long pause Wren said, "we flew the survivors out and opened the Rookery to them. Anyone who was there that night. Including the humans and a Pixie."

That explained the tracks at the site. Giant birds had come and picked up those too weak to walk out themselves. Joshua hadn't considered the possibility that the Aeros had helped. This was probably when the relationship had become so strained between the factions. This was why there were so many humans and other races around and within the Rookery.

"Serene was a guest here while she recovered." Wren stated it as if it was of no consequence. Serene being protected by the Aeros explained so much. Why the HPA had never been able to find her.

"Why did you protect Serene?"

Wren glanced at Joshua. "Because of what she'd done for my sister and because the Seer said that someone of both worlds is the key to Unmerging."

Someone of both worlds. What worlds had the Seer been referring to? Seers seemed to have much in common with the genie whose answers could be interpreted many ways. Other than her losing her pack, he knew nothing else about Serene. Perhaps the two worlds were with and without the pack. "Why would Serene be the target?"

"The child she carried was both human and Pack."

The HPA history from her most wanted file had her mated to a Pack alpha. So her child couldn't be both Pack and human, because she was Pack and her mate had been too. Given the half page sheet the HPA had on Serene's history, it wouldn't be shocking that she had a more complicated history than the HPA knew.

The word world could mean any number of things depending on how he looked at it. If the word world was literal, then Joshua qualified as being of both the Merged and UnMerged worlds. Wren and Alesia were of human and bird worlds. If Serene'd had a child who was both pack and human, that could qualify as well.

"So Serene is safe now that she lost the child." Joshua still felt like he was missing something. "There could be many who are of two worlds. Why Serene?"

"True." Wren shrugged which settled his feathers into a smoother line. "Seers can be hard to interpret."

"What now?"

"I cast a spell to send the book where it needed to be," Wren said. "I can do the same for you."

The anger fled Joshua leaving him feeling tired and confused. Why the book needed to be somewhere specific seemed odd. Where it needed to be for what to happen? For the plot to UnMerge to work? "You would cast a spell to take me where I am most needed?"

"No. For you, the spell will take you to where you most need to be to achieve your goal."

Such open ended magic was dangerous. The stories of genie wishes where you might get exactly what you asked for, but not what you wanted came to mind. "Any idea where I'll end up?"

Wren bit his lip and looked away for a moment. He seemed to be having an internal debate.

Worry pooled in Joshua's gut. If Wren was worried, this would be very dangerous. "What aren't you telling me?"

"If what you want is impossible, then you will die on the spot."

Joshua breathed out through his nose. He would need to be careful what he said he wanted to make sure it wasn't impossible. Even being careful, it would be dangerous. If he could get the book, he'd be able to secure it, even if it meant burning it. No other option gave him a better chance of stopping the UnMerge. "Do you have any idea where the book went?"

Wren chuckled a little. "Your office safe."

Annoyance flickered through his chest. "How the dragon am I going to get in? You might as well say it's on the moon."

Joshua pinched the bridge of his nose and closed his eyes. There wasn't a way to get into the building. The front entrance was locked. Any other door was one way, an exit from the building. There were no windows that opened.

Wren getting the book into the safe must have been accomplished at least partially through wish magic which meant Wren was a very powerful wizard. Joshua hadn't set the magic to prevent things from entering the safe, only from removing things from his safe. Even Wren wouldn't have been able to get the book out. So how had someone gotten into his office and into the safe to begin with?

"How did you get the book?"

"A pixie." Wren said it like he was talking about the weather. Like it was the most normal thing to sneak creatures into a rival's office.

Joshua shook his head in disbelief. The HPA building was warded against magical creatures. Had someone from the HPA assisted the Pixie? "How?"

Wren shrugged again. "That Pixie we saved that night at the HPA lab was hired to steal the book. She was let into your office, but decided I should have the book instead of the one who'd requested it."

Joshua blinked. This was more evidence that someone in the HPA was corrupt. It still didn't explain how the Pixie actually got into his office. No one but he had access. "How did she get out?"

"The top floor of the HPA had an explosion recently."

Joshua couldn't help his grin. Leave it to a people who flew to remember an explosion on the top of the building. Rose had led the HPA agents up the stairs. The explosion had been at or near the top. It must have left a way for the Pixie to exit the building. Maybe it had left him a way to get into the HPA. This seemed to be his only shot. "I have my goal. How soon can you cast the spell?"

"You are going to trust me?"

His choice was simple. Wren was the only one who knew where the book was. Wren wanted his sister safe and the worlds to stay merged. That made him trustworthy. Wren had never acted with anything less than honor when Joshua had interacted with him. If Wren could send Joshua, he could put the Book of Secrets out of the game. "Yes." Joshua looked Wren in the eyes.

"I need to get ready to cast the spell." Wren stood, "Come with me."

For once Joshua was not counting steps or memorizing floor plans. Serene had taken shelter here. She'd wandered these bright sunny hallways and had been able to heal. There may even be a room that she'd stayed in that still smelled like her. Joshua's chest and stomach felt warm. It was hard to see Wren and his people as monsters when they'd helped Serene.

"It was not easy at first with Serene. Her grief..." He said it slowly, thoughtfully and almost as if Wren knew where Joshua's thoughts were. "Aero's don't handle that sort of grief well. My sis-"

Wren cut off and shook his head, his crest raising and wings twitching. "It has been very easy today to forget that we are enemies."

"Are we really?" Joshua wanted to know. Were they really or were they enemies by habit and custom?

Wren's mouth closed to a firm line, but then the side ticked upward, the crest smoothed out on his head. "Perhaps we can address this after we stop the Unmerging."

"Perhaps." His chest warmed with kinship to this man.

They entered a large room with interlocking circles decorating the floor. Silver, Gold, and Red highlights glittered from the floor. The Aeros in the room had short robes that fell to the knee. They were very careful not to touch the lines on the floor as they scurried about lighting candles.

Some of the Aeros had talons with long blood red nails. They seemed to be guards, and stood around the outside of the room. The ones that scurried had more human feet as if the talons had merged together over time. They dodged the sparking lines and the shimmer from the large crystal in the middle of the room.

Wren snapped his fingers and pointed at the crystal. "That acts as a focus. It takes the magic and fragments it. Makes it useful and controllable"

Joshua'd never talked to a powerful spell caster. Few humans had the talent and fewer could get training. Most viewed magic as wild and evil. The HPA had very little data on magic. What they did have was about when magic went bad and the HPA had to destroy the wielder. Wren seemed far too honorable to cast evil magic. "So if I bust your crystal you wouldn't be able to do magic?"

"If I busted your hand would you be able to punch? Or draw a bow string?"

Magic did seem to follow rules and had parallels in the world he knew. It seemed to be a tool just like his bow. Joshua shook his head. "I guess I could still hit you with the bow. What do you need me to do?"

"Stand here in front of the crystal. You need to have your goal clearly in mind when the crystal starts to glow. Then when I say go, jump forward into the crystal."

Joshua nodded and half-closed his eyes. He needed to be on the roof of the HPA building. Once he was there he could get in, go in his office, or whatever was left of it, and find the book. That would guarantee the world would stay safe. That Rose, Serene, Bob, even Wren would be safe. He needed to wait for the glow and think of the roof.

"Think of it as an exercise in trust," Wren said.

Joshua glanced at Wren in alarm.

Wren shrilled a laugh in response and then addressed the Aeros in the room. "Lock the room."

The Aeros completed last minute things before filing out of the room. Joshua stood back and watched. He'd never seen live magic being worked. The guards were the last to leave, walking out awkwardly, like huge penguins strutting side to side.

<u>Whump</u>.

The thick doors pulled shut.

The air stilled, and the room grew warm. The flickering light of the candles was the only light.

Wren stood with his eyes closed. He opened his eyes and his inner eyelid stayed down. His feathers were tucked against his body. He raised his hands and then sang some ancient language that sounded like a combination of bird calls and chanting.

The crystal glowed.

It was time! Joshua held the thought of the roof of the HPA building in his mind. A wind swirled into the room, then picked up speed, making him shiver. The wind must be part of the spell. Feathers and nesting material swirled in the vortex around him. Inside of the heart of the crystal, a swirling vortex opened. Yellows, blues and reds pulled back leaving a black pinpoint. It looked like a picture of a black hole he'd had as a poster on his childhood home.

Joshua needed to focus on the roof of the HPA building.

"Go." Wren's voice was distant.

Joshua's heart took off and he leapt forward. The wind whipped his body around and he thudded into something smooth and cold.

He slid down. His fingers and boots scrabbled to find purchase.

The wall beneath his feet disappeared and his fingers dug into the stone.

32

JOSHUA

<u>Night, Luminous thirty-first, 299 years post-Merge</u>

The wind raced through the opening in Joshua's clothing to rake icy talons along his legs and back. He squinted his eyes to see if he could tell something about where he dangled. The angle was all wrong. He'd never been off the side of his building. Any building. He couldn't confirm that the brick work that dug into his fingers and scraped his nose as the wind buffeted him was even on the HPA building and not some random building that Wren's spell had cast him to.

His fingers were cold enough to make ice cubes in a glass of water. He wouldn't be able to hang on long.

Time slowed.

His fingers slipped. His heart sped. If he died now, there'd be no one to stop the UnMerging. He pushed his feet against the side and almost pulled himself off, but found a crack to put his foot into. That little bit of body weight off his hands let him let go and reach higher. He found an edge and pulled.

He gritted his teeth as he shifted up. The ache in his arms extended from his shoulders to his fingertips. He wasn't going to fail. His other foot found purchase on the stone and he pushed higher. He lifted his other hand and found a hand hold over the edge. One more push and he'd pull himself over the edge. He pulled with everything he had and landed on the cold tile of the roof.

He shook and gulped air. Where the hell was he? Standing on shaky legs, he glanced around and got his bearings. He was on the HPA roof. Hope gave him a bit of energy. Now all he had to do was get in.

Joshua stuck his hands in his armpits to warm them. The door should be on the corner. It still was, but warped and didn't close the whole way. He opened it and slipped into the stairwell. The surrounding walls were darkened, the ceiling spotted.

This was where the explosion that had helped him escape the building had happened. That seemed like a lifetime ago. Rose had survived the blast. She was the toughest and savviest person he knew. When this was over, he'd make sure he told her that.

Something in the rubble glinted. It seemed out of place, so he bent down to study it. There, peeking out from under the debris was a locket. Recognizing it as Rose's, he scooped it up. It wasn't something she'd leave behind, so he knew she must've lost it. He put Rose's locket in his pouch to give to her the next time he saw her.

The sooner he got this done and then ferreted out the evil in the HPA, the sooner he could find her. He went down the stairs. Odds were high some of the HPA agents would be out, but he needed to see how many were left.

He sent a small Soul Wisp forward into the main room. It was empty. Odd. The agents should be here this time of day. He sent it farther on and found Bob walking toward Joshua's office. His heart leapt. If Bob was here, Joshua'd have an ally.

Joshua made his way to his office quickly. "Bob."

Bob jerked and his eyes widened. A range of emotions flashed across his face too fast for Joshua to identify. "I'm surprised you'd come back after what you did to get out the last time you were here," Bob said.

Joshua paused in puzzlement. He'd expected Bob to be on his side. "Was anyone hurt?"

"Rose is still MIA."

Joshua could feel Bob's gaze on him. Bob wouldn't know that Rose had escaped and helped Serene.

"Everyone else had only minor injuries."

"Good." Joshua was glad the other agents weren't hurt, even if they'd tried to kill him. They were only doing what they'd thought was right based on the lies they'd been fed. Once they knew the truth, maybe things could be different. They could make an organization to be proud of.

"Why are you here?" Bob's tone sounded belligerent. His face reddened and he stabbed his finger at Joshua.

"I needed to get in my office." Joshua forced calm into his voice. The feeling that something wasn't right hovered near, quickening his heart and raising the hairs on his arms.

"Why?" Bob blocked the door with his fists on his hips.

Joshua searched Bob's face. Bob had always been more apt to use his persuasion skills rather than force to solve an issue. The fact he was physically blocking Joshua was very much out of character. Something big was bothering Bob. Maybe taking over the HPA and his best friend being a suspect didn't sit well with him. Joshua decided not to complicate the story and to keep it as simple as he could. "To get into my safe."

"No one can get your safe open." Bob's chest thrust forward. His nostrils flared.

It seemed weird that anyone would've bothered with his safe at this point. "I can."

With those words, the anger drained from Bob making him seem smaller. He looked more dwarf-like than ever. His smile this time, although still not friendly, was almost coy. "What's so important in your safe?"

That spot between Joshua's shoulder blades itched. The question made no sense. Why would Bob care? Joshua said nothing, just smiled at Bob.

Bob cleared his throat. "You know I was made the head of the HPA in your stead." Joshua decided that if Bob had been a bird he would've been a peacock with his fan extended fully and head bobbing. He turned and stepped through the door toward the office.

"That's great." Bob should've been the head of the HPA years ago. It'd never made sense why the committee hadn't chosen him to begin with.

"I have your office now." Bob acted like he was chatting, but something in his tone said he was fishing. "How did you get out last time?"

The question was casual, yet it set off alarms in Joshua's head. So he decided to test Bob. They'd had a good relationship when they'd been partners. Including the teasing that always went with being a partner. "Went through my safe."

Bob's eyebrows rose and then lowered. "Quit fucking with me."

Joshua put on his innocent face. He tried to widen his eyes and mimic the look the fox shifter kid had and then chuckled as if he were teasing. Bob could either go along with the teasing or demand an answer.

"It's my office." Bob emphasized the word my. Then he paused as if daring Joshua to deny it.

Everything about Bob seemed off. Perhaps he'd been hurt

when he'd been passed over for promotion. Maybe if he acknowledged the fact, Bob would relax. "Yeah, your office."

Bob nodded, but held his silence as they walked toward the office.

"Where is everyone?" Joshua asked to break the awkward silence.

"I sent them all out on a mission."

"Even the secretaries?"

"Yeah, our number one fugitive was spotted over by the Rookery." Bob glanced at Joshua.

Joshua would bet anything that he was now number one on that list. Hopefully Wren would handle the HPA with no issues. Was it possible Bob was being deceived? Maybe Bob thought Joshua was the bad guy. He'd have to prove that he wasn't. "That should keep them busy."

They walked down the hall. Black and grey coated the walls. They hadn't had time to clean up from either explosion. His office door was warped. Bob pulled the handle and turned the knob, but the door wouldn't open. He grimaced and tried again. With a grunt and a screech of wood on metal, the door opened.

"One of the things I could never figure out is how they broke into my office," Joshua said as he entered the room. It looked the same. Same white walls, same desk, same wadded up paper under the desk. Only the paper wasn't wadded. A sparkle gleamed from within. Joshua picked up the paper and found faery dust. His gut twisted. The paper shook in his hands.

"The night of the party, you brought this paper into my office." Thoughts tumbled in his head like a rock slide. It was Bob who'd stolen his book. The pieces slid into place. Bob's unusual visit to his office, the prolonged conversation at the Gala. All things that had helped him steal the Book of Secrets.

Bob closed the door. When he turned, it was as if Bob had

been replaced by a different person. His suave, jovial demeanor had been replaced by grim determination.

"You brought a pixie into my office to steal from the safe." A pixie could get into the magic of the safe, but wouldn't be able to breach the HPA protections.

Bob walked around the desk and sat down. His smug smile made him look mean.

Had Bob been brainwashed? "Why?"

Bob's face twisted into the kind of smile a kid might have when stomping on a spider. "Did you enjoy it?"

Joshua's mind blanked. Enjoy what? What could Bob be talking about? If Bob was part of stealing the book, was he also part of the kidnapping? If so, then Bob hadn't been his friend for a long time. The betrayal heated Joshua's guts. "You were involved with my kidnapping and drugging?"

Bob crossed his arms and leaned back into Joshua's squeaky chair.

Joshua directed the Soul Wisp from earlier to Bob. "I thought we were friends."

"Us? Really?" A mixture of anger, jealousy, and bitterness fed back from the Soul Wisp. And a lust for power. Bob wanted to be head of the HPA. Head of the whole city.

"We've known each other for over ten years. We were partners." Joshua could hear the disbelief in his own voice.

"That just gives us a history."

"Then what made us enemies?" Joshua searched Bob's face for answers.

"It should have been mine." Bob slammed his hands on the desk, rattling the cup.

"The HPA." Bob hadn't been okay with the council's decision. He'd probably been embarrassed and jealous. Joshua found it inconceivable that he'd been hiding those feelings this whole time.

"It was always Joshua this and Joshua that. I was always in your shadow. You laughed at me."

Bob could still be being controlled. Joshua used his Soul Wisp to search for a hook, but saw nothing. Bob wasn't being controlled. "Bob, you were my friend. My partner. One of the few people I trusted."

"I know what happens to your friends. *He* told me." Bob lowered his voice as if Bob was afraid of being overheard. Bob panted as if he had run a marathon. Sweat trickled down his shirt, staining under his arms. He was working himself up to something. Someone had corrupted him. Fed him ideas that Joshua wasn't his friend.

Bob was closer to the weapons, and if Joshua made a move toward a weapon, he'd have no chance to convince Bob that they could be friends. "It doesn't have to be this way. We could still be friends. Don't listen to him." Joshua didn't move, but put every ounce of sincerity into his voice.

"Never." Bob snatched the crossbow from under the desk and pointed it at Joshua. "Open the safe."

The Soul Wisp found no soft feelings for Joshua in Bob. Joshua knew that when the safe was open, Bob would kill him. If Joshua died, Bob and whoever he was working for would UnMerge the worlds. Everyone Joshua knew would be dead. He pushed his grief aside. To live and to protect the world and those he loved, he'd have to trick Bob and kill him.

Joshua put his hand palm down on the plain white wall next to the safe. The wall shimmered and a door with a touchpad appeared. He typed in the 59 character password and watched the second hand on his clock.

"Last chance, Bob." This was said quietly. Joshua's Soul Wisp was ready to be more intrusive, wedging its way into Bob's mind to seek the answer to who was behind this plot. He'd only have a moment.

"Stop. Stalling." Bob's voice was cold and precise.

"This is the last trap." This was Bob's last chance to change his mind. When a full minute went by, Joshua typed in an additional 70 characters. The safe popped open with a hiss. Joshua stepped back and put his back against the wall. The safe stood open in front of Bob.

"It *is* there." Bob's voice was rough with greed and glee.

"Who are you working for?" Joshua coaxed as he sent the Soul Wisp in deeper to catch Bob's response. The trap would spring as soon as Bob touched the book.

Bob stepped forward and reached into the safe. "Finally."

"Who are you working for?" The crash of Bob's emotions battered him, like an undertow at the beach. The calm surface gave way to elation, glee, fear. The Soul Wisp dug through Bob's memories, looking for a clue.

Bob must have touched the book, because a low thrum echoed through the room. Joshua's alarm-spell shrilled through his system.

"Bob, who are you working for?" The safe's final trap reared to strike causing Joshua's senses to tingle. An image of a cloaked man hovered near the surface of Bob's mind. Someone tall with blue eyes. It was the same person who'd been over Joshua during the drugging. But that person hadn't been the person in charge. The Soul Wisp dug deeper. Then an image from the party popped through: Elder Martin had nodded at Bob, just before Bob engaged Joshua in conversation.

Elder Martin was behind the UnMerging.

Joshua was stunned. It was worse than he'd thought. Elder Martin was perfectly positioned to coordinate the UnMerging, but it made no sense. He was the force that had brought the factions together. He was the one who called for peace and had damn Gala parties in support of it. He was also positioned to know every secret. Everyone owed him favors.

He was the one Joshua had to stop.

Bob grunted and crumpled to the ground. The book and the loaded bow fell from his hands. Spasms rippled across his body.

Joshua slid down the wall to sit next to his friend. There was nothing he could do about the poison. "I'm sorry."

He waited so his friend wouldn't die alone.

Bob shook and shuddered. Joshua's Soul Wisp caught the fear building within Bob.

Out of pity, Joshua used the Soul Wisp to spin a dreamlet in which Bob was a hero and saved the day. The darkness of death spread like a raging fire through Bob, extinguishing what he was.

Joshua pulled his Soul Wisp out before the darkness could touch it. He had no idea what might happen if he was in contact at the point of death.

It only took a moment more before the poison had done its work.

Joshua closed Bob's eyes and picked up what he'd need to face Elder Martin. He tucked the Book of Secrets in his bag. His safe was no longer safe. He'd have to keep the book with him.

The question that kept echoing in Joshua's mind was why would Elder Martin betray the world.

33

JOSHUA

Joshua paused in an alley to collect himself. He felt like a punching bag. Bob was dead. He stamped down the remorse and guilt he felt for his part in his death. Joshua's only ally was tending to her dying son and Rose. The Book of Secrets weighed heavily in his pack. Somehow seeming far heavier than he remembered.

Elder Martin was his prime suspect. He had to get into the rich ward with a minimum of fuss and confront Elder Martin. He'd have to take the ditch again and this time confront whatever monster called the ditch home.

He passed the guards' post for the rich section. The guard was gone. Everything had a desolate empty feeling as if the world was huddled under a blanket, hoping for the storm to pass.

Joshua pulled out his spare bow as he passed into the rich ward. He might not need his bow if he didn't find anything at

Elder Martin's. Bob could've been confused or misled. Just because Bob had believed something didn't make it true.

He edged closer to Elder Martin's house to study it. The house crouched like a toadstool growing up under a giant tree. Odd. Most of the house's defenses were down. The servants and bustling activity from the day before were gone. The Crylons no longer on the walls. They'd already gone and destroyed the LizardFolk's home. Dark windows and the balloons that had lit the night and protected the grounds were also gone.

He'd gone over every interaction with Elder Martin and had come up empty. He still had no idea why Elder Martin might betray humanity in general and Joshua specifically. As far as he could tell there wasn't a motive. Which meant Joshua was still missing big pieces of the puzzle if Elder Martin was the bad guy. It was possible he was pursuing the wrong person and time was running out.

The lack of movement around the house made the missing defenses worse somehow. Elder Martin was never without people. He liked an audience. Every action public. Anything that didn't follow the pattern made Joshua's stomach twist with nervousness.

Since there seemed to be no one around, he opted for walking in the servants' entrance. Rich folks did forget those entrances existed. The door opened at a touch. Strange.

He'd come to this entrance the first time he'd visited Elder Martin. The entryway was still small and functional. The wall filled with the things one might need going out. One door led deeper into the house, the other led to a pantry. Metal rattled on metal, behind the door he knew went to the pantry.

It was an odd sound that reminded him of bars on a cell. He held his breath and listened. The rattling stopped, but the soft sound of ticking replaced it. He padded to the door and listened.

He had no idea what might be making that noise. It sounded too big to be a mouse trap.

Joshua eased the door open and looked through the crack. In the middle of the pantry amidst bags of flour, the butler, Max, huddled in a cage. Unease flickered over Joshua. A cage in the pantry didn't mean Elder Martin was behind the UnMerge plot, but something was going on. There hadn't been a cage the last time he'd been here. Elder Martin must have done some redecorating. The ticking seemed to come from what looked like an egg timer connected by a string to an egg beater. It looked like a Rube Goldberg contraption meant to open the cage door.

Rips and stains decorated Max's formal attire. His hands were clenched and lay shaking in his lap. Max's lips were clamped together and his gaze followed something deeper in the room that lay outside Joshua's line of vision.

Joshua shifted and saw a Streg. His heart thundered. Up to this point Elder Martin could've been innocent because Bob had been wrong or misled. But actually seeing a Streg here meant either Elder Martin was involved or was being framed.

Bites and puncture marks littered the Streg's face. Muscle showed through in places on his arms. The overall conformation was human, the shredded black rags covering his torso were the same black of an HPA hunter uniform and the insignia on the pants pockets matched.

The hairs on Joshua's arms raised and his stomach dropped. He strung his bow and took aim at the Streg. His arrow with its special mixture should take the Streg down as long as he got a heart shot. He raised the bow and sighted high center mass. On his outward breath, he let the arrow fly. The arrow embedded itself in the Streg's heart.

Instead of falling over in a heap as he'd expected, the Streg tilted its head, pulled out the arrow and laughed. It was an eerie sound that sounded more like a hyena than anything that had once been alive.

Joshua took a step back.

"I bet you tought that would hurth me," The Streg said. His swollen tongue thickening his words.

Joshua's mouth dried and panic flared. Maybe they'd made the Streg invulnerable to his attacks. His stomach rolled. The thought horrified him. If that was the case, there would be nothing the living could do.

"Don't trust anything that was in your office." Max's voice was raw as if he had screamed himself out earlier.

The panic shifted. His belongings being tampered with was good news, but he was still in trouble. It left him with few options that would stop an undead.

"Thath's cheating." The Streg banged the bars.

Max whimpered in response and curled into a ball, clutching his arms over his head in the center of the cage.

Joshua was facing an unrestrained Streg and he had no tools he could trust. His skin heated and his heart hammered. His mind felt as if he were the rabbit and the Streg were the fox poised to pounce.

Joshua sent a Soul Wisp out and almost gagged on the foulness that flooded back. Rage rippled under the Streg's surface. What could cause this much damage in such a short period of time? Joshua shifted through the cesspool of hate and rot and found a hook that held back the madness. A psychic hook driven into a Streg's essence acted like a muzzle. This was how the Streg were being controlled. Was this the work of the Conduit?

Stregs were known for being crazy killing machines. The hook must not only control them, but hold back the madness. Perhaps he could use the hook to control the Streg and lock it somewhere. There had to be a cabinet or barrel he could use.

The Streg gathered itself for a launch at Joshua.

In desperation, Joshua pulled on the hook, trying to take control, trying to hold the Streg back. The Streg fell back away from Joshua, but was up a moment later, its face twisting with frustration. The rage pulsated in Joshua's head like a heavy metal song. Joshua couldn't control the Streg only hold him back. So trying to get him into a place Joshua could lock was going to be tough.

The timer dinged, the egg beater twirled pulling a string, opening the door of the cage. The cage was perfect. If he assumed a maddened Streg would go straight for a living person, then he just had to get Max out of the cage and behind it. His plan fell into place in his mind. If only he could pull it off. Joshua needed to convince Max to cooperate while Joshua held the Streg at bay.

"Max, you need to get up and out of that cage now." Joshua used his most reasonable and level voice. Max would never believe Joshua if he couldn't see his face. Joshua would rather save Max than have his death be the Streg's distraction. There'd already been enough death.

Joshua concentrated on the hook and holding the Streg back.

Max lifted his head and moved his arm to glance around the room. His eyes rounding even more when they landed on the Streg on his back on the floor and scrambling beyond the open cage door.

"You have to trust me."

The Streg jumped to his feet at the slight dip in Joshua's concentration. He'd lose his chance if Max didn't cooperate immediately. "Please. Get behind the cage."

Max gulped, his Adam's apple jerking in response. He gathered himself up to his knees and crawled out of the cage and then around to the back.

Joshua hoped the Streg would go for the nearest living being when Joshua let go.

When Max was behind the cage, Joshua let go of his control on the Streg and twisted out the hook, leaving the Streg in his raging form. The Streg jumped up and pounced toward Max, slamming into the back of the cage.

Joshua leapt forward and snapped the lock back into place.

The Streg shook the bars, snarling and snapping. The Streg was unable to open the locked cage at this point as the rage pushed back whatever remaining intelligence it had.

As long as no one was stupid enough to let it out, it would be stuck in its cage until they had time to deal with it.

Sweat dripped down Max's face, he trembled. "I almost died."

"But you didn't die. Is anyone else in the house?"

Joshua hoped Max would be an ally now. If nothing he possessed would work on Stregs and Elder Martin was behind this, Joshua would need help.

Max paled, but nodded.

Good. Max was responding. "Where's Elder Martin?"

"Top floor, observatory. first door."

That seemed oddly specific. "How do you know?"

"He's been going every night since I started here."

What an odd thing for Elder Martin to have done. Did it mean that Elder Martin had been planning this the whole time?

Joshua led Max to the servant door. "I need you to find Walter or Wren. Do you know where they are?"

Max nodded.

"Tell them everything. Everything you know. Can you do that?"

Max nodded more decisively. Then he bolted out the servant's entrance.

Joshua wished he could leave as well. The house creaked

and moaned. Joshua took the other door which should lead to the main house. Before he got to the rest of the house there was the entryway he'd come into for the Gala.

The chest in the corner drew his eye. If he still had the key, he'd be able to even the odds of his survival against more Streg. He patted himself and in his pocket, he found the key.

He knelt at the chest and inserted his key, when he turned it, all of his items were there. Relief filtered through him. He wouldn't be completely helpless.

The main house would be through the next door. A formal stairs with a glittering chandelier swept upward. A man sat on the top stair with his feet dangling two stairs down. His torso was still taller than most.

Joshua slowed his steps, surprised to see a man just sitting there. The sensation that he'd seen this man recently scratched at the surface of his mind. He shifted through memories but couldn't figure it out. Something about his height and his blue eyes seemed familiar.

When he spotted Joshua, he gave a little wave.

"What's your name?" He sucked in a breath as recognition hit. "I know you." If Elder Martin were guilty, this man could be a likely accomplice. If Elder Martin was being set-up, then this man was likely the one behind it.

"Andre." The man leaned forward and pinned Joshua with an icy stare. "Probably not. I am more of a behind the scenes person." The tall man smirked reminding Joshua of the man who'd stood near Elder Martin at the Gala.

"You entered the party before me. You were also with Elder Martin at the party just before I found him." That could make this man a key player in what was going on, but there was a more elusive memory about this man's eyes. A memory associated with fear and helplessness.

"You did spot me. Elder Martin said you noticed more things

than you let on." Mist emanated from his hands and filled in the stairway, rolling down the stairs in a faint blue glow.

Joshua backed away. Glowing mist had to be some sort of magic. The first trickle of fear scratched at the back of his neck.

The pictures on the walls and dark paneling blurred. He rubbed his eyes. The chandelier morphed into a thatched roof above his head. Joshua's heart beat a little faster. He blinked and then he could feel the press of a floor at his back. A fly buzzed toward his hands. Joshua's hands were smaller, freshly scarred, with ragged dirty nails. He pinched himself and felt the pain of the pinch.

He wasn't dreaming. Fear pulsed harder with each heartbeat.

He clutched a straw doll, instead of his bow.

Delilah's doll.

A mix of fear, regret, and exhaustion filled him. He tried to bring the staircase back, but nothing happened. He knew he had a mission and that the world was counting on him, but the doll in his hand was so real. Everything was so real.

He tried to stand, but his body was as useless as a vat of wet noodles, unresponsive to his commands. Delilah stepped into his line of sight. She watched him with a strange expression on her face. His younger self had no idea what that look meant, but the older one knew: Love. Delilah had loved him.

<u>Cloup-Cloup</u>. <u>Cloup-Cloup</u>.

The Yarg were here for their sacrifice. He was the sacrifice.

Even in his weakened state the fear rushed through his body in waves, dropping his stomach and raising the hairs on his arms and back. Everything in him wanted to grab Delilah's hand and run.

But, he couldn't move his head. Couldn't look away from what he knew was about to happen. Fear for her hammered his heart.

He knew what would happen before it unfolded in front of

him, slowly, second by painful second. Delilah would throw herself in front of the Yarg before they could reach him. She'd raise a sharpened stick and strike the leader in the face. She would die.

Joshua studied her face. Her teeth caught her lower lip and pressed down enough to leave a mark. The dirt looked darker on her pale face, but her little chin jutted out as it always had when she was determined to get her way.

The Yarg stepped into view. A big ram's head filled with the sharp teeth of a carnivore.

Her body tensed. This was the last moment that he could save her. In less than a second she would leap. Guilt and Fear tugged at him. He struggled against the weight pressing him down. It felt so real. Deeper and more vivid than any of the dreams. He'd do anything to save her.

She stopped breathing. Everything froze.

"I could change it." Andre's voice slithered through Joshua's system. "I could change what happened so that you were not the cause of Delilah's death." The word death echoed in Joshua's head.

If he could undo his mistake and save Delilah, he'd do it. Magic was a strange and wonderful thing. Maybe the only way to travel back to the past was with magic. If they could go back, he wouldn't use his power to scout a way out of the village. Then he wouldn't be weak and they could flee. She wouldn't die because of him. They would be free.

He'd come to learn that magic had a price. That magic followed rules, maybe not like science, but rules nonetheless.

What would be the price for saving Delilah?

34

JOSHUA

<u>Night, Luminous thirty-first, 299 years post-Merge</u>

Joshua was still in the hut from so long ago. The offer to fix his mistakes and save Delilah still hung in the air.

There was no hint of time travel in any of the records. He'd looked. None of the lore of any of the species had anything consistent or useful. The only thing that had come close, was when the worlds had Merged. This had to be a trick.

"That's not possible," he whispered. But doubt and remorse weighed heavily on him. If only he could have moved he could've saved her. If he weren't weakened from playing with his powers, they could've escaped together. If it was possible he'd have one less person's death on his conscience.

"It is not your fault the girl died." This voice whispered up from inside of his core. A friendlier voice. The voice from the ghost pack's Alpha. "It was her choice. She would have made it with or without you having powers. You both would have died trying to escape. Didn't it take four HPA teams to rescue the humans from the Yargs? What chance did two kids have?"

The knot untwisted in his gut. Could it be true? Perhaps he hadn't been the sole cause. A factor, but not the cause? The weight of her death loosened, just a bit.

"All you need to do is let me in, and I can fix everything." Andre's cold voice broke in, seemingly unaware of his other conversation or the change within Joshua.

"We cannot save her, but we might be able to save you. But you have to trust us," the Pack Alpha whispered.

Which voice should he trust? Even though it was cold, Andre's voice might rid him of the guilt and anguish that had started the day Delilah had died. Was it really possible or was it a trick? If it was real, he'd do it. He'd save her and by saving her, he'd save himself. Or should he trust yet another Other? The Alpha of a long dead pack. Serene's mate.

"Look at yourself then." The Alpha's voice was joined by many sub-notes running through it. The rest of the pack must've joined in. Could it hurt to listen to them for a moment? They asked him to look at himself. It must mean the him from back then.

That command allowed him to separate from the vision of the past. He saw what he must've looked like. So young. So scared. So lost.

That boy had done the best he could in the new world. He'd seen people killed trying to escape the village. His use of power had been the one shot at he and Delilah leaving the village without dying. He hadn't known the rules of his powers, that they would make him weak because he hadn't yet learned how to recharge himself. No simple change would fix that scenario. And how many people would die if he exchanged his life for hers.

He'd trust the pack.

The Alpha's voice howled as if calling him home. "Bring the other with you."

"What do you want?" Joshua projected to Andre.

"Entry." A tendril of Andre's thought, which looked like a green hand in his vision, reached out to Joshua.

The Pack had said to bring the other, maybe if Joshua grabbed Andre's hand he could take him to the Pack.

Joshua's ghost-self grabbed the hand. Andre's mental energy was layered, with a core of ice and it had a brush of sickly sweet rot.

"Bring me to your inner pool," Andre demanded.

The pool had been the last place Joshua had seen the Pack. He surmised they must have stayed hidden within him.

He descended to his pool, taking Andre with him. Joshua opened his eyes, expecting to see the bleak walls that he'd seen when painting in the Archive. But something was different. Colors pulsed through the rock and swirled just under the surface. The impression of picture frames hung on his walls.

White capped waves covered the pool as if it were an ocean in a storm.

Next to Joshua, Andre, the tall skinny man from the stairs appeared. The way his eyes looked reminded Joshua of the other place he'd seen Andre. Andre'd been the one to drug Joshua the night of the Gala. He was the one from Bob's vision. The one Bob had feared, but Andre hadn't been in charge. Adrenaline crashed through Joshua's system as he waited for Andre's next action.

Andre's gaze swept from the walls to the pool of Joshua's inner room. Then Andre turned and hurdled a black net with sharp hooks around the edges at Joshua.

Joshua rolled out of the way, landing flat on his back near the pool's edge. The net writhed, edging closer. The net looked like a more complicated hook. If it had touched Joshua he probably would've been trapped. Droplets from the violent sea in his pool pummeled him. Andre was fast, seemingly used to fighting in this soul-scape.

Andre leapt over and shoved his knees in Joshua armpits, pinning him. "Where were we?" His hands glowed black with red and blue undertones.

Joshua shoved his body up, but he wasn't as strong in this body as he was in his real body. Andre didn't even budge. Fear hammered at Joshua. "What are you?"

"The Creator. You will join my Streg army and we will rule after the UnMerge is completed." Andre wrapped his hand around Joshua's throat.

The journal Serene had found had mentioned Andre, the Creator. This was the person who'd been creating the Stregs. He was probably the person Joshua had sensed muzzling the Streg when Joshua had first encountered them. But none of that knowledge helped. Joshua was trapped with no options.

"Touch the water," the Alpha whispered.

Joshua reached back and dunked his whole hand into the pool. A blast of power blew the Creator off of Joshua and bounced him against the wall.

Andre twisted like a cat and landed on his feet. He snarled.

The Alpha stood protectively above Joshua. Awhhooooooooo. The deep tones of the pack's Alpha call resonated through the room.

Andre flinched and shifted back.

Pack members shimmered out from the walls and joined their leader's song. They surrounded Andre, circling him.

"We'll take it from here," the Alpha said.

The Pack attacked as one, leaping upon Andre and pinning him.

Andre punched and kicked, but there were too many of the pack. They lifted him into the air.

Andre wailed long rasping notes. "You'll never control my army. I am the Creator."

Joshua clenched his fists. He'd heard that tone in other fanatics.

The Pack lifted him above the water and then dropped him in.

Andre struggled against the water, but the surface acted like a Venus Flytrap enclosing Andre and holding him tight. The ghost pack circled above.

Andre managed to rise above the surface, but the Alpha rushed in and dunked him. Andre rose quickly sputtering and lashing out. The Beta dodged the blow and landed with all four paws on Andre's head. The Beta leapt up, forcing Andre's head below the surface.

The pattern set, each time Andre rose, a pack member was ready. Time and again until Andre didn't break the surface.

The Alpha circled above the pool. The waves calmed and the pool reverted back to its calm state.

"She is nearby. Protect her." The Alpha howled and the rest of the Pack joined their voices with his. Joshua recognized it as a goodbye to a Pack member.

The wolf pack bowed and disappeared.

Joshua came back to his physical body on the bottom stair of the sweeping formal stairway. He shook his head. His real body felt heavier than his mental one. He climbed to where Andre's body slumped on the carpet, water streaming from his mouth.

He needed to find Elder Martin before he attempted the UnMerge.

There were four doors on this level, the only one of interest was one that led to the back and up the stairs. When he pushed open the door the wind howled in agreement.

Joshua followed the path, still not seeing or hearing anyone else in the house. A shutter banged on the outside. The wind whistled through gaps in the windows. The wind seemed stronger than before. The strong wind could mean the moment of the anniversary was close. If the time matched the Merge, they'd have until just after 2AM to stop the UnMerge.

The floor creaked with each step down the hallway. A single closed door was at the end. This is where Max had said Elder Martin would be.

He pushed open the door to reveal a dark room. He peered into the darkness. Where was he? Elder Martin must be here somewhere.

He stepped in and closed the door, waiting for his eyes to adjust to the darkness.

35

JOSHUA

Joshua stepped back so that his back was flat against the door. The room looked as if it had once been a rooftop garden or observatory. Huge glass walls and curved glass ceiling showed the dark night sky. Darkness wrapped the room except for a red pulsing light from a large crystal suspended in the middle of the room. The wind howled outside, shaking the glass. He shivered.

The red light from the crystal shifted casting light on the far side of the room. On the other side of the crystal in an ornate bird cage Serene stood in her human form. He gasped and stepped toward her.

There must not be enough room in the cage to sit because she slumped against the bars. Her face pressed toward him and her eyes were closed. He couldn't tell if she was dead or just unconscious. His stomach tumbled. If Elder Martin had her, she was in deep trouble.

Elder Martin stepped from the shadows on the right. "That was unexpected. I did not think you would survive Andre." His tone was monotone as if his interest wasn't in the room. He stared at a spot to the left of Joshua's shoulder. What could drive a man like Elder Martin to such lengths?

"I'm here to rescue Serene." Joshua projected the words, using a voice usually reserved for emergency operations. He hoped his voice might roust Serene, but she didn't even twitch.

Elder Martin threw his head back and laughed in long, loud, shouts of laughter that echoed through the mostly empty room. He leaned against the wall shaking with fits of mirth.

The lightning flashed, burning away the shadows for a moment. Stregs stepped up, surrounding Joshua. Joshua jerked back. There were too many, too close. Their twisted faces and bared teeth were so close he could feel the heat of their breath on his face. They were all human and some still wore remnants of the black uniform that could mean they'd been HPA agents.

Even without his Soul Wisps out, Joshua could feel the barely controlled rage. A force held them in check, muzzling them. Who held the leash now that Andre was gone?

Two Stregs grabbed Joshua's arms. He pulled away and could almost feel the control of the muzzle break. One snarled and snapped inches away from Joshua's face.

Joshua flinched back, heart pounding.

"If you struggle they will tear you apart," Elder Martin said.

Joshua's heart thundered in the effort to hold himself still as they dragged him to the center of the room. One ripped off his backpack and tossed it to Elder Martin. The other pushed him to his knees. They backed away and were lost in the shadows.

Elder Martin pulled the Book of Secrets from the pack. He moved to a stone altar Joshua hadn't noticed near the cage. Placing the large, brown carefully on a stand, Elder Martin arranged two cups on either side of the book and placed a stylized dagger just below the book.

Something about the way Elder Martin moved reminded Joshua of someone. The sense that it was important pricked at his mind. He needed some angle to help control the situation. Elder Martin must be using Serene, the book, and the crystal as a part of the UnMerge spell.

"Why are you doing this?" Joshua asked, "You'll lose everything."

Another flash of lightning revealed two dozen Stregs pinned to the outside wall, as if by some invisible force. They snarled and pushed but weren't able to break the bond that held them there. The curtain of darkness fell, leaving the angry red light.

Joshua saw uncertainty on Elder Martin's face as he opened the book. He shuffled through the pages and seemed to find what he was looking for. He ran his finger down the page and murmured something. A light pulsed from the book and a high pitched scree ripped through the room.

"I have to correct the mistake my ancestor made that doomed all family members to purgatory when they die. Never to reach the side of the maker or to be eligible to try again with their lives, to be forever ripped from the tapestry of the world."

Joshua knew nothing about Elder Martin's family. He was in a position of power, how could his family be doomed? There was something about the way Elder Martin spoke about his family that seemed familiar. Maybe this could still be handled by talking with Elder Martin, showing him that starting the UnMerge wasn't the answer. If Joshua could find out the root event, maybe he could help Elder Martin.

"What could your family have done to deserve that?"

Elder Martin stood for a long moment staring at the book. "Jedidiah Rue, my great-great-great grandfather, was the person that caused the Merge." Elder Martin's words echoed counterpoint to a high pitched whine.

Joshua's stomach dropped. Even the wind seemed to pause in shock. Could all the loss of life from both worlds and his own haunted past have been caused by Elder Martin's ancestor?

"It was an accident really." Elder Martin arranged the candles into a circle and lit them one by one. He paused in between and referenced the book. "He was a scientist with the heart of a wizard and played in areas man was not meant to play in."

"If you continue with this, you'll be making the same mistake that your ancestor did."

"Not really. I'll be freeing my family from purgatory. That is not a mistake." The hardness of his face said that he was resolved. This wouldn't be solved with a conversation.

The only thing Joshua could do was try to interfere with the spell. If he could take out one of the elements, then maybe that would disrupt the spell. He glanced at Serene. Even after the drug had cleared his system he still felt protective of her. He had to get her free. He did still have the necklace from Wren. Could he use it to save Serene?

The space between them seemed too big to conquer even if it was only feet away. He needed more time to come up with a plan.

"This isn't you. Killing humans, working with Streg. You are a man of honor," Joshua said.

"You only think you know me. You have not seen who I really am."

Elder Martin seemed more upset than he should be about Joshua's statement. Joshua thought that maybe he should push harder and see what happened. "I know you. Nothing you can say would change that." Joshua made sure his tone was dismissive.

"You think you know me?" The air shimmered and Elder Martin's face plumped up and the gray faded from his hair. The face that was left looked like an older version of his dead friend Marvin. Except he didn't look dead. "What do you think now?"

Joshua's hands shook and his breath came in raspy pants. The air was too thin. The boy he'd mourned for so long, that he had broken his friendship with Alex over, had been alive this whole time. Alive and plotting to UnMerge the worlds. How was Marvin still alive? "You're alive. What happened? How did you escape?" Joshua touched the mirror necklace still around his throat.

"I was never trapped. I left before you got out. I told Alex to shatter the mirror so you could never put the book back."

Joshua gasped. All this time he'd blamed Alex for Marvin's death. Not realizing that Marvin had put Alex up to breaking the mirror. Marvin had been manipulating them both the whole time. "Why?"

"Do you know what I saw that night?" For the first time Marvin looked at Joshua. His eyes were wide, pupils dilated. His careful control was shattered.

"What did you see?" Behind Marvin, a ribbon of white slashed the dark sky, then another. Meteorites. The red crystal pulsed.

Joshua was running out of time.

Marvin seemed to try to sneer, but it was ruined by the light in his eyes. He looked as if he couldn't wait to tell his story. To gloat. But the moment passed.

"I want to believe you." Joshua said it sincerely. If Joshua could distract Marvin and forma connection, get him talking, maybe Joshua could rescue Serene. Without Serene, Marvin wouldn't be able to UnMerge. And maybe there was enough of his friend left that he could reach him. His only chance was to try and replicate what the necklace had done for him when escaping the HPA headquarters. Maybe he could project an image to Marvin.

Marvin shivered and the arrogance fell away from him making him look more hopeful and childlike. "I saw them." It was a whisper that barely carried.

"Who?" Joshua sent a Soul Wisp out and made an image of himself standing in front of where he knelt. Then created another image of a Streg that he could use to hide behind. The Stregs were the only things, besides Marvin, that had moved in the room.

"My ancestors. I-I never thought I would see dad again after he died, but he was there with the rest of the family. They were waiting. Waiting for me to finish my quest."

"Where did you see them?" Poor Marvin. It would be horrible to see his family in pain. Joshua knew his parents were dead. He knew how hard it was to lose family. He kept the image of himself standing steady and walked behind the image of the Streg to block Marvin's view.

"I can see them whenever I have doubts. When I wonder if what I am doing is right." Marvin nodded to himself and cocked his head as if he were listening to something.

Joshua remembered Marvin's father. Small, pinched, bitter. Marvin's father had drummed into Marvin that he was the last hope of the family. That they would be trapped in purgatory until the end of time because of the sin of an ancestor. Once his father had died, Marvin had become obsessed with proving him wrong.

Marvin's face hardened.

If Marvin looked up at Joshua, he might be able to see through the Soul Wisp illusion. Joshua needed to distract him for a few more moments. His gaze fell on his pack which was still crumpled on the side of the desk. He tried to project his voice from the Soul Wisp "There is something else in the bag for you. I saved it all these years."

Marvin glanced at the bag, reaching out. But he stopped part way there.

"Please."

Marvin reached into the bag and pulled out the picture of them as teens at the HPA Archives. He gave what sounded like a disbelieving snort.

Joshua inched closer to Serene, not able to go quickly and maintain the two images.

"You kept it this whole time?" Marvin wouldn't look at the image of Joshua. Which was good, since he might be able to see through it if he concentrated.

Joshua reached the cage. His hands wouldn't fit through the bars. There was a tiny door. He opened the catch on the door and was able to slip one hand into the cage. The scent of peppermint and lavender came out as he eased her hair away from her neck.

He tried the clasp, but it slipped from his hands and he almost dropped the necklace. The clasp was too small for him to open with his shaking hands. He would have to wrap it around her wrist and hope it still worked.

He needed to distract Marvin for just a few moments longer. "I did. You were my best friend."

Marvin sighed. "You were mine."

Marvin's words sent an ache of regret through Joshua. If only things could've been different, they might still be best friends. Joshua wrapped the necklace around her wrist and back inside itself to form a cow hitch. He could feel her weak pulse under his fingertips. Relief warmed him. He just had to turn the key to send her back to Wren's.

Joshua tried to create another image to camouflage the moment when Serene would disappear, but the image sputtered. His talent was stretched to the limit. It was more than he could do.

If he sent her away now, he'd lose any chance he had at repairing his friendship with Marvin. If he didn't it would leave Serene in danger and the spell still viable.

But if he sent her away, she would be safe, the spell would be broken, and he would be left with a very pissed off Marvin and his Streg army. Even so, he knew the right choice.

He twisted the pendent the way Wren had shown him. Serene vanished with a small pop. Joshua lost control of the projected images.

The Streg lifted their heads and howled, but stayed stuck to the walls.

Marvin screamed, "NO," and fell to his knees.

36

SERENE

<u>Midnight, Luminous thirty-first, 299 years post-Merge</u>

S erene felt a breeze across her face, bringing the faint smell of feathers. Her head pressed into something soft.

She opened her eyes. Wren stood at the foot of the couch she was on. His wings opened wide and they fanned her gently.

"Where is she?" Wren demanded.

Serene stared at him. Her mind was slowly turning through possibilities. He must mean Alesia.

"I don't know." Her voice cracked at the end and she cleared her throat.

His feathers rose in his crest and he cocked his head to the side. "You had no right to interfere."

Serene couldn't think of how she might've interfered. Alesia had decided her path. Serene may have taken Alesia to Walter, but that had been with full support of the Seer. "What did she tell you?"

"She didn't even leave a note that said she was leaving."

"There was no time."

He shook his head, his shoulder feathers puffing up. "The only thing that makes any sense...." He stopped and took a breath. "Is that she's doing some fool errand for you."

Serene blinked. Alesia hadn't told her brother about being a Seer. If she had, he would've known that it was not a fool's errand. "Did you know your sister is a Seer?" She kept her voice soft.

His eyes widened, but he wouldn't meet her eyes. Could he have known Alesia was a Seer, but not known that Serene knew? Maybe the Seer had already revealed herself to Wren. "How could you use that against her?" His words were gruff.

Serene understood how he felt. Her son's habit of taking risks in an effort to help people worried her. But how could she interfere with his calling? If it made him happy and gave him purpose, would it be fair to stop him? "She's not your grandmother. She'll be back and will still be sane."

"You don't know what I went through to protect her." The hiss came after his words, as an expression of his pain.

"She loves you." She held Wren's gaze, hoping he could see that she too cared for and was worried about Alesia. "The Seer in her heard the calling and went."

"Do you know where she went?"

"No, I just know that she'll be fine."

"How can you say that?" The pain in his voice pulled at her heart.

"The Seer said so herself." She pushed down her own worry for Alesia. Serene had to believe the Seer. The fog lifted from her mind. Joshua was in trouble. Worry and admiration twined in her chest. He'd risked everything to save her and stop the spell. But he didn't know that he too could be used to fuel the spell. She had to do something to help him, but first she had to wait for Wren to see the truth.

Wren stared at Serene for a long time. The weight of his stare pushed at her. Part dominance and part fear, and more emotions played across his face. Finally he nodded and slumped. "All I can do is trust in the Seer to keep her safe."

Hope filled her chest, perhaps now he'd be willing to give Joshua the help he needed. "There is another you must keep safe."

He scoffed under his breath and walked to his desk and sat, turning his back toward her. He was going to ignore her now. It was a clear dismissal. Her stomach twisted. She needed to reach him somehow. Show him that helping her was helping his sister.

He snatched glasses and opened a book.

"Joshua needs your help."

Wren turned and his little spectacles glinted on his hawkish nose. "Indeed."

"Yes. He is at Elder Martin's mansion."

"And what if I do not choose to care about that fact?" His eyes and tone were so cold, it sucked the air from her lungs.

How could he be so cold? But she knew his reasons. She knew he was worried about Alesia. But this was bigger than her friend. Yes, she was worried about Alesia, but if Joshua failed then Alesia and everyone else she cared about would die.

Her worry about her son, Rose, Alesia, and Joshua congealed into determination. Serene needed to spur Wren to action. "Joshua uncovered a plan to UnMerge the worlds."

Wren flipped a page. "We all save the world in our own way."

She needed him to understand that all of them were involved. "Do you think Alesia will survive if the worlds are UnMerged?"

Wren leaned back and blinked again.

"I was kidnapped by Bob and brought to Elder Martin's as the sacrifice." Unease tightened her stomach. The humans had been too close to her son.

"You are here. So the worlds are saved."

"I heard what they said was needed. A person of both worlds. They thought me being a transformed human would be the key, but I think it's Joshua living before and after the Merge."

Wren's face took on his long distance stare that meant he was thinking about what she'd said. Would it be enough?

37

——————

JOSHUA

<u>Early wee hours, Primum first, 300 years post-Merge</u>

Joshua scanned the floor for a weapon. Now that Serene was gone and the spell couldn't be cast, Marvin was likely to kill Joshua for his interference. He braced himself for the attack that would come. Marvin's face was still twisted with shock and anger. The Stregs still growled from the darkness around him.

A broken piece of wood a bit longer than his arm lay on the floor near the cage. He snatched it up and faced Marvin.

Instead of the rage filled expression Joshua expected, Marvin's face had twisted into a grin. Chills rose up Joshua's back. Marvin's look meant he thought he could still win.

"If you think that you have made a difference, you have not." There was a tremor in his voice. "The spell requires someone of both worlds, I thought it was Serene because she was human before she was converted to Pack, but now I think the key is you." Marvin's eyes were wide, his face pale. Joshua realized Marvin was prepared to kill him to UnMerge the worlds.

300

"Why would it be me?"

"As far as I can tell you are the only person living today who has lived in the Merged and Non-Merged worlds."

A fear slithered down Joshua's spine leaving chills in its wake.

Two Streg stepped out of the shadows. Joshua backed up. All he had to protect himself was a broken piece of wood. He backed up until he was in the same place Serene had been. The cage locked around him, and the Streg backed off growling and howling. Marvin stood motionless. His face was a mask of concentration. A bead of sweat trickled down by his ear. Perhaps Andres just made them and set the hook, but left the control to Marvin.

"You are controlling them."

Marvin smirked and went back to his book.

Joshua struggled to understand how he was controlling the Stregs. The only way to control a hook was to be able to see it. Which meant the person had to have powers or magical sight. Marvin hadn't had either. "How is that possible?"

"You think you were the only one able to hide your powers?" Marvin sneered.

Joshua had always been envious of how normal Marvin was. "But you are human."

"Yes, and so are you. At least mostly. Are you really an Other? Were you changed by the very event that caused this mess to be something more, something different?"

A week ago, Joshua would have worried about that label. He would've been distracted by the idea that he wasn't human. Now, the label didn't matter. He was just Joshua Lighthouse. And he was meant to protect. To help. To guide.

It didn't matter what they called him. What mattered was that he was here to save the people of this world. All of them. The Others he had met had proven to be great allies, and if he survived this, he'd consider some of them friends.

"Something not quite human. Something evil?" Marvin said with another sneer.

Now that he was no longer so internally focused, something about the way Marvin was talking seemed off. Like he agreed and disagreed at the same time. Or Marvin was just dragon shit crazy.

Marvin flipped through the worn pages of the book quickly, seeming to find what he needed easily. Too easily. The book was usually tricky. How was this possible?

Unless.

Unless.

The Book of Secrets wanted the UnMerge to happen.

Perhaps the book was actually part of this. The book might even be the one behind everything. If that was true, then maybe Joshua still had a chance to fix this. He needed to find out.

"Marvin? How did you survive that night? Did you read the book?"

Marvin paused mid page turn and looked up at Joshua. His eyes were haunted. "Yes." It was a whisper, one that barely touched the flickering flames of the candles.

"I found you in the room with the book. What did you see?" Joshua softened his voice.

"The book was open to a spell."

"What was the spell?"

"To show me my family." Marvin shook his head. "I saw them. I saw my family and how they suffered. And I..." He wore a puzzled frown as if he couldn't quite remember. If the book had been manipulating him this whole time, maybe the beginning had been manipulated as well. The worst thing for a person who cared about a tragedy which befell their family was to be spared the same tragedy. Survivors' guilt was a powerful thing.

"And you weren't suffering."

"Yes, that is exactly it. Here I was the only person who could save them and what was I doing? I was squandering that chance with you and Alex in the Archive."

They'd been kids still. The book must have planted the idea. "And the book showed you how to UnMerge the worlds?"

Marvin looked at Joshua out of the corner of his eye and then turned to look at him fully. "Not at first. The book opened to another spell."

Joshua needed more, because the picture still didn't make any sense. "What spell?"

Marvin flinched. Could he be remembering the pain of a hook lodging deep within him? Had the spell in the book given Marvin a hook so that the Book of Secrets could control him? That could explain how the book knew things, not because it could truly see into the future, but because it was connected to Marvin. "It gave you the powers you wanted. Needed."

"You had them, why shouldn't I get them too? Especially since I suffered for them." His lips pressed tighter together and sweat trickled down his face.

"I never wanted my powers." Joshua whispered. "I was embarrassed by them and ashamed." At that point he had desperately wanted to join the HPA, to fit in. And the only way to do that was to be human.

"I wanted powers and when you wouldn't give them to me, the book did. I knew you were secretly laughing at me because you had the things I was supposed to have." Marvin's voice became clipped.

Marvin had been his best friend. Joshua hadn't ever laughed at who Marvin was. Marvin had seemed so much more in tune with this world. Joshua had wanted to be more like Marvin.

Maybe he could reach Marvin. "The book is using you. You have to know that."

"The book will give me what I want to save my family by UnMerging the worlds."

Elder Martin had been known for tradeoffs and finding out what people really wanted. Maybe Joshua could help him see that the book was not innocent maybe also not without its own motivation. "Why? What does the book get if you do that?"

A flicker of unease skated across Marvin's face. "It doesn't matter."

If the book was behind everything, it must want something. But, what? He thought back over what he knew about the book. Joshua had locked the book away because it had tried to take him over. It was behind creating Stregs which, according to Serene, was a brutal process. It was behind the murders of the little girls and their families. Even if getting components for the spell was its goal, it could have gone about it with less effort. It was almost like the book liked suffering. The book had become more powerful over time, perhaps it fed on suffering. Joshua gasped, that was it.

"It does. It feeds on suffering. The linked Stregs, your quest, what I was suffering for my own guilt all was feeding that damn book." Joshua's voice rose with each statement.

"You can say anything you want, it does not change the facts." Martin glanced at the book.

"What facts?" Joshua asked. "That the book doesn't care about any of us. The book has used each of us?"

"No. That you will soon be dead." His voice had steadied, but his eyes still seemed a little panicked. A little too wide and dilated. The hook was winning.

Joshua sent a Soul Wisp to touch Marvin. A thick black cable which pulsated red pierced Marvin and snaked over to the book in front of him. Chills crossed Joshua's back. The hook must've been growing for years. All of his efforts to lock the Book away in his office had been pointless. It'd been living and growing its influence by transforming Marvin to Elder Martin.

Marvin raised his hands and chanted. "Dè a chaidh a chall aig aon àm, lorg e."

The Streg howled in counterpoint to his words.

Joshua didn't know how to take out a hook that big without ripping apart his friend.

"Seall dhomh na snàithleanan a bhios a 'cumail nan saoghal còmhla"

Outside the curved glass of the observatory, bright orange lights crisscrossed the sky just as they had during the Merge. Joshua's scars ached. This was real. Marvin would rip the world apart if he were able to finish the spell. Everyone Joshua knew would die, and Joshua would already be dead.

Joshua reached out with his mental hands and grabbed the hook and pulled.

It resisted, flailing and twitching like a giant snake.

Joshua funneled his fear for the people of this world, and his worst nightmares into his Soul Wisp and gave a huge pull. The hook pulled out like a stake, and spirit blood gushed out.

The bloated hook collapsed under its own weight. It didn't seem to be able to move as the one on Alex had.

Marvin fell back away from the book, leaving the last words of the spell unspoken. The unspent energy crackled in the air. Marvin gazed at Joshua with clear eyes and mouth opened. "What have I done?"

Marvin stared at the book. With his Soul Wisp Joshua could see that the book was trying to take Elder Martin back over. The hook swatted out, slow and fat, but Joshua made the shield he'd used the last time he'd battled a hook and blocked it.

"Get out of here." Joshua wedged the piece of wood between the bars of the cage and pulled. The bars creaked, but held.

Joshua mentally shield bashed the hook away. If Marvin fled, his friend could live. Reinforcements were coming so Joshua might even survive.

"If you die, the spell will be complete." Marvin paled, but picked up the dagger.

Dread settled in Joshua's gut. The book could still win. And Marvin might choose anything at this point. He looked horrified, but maybe he still believed that UnMerging the worlds would absolve his family and free them from purgatory. Joshua leaned on the wood he'd placed between the bars. A sharp crack sounded, but he couldn't tell if it was the wood or the bars.

Marvin's soul image listed toward the book as if it was no longer stable. If his soul image shattered, the book would have an empty vessel to take over even without a hook.

"Get out of here," Joshua shouted.

Marvin grinned. It was the grin from their youth when Marvin had gone against his father. "I'm sorry. You and Alex were right and I was just not old enough."

"Wait-"

Marvin threw the dagger up at the crystal high between them. It lodged for a moment and then a shriek pierced the air, shattering the glass of the observatory.

Joshua covered his head and ducked. His heart thundered as he waited for the glass to cut him. But, the cage protected him. An avalanche of glass slid down around him. The shards rang as they cascaded down.

Marvin lay on the ground, pierced by a large shard of glass.

Joshua threw all his weight on the wood and the cage shattered. He scrambled to Marvin. "Hold on buddy. I have some stuff that might heal you."

Marvin coughed. Blood seeped from the corner of his mouth. He shook his head. "You have to finish it."

"It's done."

"This was not the only spell in the book to UnMerge the worlds."

The room shook. And the orange lines faded from the sky.

The Streg freed themselves from the wall. They snapped and snarled at each other and then turned to the only two non-Streg; Joshua and the dying man on his lap. Even though he couldn't see the hook beneath the glass, he knew it was there, waiting to attack.

38

SERENE

<u>Wee hours, Primum first, 300 years post-Merge</u>

Serene pressed her body into the warm feathers of her mount. She hugged the sturdy chest and flexing muscles. The giant bird was in the middle of armored Aeros. Wren had brought a whole flight to help.

The orange lines cross-crossing the sky sent shivers down her spine. The feel of the air and everything seemed so wrong.

"There." It could have been Wren speaking. The bird she was on dove. Her stomach dropped and the air whistled by her head. She squealed and held on as hard as she could.

The bird landed lightly and she lifted her head. They were at the top of Elder Martin's house. The orange glow had begun to fade, but it still showed the catastrophic damage to what must have been a greenhouse. It had been demolished.

Snarling and howling filled the air. Broken glass glittered in the remaining light. Shards of half broken sheets of glass pierced the air like set spears. The Aeros swooped in and were attacking what looked like Stregs.

In the middle of the open room, Joshua had a man she didn't recognize on his lap. A three foot shard of glass impaled the man. Joshua's head was bowed over his unmoving chest.

Had Joshua prevented the UnMerge?

The inner house door burst open and Lizardfolk charged to battle the Stregs. Intermixed were the black garb of HPA humans who attacked the Streg as well.

They were all focused on killing the Streg.

She struggled with the knot holding her to the bird. The strap had tightened with her death grip. The bird turned its head toward her and cawed in question.

"I'm getting it." She pulled and twisted it. Finally she just transformed a hand and extended a claw to cut it. She tumbled off the bird and it launched into the sky, flattening her to the ground with the thrust of its wings.

She was woefully ill prepared to fight the Streg. She watched for a moment to see what she could do.

The Streg didn't go down when cut. They kept fighting and biting. They didn't bleed. Only when they were decapitated did the body stop fighting.

She kept glancing at Joshua. He hadn't moved since he stood up. His hands were clenched and his eyes were closed as if he were concentrating. A pulse throbbed on his neck and forehead.

The feeling that something was wrong caught her. She scanned the room trying to figure out what it was that made her so uneasy.

A Streg rose from the ground by the far wall, but instead of attacking the back of a nearby LizardFolk, it stalked toward Joshua. It avoided the direct route to circle other targets as if it was deliberately positioning itself to attack from behind.

No one else seemed to notice.

39

JOSHUA

<u>Wee hours, Primum first, 300 years post-Merge</u>

Joshua closed his eyes when Marvin took his last breath. He kept waiting for another one, but it didn't come. The sounds of combat surrounded him. Battle cries of Aeros, Lizardfolk, and HPA humans had never been on the same side before. Even during the last attack from the nearby town many had chosen to remain neutral instead of fighting on the same side.

Grief welled in his chest. He needed to figure out how he was going to defeat the book. He felt that if he didn't move then the battle would not come to him.

That feeling was shattered by a crash behind him. Serene had launched the bird cage at a Streg at Joshua's back. The cage fell on top of the Streg trapping him within the bars. The weight of the cage seemed to keep the Streg stuck.

"Thanks." He nodded at Serene.

"What the hell are you doing?" Her gaze darted between the fights around him.

"The book has to be stopped."

She tilted her head, and stepped closer. "Then stop it."

"How? The damn book is indestructible and even locked away it was still able to control people." He ran his hand through his hair.

"Didn't you say some kids found it?"

"Yeah." She had no idea that he was the one that had found it.

"Can you put it back wherever they found it?"

Joshua gasped. He remembered the morning he'd found the book. The guardian had said that something broken could be fixed. Maybe the guardian had meant the mirror. Joshua still had that shard from the mirror Alex had broken. Could he get the book back in the mirror through its remaining shard? But, the book was physically too big to go into the tiny shard he had.

If he couldn't get the book in there physically, maybe he could still trap its essence. Maybe he could use the hook's attack to suck the book's essence into the mirror. What did he have to lose?

But first he had to see if the shard would open the way the full mirror had in the Archive when he had touched it with his powers. He sent his Soul Wisp to touch the surface of the shard. He held his breath. If this didn't work, he had no idea how to contain the book.

"You are a guardian, you may enter," a voice inside his head said.

A crack sounded in his head and a line formed in the broken shard of the mirror. It thickened, becoming a door within the glass. He touched it, opening the glass and revealing a dark void like he'd seen all those years ago. He used the Soul Wisp to make the shard look like normal glass.

Relief warmed him. He had a chance. If he could get the hook to attack him just right, he could direct that attack into the shard. But how could he get the hook to attack where he wanted it to? If the book realized that he still had part of the mirror it had been trapped in, who knew what it might do.

Serene dodged back from an Aero dive bombing a Streg, and brushed against him. Even though her hair was mussed and she had a feather just above her left ear, she was beautiful.

Then the idea solidified. He could pretend to give into his attraction to Serene and lose himself in a kiss. He'd have to let his shield drop in the middle of the kiss, that might entice the book to attack his back with a hook. If he could time it correctly, the tiny mirror would suck in the hook first, which should drag the book in.

Joshua turned to Serene, making sure that his back was toward the book. "I need you to trust me," he mouthed.

Her mouth creased into a puzzled frown, but she gave a small nod.

He stepped into her personal space. Her lavender and peppermint scent surrounded him. Her eyes widened. He smiled in a way that he hoped communicated that he did find her attractive. He stroked her cheek and then leaned forward, closing the distance between them. Her breath hitched.

He pressed a small kiss on her lips waiting to see if she would pull away. He held his breath, wondering if this was too much to ask of her. She returned his soft kiss and twined her arms around his neck. He deepened the kiss and dropped the shield. It would be easy to lose himself in this kiss because everything about her from her scent to her bravery pulled at him and made him want to spend time with her. He promised himself that once this was all over, he would pursue a formal relationship with her.

Even as he reveled in the softness of her lips and the rightness of the kiss, he used a Soul Wisp to watch for the hook he expected would strike from behind.

He was beginning to wonder if this tactic would work when he caught sight of the hook coiling in preparation of springing. Just as it would've reached him, he spun, thrusting Serene behind him as he held up the necklace. Quickly, he shaped the Soul Wisp into a funnel.

The hook slid into the funnel and into the piece of the mirror and the book lifted and careened from its place on the table. Joshua kept Serene at his back, protected by his body.

<u>Wham</u>.

The book slammed into his chest, pushing him back. The gold chains flailed, looking for purchase. The book's skull eyes widened as his Soul Wisp felt the book's frantic struggle as the shard slowly sucked it inside the mirror.

He blinked and the book was gone, drawn into the tiny shard of mirror.

Joshua helped Serene up and then hugged her. "Thank you."

He held out the necklace for her to see. It was now the color of the closed door. "The mirror is closed and the book is trapped. I never could've done it without you."

40

———

JOSHUA

<u>Dawn, Primum first, 300 years post-Merge</u>

The battle wound down around them. The forces of good had won, but Serene didn't seem happy. She had an uncertain frown on her face and kept glancing at him and then looking away.

"You okay?" Joshua asked.

"The kiss was just to make the book think you were going to be easy prey?" She seemed hesitant.

"Yes and no." Joshua grinned. "I did use the kiss to make the book think I'd be easy prey, but I also really wanted to kiss you again."

She tilted her head and grinned back.

Wren landed near Joshua and Serene.

"Thank you." Joshua held out his hand. "We make a good team."

Wren cocked his head but then accepted the shake. "We do. We should do it more often."

Wren's gaze shifted to something behind Joshua's shoulder. He seemed distracted and his crest puffed.

Joshua glanced behind him and saw Walter loitering by the door. A touch of red fluttered near his throat. Alesia was nowhere in sight and he wondered whether she was still with the LizardFolk. Perhaps that's why they were both so agitated.

Joshua stepped to Walter and shook his hand as well. "Thank you."

"You will owe me," Walter said, but avoided meeting Joshua's gaze.

Joshua shrugged. Whatever Walter asked for would be worth it. The book was locked away. The Streg had been eliminated. The bad elements in the HPA had been removed. No more innocent blood would be shed to make Stregs. The biggest open issue was Rose and Serene's son. Whatever was going on between Wren, Walter, and Alesia was their business for now. If anyone called a feud, Joshua would try to help.

"Alesia's okay?" Serene asked Walter softly.

He nodded his gaze flicking to Wren for a second before returning to her face.

"We need to check on..." Serene and Joshua said at the same time.

"Let's go." Joshua put his arm around Serene and gave her a gentle squeeze.

They left Wren and Walter alone to deal with the awkward silence between them.

He and Serene made it across town in record speed. There seemed to be an air of holiday, as if humans and Others alike knew that a catastrophe had been averted. They mixed on the street. Some sang songs and danced. Others hugged anyone going by. A few peered out from behind half closed shades as if they were uncertain it was truly over.

Serene led him through the maze of illusions to a door with

the Jolly Roger pirate flag. She stopped and gripped his hand. He could feel the fine tremors through her fingers. She was afraid of what they might find.

He was worried as well. Worst case they were dead, his stomach twisted. There'd already been too much death. The best case they'd gotten his blood in time to save all three. He knew which path he was rooting for.

Her son had helped him when no one else would've. He'd risked his life to save a man consumed by the Streg sickness. Not many people were as dedicated to being a true healer. The world needed people like him.

And then there was Rose, his friend. Who perhaps didn't realize how much he valued their friendship. He took a deep breath to ease the ache in his heart. He'd make sure to be a better friend to her, if he was fortunate enough to get the chance.

"Ready?" Joshua squeezed Serene's hand.

She shivered and then straightened up and nodded. She knocked on the door in an obvious code.

A moment later Rose opened the door. Her eyebrows rose as her gaze darted to Joshua and Serene's joined hands. Joshua closed his eyes in relief. If Rose noticed hand holding, then everyone was fine.

"He's in his room resting," Rose said.

"Is he...." Serene stopped and swallowed.

Rose opened the door wider. "He's going to be fine."

Serene let out a breath that sounded like a sob.

"Go see your son." Joshua urged and she bolted through the bedroom door.

Rose was motionless as she always was when she expected the worst. She needn't have worried. He already knew there was something special about his friend. Otherwise, how had she gotten away from that blast that had incinerated the top of the

HPA building? How had she always seemed to know what the bad guys were going to do? How had she so easily helped him escape? She'd supported his weight with ease. None of it mattered. Friendship was his choice.

He took out the necklace that he'd found in the stairway and held it out to her.

Rose bit her lip and her face paled. "Where did you find it?"

"In the stairway at the HPA."

She snatched the necklace, cradling it in her hands. "Thanks." She didn't meet his eyes.

"I don't care what your secret is. You're my friend. When you're ready to tell me, we'll still be friends."

Rose met his gaze and gave him a tentative smile. Maybe she would trust him with whatever was going on with her necklace.

EPILOGUE: JOSHUA

Mid-morning, Primum tenth, 300 years post-Merge

Joshua hesitated across from the HPA headquarters. The city council had locked the HPA down the night of the foiled UnMerge plot. It had been nine days since anyone, but Council's clean up agents had been allowed in.

Serene caught his hand. She didn't have to say anything. He knew she believed in his vision for what the HPA could be. He kissed her, keeping it short. It was far too easy to lose himself in her kisses now.

The first thing he'd done was give the shard of mirror to Alex at the Archive for safe keeping. Then he'd spent the time confronting the council with the truth about what had happened in the HPA. At first, he'd been treated as if he were dangerous, but Serene by his side had made an impression on the Council. They'd cleared his name and had even been receptive to his ideas about reforming the HPA. It probably helped him that many evil creatures still terrorized the city. The city desperately needed protectors. He'd then met with the faction leaders, looking for some seed agents.

He knew that he needed to approach the HPA agents with care. While many of them were solid agents, he was unsure how they'd respond to his unification ideas. He'd gotten Joe to spread rumors of the meeting planned for tonight. Now it was time to see if he could rally the HPA agents to his cause.

He took a deep breath to ease his queasy stomach. Still he worried that all of his work would be for naught. If the HPA agents decided they didn't believe in his vision for becoming city protectors, he'd have a hard time building a strong organization quickly.

He crossed the threshold. Everything inside looked the same and yet so different. The K2300 Detector still stood in silent vigil in the hall. The faint smell of new paint brought his gaze to the walls. At his request, they'd been stripped of the trophies and placards and repainted.

And like that morning not so long ago after he'd been betrayed and drugged, the waiting crowd parted before him, making him first at the scanner. But this time the crowd was not just the remaining HPA staff and agents, but a slew of other species curious to see the spectacle.

A new cop stood as Joshua approached the grey box. The new cop was a shifter who happened to be Michael and Lissa's father. Joshua saving his children had established trust. It had also helped that Master Phil had vouched for him.

Joshua stepped into the K2300 Detector and placed both of his hands down on the sensor. It glowed a faint light blue and then turned green and chimed once. Joshua walked out of the other side, but instead of going to the elevator, he hopped onto the security officer's desk.

"We are making some major changes to the HPA." He waved

at two technicians that had followed him and they opened up a panel on the detector.

Thomas stepped forward. "And what might those changes be?"

"A new mission. To protect all peoples from true evil and promote understanding between the species."

Thomas nodded. "A lofty goal."

"It will only work if we can find strong people of all species who wish to protect everyone in the city, regardless of species." Joshua paused at the shocked whispers. The HPA had been inundated with anti-Other sentiments. His own mistrust of Others had been evident. This hadn't been what the agents had expected.

"This machine is being recalibrated. It will make sure that no one can sneak in as something they are not."

"Why do you care?" Someone shouted from the back.

"Because I don't want this organization built on lies and prejudice. We are conducting interviews for anyone who thinks they have what it takes to join us." This was the moment. With his heart thundering in his ears, he asked, "Who's interested?"

Serene raised her hand. Warmth filled his chest. He'd known he could count on Serene. She was so in that she'd even moved into Kraft tower with him.

Thomas raised his hand. All across the room, hands raised in support of his vision. Then the cheering began. The new organization looked like it would have a bright start. He hadn't even mentioned the proposed new name. Blades of the City. Agents would be called blades. The idea was to cleave the true darkness.

Michael and Lissa's father chuckled. "That's a lot of people to interview."

"It is. But I've many friends to help me." Serene, Wren,

Walter, Master Phil, Joe and so many others he'd met along the way.

He scanned the crowd searching for the one person he hadn't seen in a week. After returning Rose's necklace, he'd expected that she would share her secret. Instead, she vanished.

Where was Rose and what was she hiding?

THE END

Congratulations on reaching the end of Joshua and Serene's journey! Stay tuned for a sneak peek of the first chapter in the next installment of the Merged Series: "Thorn of the Rose".

Find out what Rose's secret is.

Enjoy this book? You can make a big difference...

Reviews are the most powerful tools when it comes to getting notice for my books.

If you enjoyed this book, I'd be so grateful if you'd spend just five minutes leaving a review (as short as you like!).

Thank you very much.

Eager for exclusive content? Want to be the first to know about upcoming releases and get a free short story?

Sign up for Claudia Blood's Newsletter at https://dl.bookfunnel.com/u5nf3wa84m

You can unsubscribe at any time.

BOOK 2: THORN OF THE ROSE

Excerpt from chapter 1

Dawn, Primum second, 295 years post-Merge

Rose Callahand opened her eyes. The shield protecting the town of Hope glimmered like a soap bubble. She'd made it through. Relief filled her chest with warmth. Her mission still had a chance.

She didn't remember actually crossing the shield. Her last memory was touching the shield at high sun, but now the dew on the grass and the first hint of light made everything seem gray. Had it taken all afternoon and night to cross? She shivered. The trees loomed above her. Nothing moved. The silence weighed her down.

Mistress Yaneli had determined that the shield was corrupted and was the reason for the sicknesses running rampant through Hope. Rose's mission seemed simple: take the stone necklace with the fire symbol to the man who would be waiting for her outside of the shield. Giving him the stone would allow him to break the shield around Hope.

Rose got to her knees and touched her neck where the stone should be.

There was no necklace.

Panic added a beat to her heart. Had she lost it? She slapped at her pockets. Nothing. Without it, her mission was a failure and her girls were in danger. Fear and failure crept up her back. The panic doubled.

No, she couldn't have failed.

The silver stone had been on a piece of twine. Perhaps the twine had broken in the crossing. She scanned the ground near her and saw a glimmer of gold. A different necklace with a thin gold chain and a locket sat in the grass. It wasn't what she was looking for, but she picked it up anyway.

The necklace stung her finger. Pain radiated up her hand, making it clench on the chain. The pain passed after a moment, leaving her dizzy. Someone else must have lost this necklace; she could try to return it.

Rose put on the chain. A strong urge to open the locket tightened her fingers. She ran her fingertip along the seam. The urge she felt was unnatural in its strength. The mission was more important than what was inside the locket. She would look inside later after looking for the stone necklace.

She dropped the locket, and when it hit her chest, a sudden foreboding struck her along with the sense that once she opened the locket, she would never be able to put back what she released into the world. This was her Pandora's Box. She shook her head to dispel the feeling. The mission and her girls were more important.

As she searched more ground around her, she resisted the urge to look inside the locket. But the necklace warmed against her chest and pulled at her imagination. What would be within it? Could it help her find the stone and salvage her mission? Could it help her protect her girls from Mistress Yaneli?

The last thought brought her up short. There was much she would risk, including this mission for Mistress Yaneli, to protect her daughters.

Finally, she opened the locket, revealing a photo of her two daughters grinning at the camera with their brown hair curling around their faces. She didn't remember taking such a picture. On the other side was engraved, "So we can see those we have lost". The dizziness returned, her chest burned, and she leaned heavily on one arm.

Suddenly, the knowledge that her daughters were dead hit her in the heart. *My girls are dead.* Loss, sadness, and regret throttled her heart, squeezing it until she couldn't breathe.

Hope had killed her girls. She was sure of that. The thought echoed in her head and fear rose from her burning chest. Overwhelming, crushing fear brought tears to her eyes and blurred the world. She had to get away from Hope and never go back.

Rose stumbled to her feet, gasping for breath. The smell of the loam with its hint of decayed leaves filled her nose.

Hope was behind her, so she scrambled forward.

She stumbled, landing hard against a tree. The bark was rough against her fingers. Her breath caught in her lungs, producing short, choppy sobs in her throat.

She pushed forward blindly, tripping over something, then she toppled. The ground rushed up to meet her. Dirt dusted her mouth and pain lanced her hands and knees. She had to keep moving. The desperate urge to distance herself from Hope spurred her forward.

Rose crawled.

The sound of her own breathing echoed in her ears. She crawled until the ground gave way in front of her, and she tumbled forward and landed hard. The fear loosened its hold on her chest, but it still stalked too close.

She took a pull of cool air and worked to calm herself.

A crunch sounded next to her. She opened her eyes to a pair of boots. Crouched next to her was a young man with scars covering his face. The man tilted his head, evaluating her with eyes that seemed far older than his young appearance. "Are you okay?"

She nodded even though she wasn't sure if it was true. The fear was still there in the back of her mind. It was smaller and more manageable. But the sense of grief from losing her girls still weighed her down. She tucked the necklace under her shirt and tried to focus on survival. She couldn't go back to Hope. Even thinking the town's name brought the fear closer.

"Need help standing?" His gaze traveled from her skinned knees to her nose and eyes. His scarred face twisted with sympathy. He had the look of a man who was distressed by a crying woman.

"At some point." She lifted her chin even as the tears fell down her cheeks. She didn't feel threatened by him, but the wretched sadness that crawled up her back made her glad she wasn't alone.

He handed her a handkerchief and looked away, giving her some privacy.

She blotted her face and then blew her nose, taking her time to evaluate him. Everything said that this man could be trusted. She took a breath and worked to lock down her feelings. It had been a long time since she'd been this out of control.

"I'm Joshua Lighthouse," he said as he sat next to her on the ground. He dug into his pack. He pulled out something wrapped in leather and offered it to her.

The food smelled of strange spices and it made her mouth

water. How long had it been since she'd eaten? She took the food. "Thank you."

She took a bite and focused on the spice. Since she had failed her mission and didn't want to go back to Hope, she needed a place to stay and a job. "Is there a town nearby?"

She'd already decided that there must be. Joshua didn't look like a farmer or a huntsman.

"New Nadezhda is near." His brow furrowed, but he didn't ask her where she was from.

"What sort of skills do they value there?" she asked. Since she was one of the few non-magical people from Ho—her hometown. If this new town only valued magic, she could be in trouble.

He shrugged. "What are you good at?"

"I know Hapkido." Seeing his blank expression, she added, "It's a fighting style."

He nodded, looking thoughtful. "I could use some back-up on what I'm currently working on."

Rose evaluated his face. She'd always had a sense for knowing when people were lying. Joshua was not lying. He could use the help. She didn't have many options, and he had been kind. Perhaps she could prove she was more than a sobbing woman.

"What do we need to do?" she asked.

"There is a vampire near here who has been killing in the city. I'm here to persuade him to stop." Joshua said it calmly, like it was a normal day for him to walk into a vampire's lair.

She studied his expression and the way he held himself. He acted as if he believed vampires were real.

"Do vampires really exist?"

Joshua nodded. "They do."

She thought about everything she had seen and heard about

the myth of vampires. "So, he's undead, and only a stake through the heart can stop him?"

"There are other ways, but that's the most reliable one. I also have this." He pulled out a vial. "This has holy water and other things and will harm the undead." He tucked the bottle back into his bag.

Even though he seemed to be telling the truth, she still thought he must be joking. There was no such thing as a vampire. Was there?

His face and everything about him supported his words. The shield had been put up to protect Hope hundreds of years ago. Could it have been used to prevent things like vampires from entering Hope? Was that what Hope's founders had seen, what caused them to put up a wall? Why hadn't New Nadezhda put up a shield?

"I'll go, but I have questions."

"Shoot." He led her along a path near the edge of the woods.

How else was this world like Hope? "Are there many mages in the city?"

"Some. Mages are relatively rare."

Hope was full of mages. She and Max had been two of only a handful of people without magic. "And are there many creatures like the vampire here?"

Joshua raised an eyebrow at her. "Yes, there are many types of undead. Most are not intelligent. Vampires are." His tone had stayed even, but something about the slight downward curve of his mouth made her think Joshua didn't like the undead.

"Are there other things?"

"All the creatures from Earth came into this world with the Merge." His face twisted as if he was remembering something unpleasant.

She followed Joshua, barely keeping track of where they were going.

The shield had protected Hope from the Merge. She would have to get used to many different creatures. She hadn't read much about fairytales. That had been more Max and her husband's thing. The ache of grief closed her throat for a moment. She forced the emotions away.

"We're here," Joshua whispered.

A small tower, perhaps two stories high, squatted in a clearing. It didn't seem to have any windows. But that made sense. Didn't vampires have an issue with the sun? The surrounding vegetation looked like it belonged in a fairytale, dark and twisted and full of thorns.

"One of the agents at the Human Protection Agency, the HPA, swears he got in a killing blow when he rescued the woman the vampire was trying to kill." He turned back to look at her. "Sorry, I had forgotten you were without a weapon." He handed her a long dagger.

She took it, did a practice swing, and assumed her first stance. The dagger was a few inches shorter than the sword she had trained with, but would work.

Joshua grinned at her. "Ready?"

She nodded.

At Joshua's touch, the door creaked open. The smell of decay tickled her nose.

Joshua lit a torch. The room seemed to be the full length of the tower. A staircase extended down into murky darkness and up to the next level.

The smell of decay was stronger up here. "Which way?" she whispered.

Joshua pointed down.

The first stirring of unease hit her. She knew what he was hunting was upstairs, but perhaps he had a reason to go down? She wasn't sure, so she kept quiet.

Rose crept behind him, trying to make no sound.

"*Why are you with the human?*" The voice in her head sounded male and old.

Her heart picked up speed. She'd never heard a voice in her head before.

Something pungent clogged her nose. The sense she and Joshua were heading into a trap pressed on her chest. She grabbed Joshua's shoulder.

He stopped and glanced back. "What's wrong?"

"The vampire is upstairs..." She wasn't sure how to explain that going down was a trap or that she knew the vampire was upstairs. But she did. She was confident in her conclusions.

He glanced down for a moment. His breathing changed, and then all the color left his face. He took a shuddery breath. "Go back," he mouthed.

She went back up the stairs, and then Joshua led again, going up to the second floor.

The room was almost as dark as the room below, which made sense if there were no windows. It would be like a big cave.

A massive bed was just visible in the gloom. The decaying smell came from the bed.

Joshua lit a torch and brought it to the bed. The man who lay in the bed was desiccated. Dry skin stretched across his bones. A gaping wound lay open on his chest, but the wound didn't bleed.

"Lighthouse. Come to put me out of my misery?" the man hissed.

"If you agreed to not harm humans, I'd have no issue with you."

"You wish me to starve." The man leapt out of the bed, flying toward Joshua.

Joshua's first arrow hit the vampire in the throat, but the second went wide. It was enough. The vampire slowly disintegrated.

"*He will kill you, too, when he finds out.*" The old male voice reverberated in her head. It must have been the vampire.

The words in her head confused her. Why would Joshua kill her? She wasn't undead.

Read Now!

ACKNOWLEDGMENTS

Thanks to my hubby and family who allow me to wander away when I need to write.

To my VA Kelly I can't thank you enough for your undying enthusiasm and design sense. Social media is way less scary with you on my side.

To my amazing developmental editor Dawn Alexander who helped me organize my chaos and keep my inner achiever from getting too enthusiastic.

Thank you Fenley Grant for your amazing editing skills and for working me in when I am inevitably late.

Thank you Wendy for reading and giving feedback to my writing since college. (A scary number of years ago) You were always able to find a nugget of good that kept me going.

Thank you to the ladies at Lakehouse Writers group, Tammy, Val, MaryAnna, B, Jay, and Kim who have been a constant source of inspiration, motivation, and sanity checking.

Thank you to Val and MaryAnna who kept me honest on our accountability texts and for helping me figure out the end of this book. You both were so patient with my what-if-ing.

Thank you Antha and Christine for the many, many, many writing sprints. Without you guys I never would have gotten the book done.

Thank you to Calley for the daily checkins. Cookies!

ABOUT THE AUTHOR

Claudia Blood writes mystical realms and futuristic worlds, where underdogs defy authority, defeat demons, and discover their destined family amidst the chaos.

Her love of Epic Fantasies led her from life as a research scientist right into that of an award-winning author. With works such as the Renegades Rising, *Relic trilogy*, <u>Merged series</u>, and the <u>Supernatural Detective Agency</u>. <u>Claudia Blood</u>'s works cover a wide range of genres and themes that have captivated many.

Juggling her roles as a wife, mom, business analyst, and pet wrangler doesn't leave much free time, but what Claudia has is filled to the brim with creating sci-fi and fantasy novels set in worlds that may be slightly familiar and some that are totally unique and new. Taking inspiration from all kinds of media from *Dungeons & Dragons*, *The Dresden Files*, Alan Dean Foster, and so much more, Claudia Blood crafts stories that entice and keep the reader wondering what will happen next.

For her latest release, visit her at
<u>www.ClaudiaBlood.com</u>

www.ingramcontent.com/pod-product-compliance
Lightning Source LLC
Chambersburg PA
CBHW052026220726

48293CB00015B/286